Katherine Warwick
SAVAGE

Grove Creek Publishing

This is a work of fiction. Names, characters, places and incidents are either a product of the author's imagination or are used fictitiously, and any resemblance to actual persons, living or dead, business establishments, events or locales is entirely coincidental.

A Grove Creek Publishing Book / published in arrangement with the author.

SAVAGE
Printing History

Grove Creek Publishing edition / March 2008

All rights reserved.
Copyright © 2008 by Katherine Warwick

This book may not be reproduced in whole or part without permission. For information address: Grove Creek Publishing, 2 South Main St., Pleasant Grove, UT 84062

Cover Design by Jennifer Johnson
Image purchased from istock photos
Book Design and typography by Julia Lloyd

ISBN- 10: 1-933963-92-1
ISBN- 13: 978-1-933963-92-1

Printed in the United States of America

A special thanks to Chance L.

Katherine Warwick
SAVAGE

Grove Creek Publishing

SAVAGE - *Katherine Warwick*

ONE

He hated dancing. Couldn't do it, for one thing. Besides, the seductive ritual of foreplay was a waste of time. Why not just get right to the good stuff? To counter his feelings with the only thing that would subdue them, he waved the bartender over and slapped a palm on the top of the bar giving his order for another beer.

To his right a little blonde bumped into him, smiling. Of course he smiled back. She kept nudging him; nearly causing him to spill the beer the bartender had just slid his direction.

"Hey," he said, grinning down at her.

Her eyes brightened, though he couldn't tell the color of them at the moment. She turned, facing him, exposing a low-cut, tight blue tee shirt.

"I'm Missy," she said.

Nope, she wasn't *missing* anything. His gaze lingered up her pale throat, finally landing on her face. "I'm Chance."

Her head tilted in surprise. It was the reaction he had been getting to his name since he was old enough to decipher the language of facial expressions, knowing they could be just as enlightening, just as damning as words could be.

She eyed his mouth. It sent a warm thread through his blood. "You have a great smile," she said. Another thing he'd been hearing since he'd known he could smile and get anything he wanted—except what he really needed. "I love your dimples."

Chance raised his bottle. "Thank you." Then he drank it down. He still hurt inside. Another bottle would do him some good. With a clank to the bar that was swallowed up in the noise, he waved to the bartender.

"You've had a lot of those." Missy glanced at the empty bottle.

Leaning his elbows against the soft padding of the bar, Chance avoided his reflection in the mirror that ran the length behind it. "You going to be my mother or have a drink with me?"

"Sure, I'll have a drink with you."

The bartender was waiting. "She'll have a..."

"An Amstel light," Missy answered, edging even closer to him. She crossed her arms, resting them on the bar so that her breasts pinched in the center, giving them more fullness. His gaze fell back to them.

"I'll have another Hoegaarden. Quite a shirt you have on there, Missy." Chance took the bottles from the bartender when he came back. He handed Missy hers.

"Glad you like it."

What's not to like? he thought, taking her in. She had it all—handfuls, from what he could gather—a study in feminine flirtation.

Even though he didn't particularly feel like indulging in company at that moment, he'd learned that if getting completely wasted didn't dull what was raging inside of him, being with a woman could do the job.

He lifted the bottle to his lips in hopes the desired effect would drown him soon. This time he caught his reflection in the mirror, and hardly recognized what he saw.

The young man staring back at him looked older than his twenty-seven years. Rough, scraggly, with dark smudges under two angry eyes. When was the last time he'd had a haircut? He couldn't remember—the fog in his brain too thick. But the damned hair was everywhere, dark curls and waves that had never done anything but what they wanted to. He thought he'd shaved. Maybe that was the other day. The shadow along his jaw made him look like he'd been holed up somewhere—neglected.

But then he had been.

It was hardest to meet his eyes. To look at them and know he couldn't escape what he saw: Chance Savage.

A roll of self-disgust started low in his gut and he lowered his head to the counter. He took deep breaths, the sour stench of his own inebriation nearly gagging him. Then he felt a hand on his back, a soft breast pressed into his arm.

"You okay?" Missy asked.

He closed his eyes, kept his face buried in his crooked arms for a moment. "I'm fine." The music drove through his head like a boxer pounding a heavy bag. He was sure she hadn't heard him. She was a stranger, she didn't really care about what was wrong with him.

She just wanted him to take her home.

Thrusting himself up, he faced his reflection in the mirror with a determined scowl before jerking toward Missy with another smile. "Hey." He was beginning to think she was just what he needed. Yeah, he could bury himself in all of those soft, round curves. That would do it, at least for tonight.

He'd worry about tomorrow later.

"How about we dance?" Missy asked. He could see it in her eyes; she wanted to get him away from the bar – for his own good.

He resisted. Resisting was his middle name. "I don't dance." He finished the bottle he'd been drinking with a thud to the bar.

"We can just rock." Missy took his hand in hers. It was soft, warm—inviting. Like the rest of her.

Rock? He could rock.

Chance let that warm hand lead him through the crowd. He scanned for his friends, saw them scattered and called out to them with careless abandon.

The dance floor of Bruisers was lit from underneath and the pulsing lights hurt his eyes. He stopped a moment, reeling from the flashing colors. He was feeling a little better now, lighter, giddier. He laughed at his own discomfort, at his being there and wondered why he couldn't just shove everything clawing at him aside and lose himself, like everyone else around him.

Missy tugged him deep into the center of the crowd and slid her arms up around his neck and since he had no idea what he was doing, he did just what she'd suggested – he rocked. It was incredibly dull and he was ready to ditch the dance floor when his roommate, Justin, elbowed him with a look meant to chide because he'd sworn he wouldn't leave the bar.

The look of sheer happiness on Justin's face struck Chance's belly as if he'd been slugged. He was envious. In the years he'd known Justin, the guy had never let life tear him apart. Chance admired that. But then Justin came from a solid family, not a lion's den.

The music slowed to a thudding, sensual beat. A couple caught Chance's eye. They were talking to Justin as they danced in the center of the floor. Chance had never seen the guy before, but he wasn't concentrating on him: his eyes fastened on the woman with him.

She looked completely out of place, like she'd just been plucked from the pages of *Town and Country* or *Society News*. There was nothing of the midriff-baring, provocative attire he saw on most of the women in the place. She wore one color – a soft shade of lavender – from head to toe in a suit with the careful fit of someone tuned into a sense of self rather than to please an onlooker. Her shimmery blonde hair was a mass of soft curls she made no excuse to straighten like so many women did.

But her face was what captured his eyes.

She was classically sculpted, like a seventeenth century aristocrat. Her smile was as fresh and innocent as a virgin on communion day. Her eyes, though she was a distance away, were big, expressive, the color of which he strained to see.

Determined to see the woman up close, he moved through the crowd.

The man and the woman in lavender danced with perfect movements Chance suspected had been learned. Since the two of them had been talking with Justin, he figured they were part of that dance group Justin hung around.

Like a statue in the middle of the floor, Chance stood watching the stunning couple as bodies moved all around him.

"Hey, where'd you go?" He heard Missy's bright voice but didn't look down at her.

"I told you, I'm not much of a dancer." His eyes were still caught on the elegant woman in the arms of another man. She held that head of hers with a tilt that whispered untouchable. In fact, everything about her looked entirely out of reach and Chance's eyes narrowed. Stirring deep inside was the all-too familiar feeling that clutched at him when he felt challenged and in need of proving himself.

"You know them?" Missy asked.

Not yet, he thought. He took Missy's hand and led her near them. His heart pounded as he saw the woman more clearly.

"You're staring at her," Missy said, breaking free of his bear-hug.

Chance looked at her for a brief moment. "Maybe this dance is over."

Her eyes widened and she sneered at him before she disappeared in the crowd.

Chance dodged bodies as he trailed the picturesque couple. He tapped the guy's shoulder and they slowed to a stop. Because he was so close to her, he barely glanced at the man who held her, enchanted by her face. Her skin was pale, smooth, the blue of her eyes startlingly dark, sharp and penetrating. Something flickered in their depths, warning, wonder, he wasn't sure but the low heat in his gut pulsed, discarding sensibility. "I'd like to cut in," he said, still not offering more than a glance to the man.

Her partner hesitated and looked at her with question. She seemed too taken aback to reply, and Chance's itch to touch her intensified.

Finally, she nodded and her partner left the dance floor. She stood waiting for him and he had to blink hard, sure this was just a figment of his ripe brain.

Never at a loss for words when it came to women, Chance couldn't think, let alone speak. She was looking at him so intensely, he was sure she could see right through him. She'd run if she saw what was inside. She'd certainly never let him touch her.

"Are you going to dance with me?" Her voice had an air of confidence that instantly set him on guard. But he nodded, taking an unsteady step toward her.

She had the body and bones of a polished ballerina. Everything about her was refined, yet he'd just seen her dance with remarkable presence. He felt the first stirrings of incompetence fight with his need to prove to himself he was still alive inside.

"I'm Chance."

She extended her hand to shake his and he studied the delicate perfection of her fingers, her palm. Then he slid his fingers around hers.

"Avery."

Chance held out his arms, even though he had no idea what to do with them other than to wrap them around her. But that would be enough. He'd be able to feel those bones move, close his eyes and see her muscles working. He was disappointed that she kept her arms in the traditional dance position.

He'd never learned how to dance.

As they moved, she looked off over his shoulder so he stared at her. The perfection he'd first seen was not a figment of his inebriated mind. The luminous glow was real, radiating from features that looked to have been hand carved by Michelangelo.

She knew he was watching her and he was glad. "What are you doing here?" he finally asked.

"Dancing—like everyone else."

"But you're not like everyone else."

Usually, a stare that intense spoke of only one thing to him, but not with her. He saw no lust in her eyes at all. It relieved him, and he pulled her closer.

"Your eyes are incredible," he told her.

"Thank you." Her response was smooth enough to tell him she was used to being complimented.

"Is that your boyfriend?"

"He's my dance partner."

"So he's not your boyfriend?"

Her smile was too brief. She looked at his mouth, then back at his eyes before she turned her head away.

"You're a professional dancer, right?" he asked.

That she kept her cordial gaze over the crowd instead of looking at him bugged him. He wanted to memorize the flecks in her eyes, the smooth contours of her face. More than anything, he wanted to let his hands roam her lovely limbs, trace her ribs, and explore hidden places.

Not used to being ignored by women, he turned her in what he hoped would be a deft move, but ended up twisted in a toe-stepping embarrassment. She shot him a look then, lifting her brow in what Chance assumed was annoyance.

"What? Can't professionals dance with ordinary folks," he asked, more snap in his tone than he intended. "Or are you too good for that?"

"I happen to teach ordinary folks to dance."

"Teach me something."

The song had changed. He felt her draw back as if she was ready to leave him and he held on, not ready to relinquish her to her partner, now standing at the fringe of the floor, watching.

Chance moved, blocking her view of the man.

"I have to go," she said, craning to find her partner. It lit Chance's frustration, brittle as it was, and he was just careless enough to pull her against him, sending a fast, hot thrill through his veins as he felt her resist.

"Not until you teach me something," he said.

"This dance is over."

"I thought you said you were a teacher."

"Let me go now," she said, looking him straight in the eye. She took a step back but he held her hands tight.

Chance let out a laugh of feigned indifference meant to cover up deeper bruises. When his eyes met hers again, he could see she was furious. He brought himself flush with her again, acutely aware of her warmth, of the hard, long line of her body next to his.

Within seconds she would be gone.

"You are too good for me." He pushed himself away with more force than he intended and instantly regretted it, reaching out to snatch her back, but she kept herself out of reach.

Chance braced for a slap—he deserved at least that. She merely tilted her head, and the pity in her eyes stole his breath.

Without a word, she turned, leaving him in the middle of the floor. Her lavender form weaved through the mass of bobbing bodies and he tried to follow her with vision losing its clarity. She went directly to her partner who shot Chance a nasty glare before the two of them were lost in the mass.

He'd been an idiot, he knew that. He'd had no business touching a Michelangelo when he was no better than street scum.

The room swayed as he turned around. Pushing his way through the crowd, he kept his eyes on the bar.

TWO

Chance could barely move. Each limb felt weighted with iron and leftover echoes of music still jack hammered into his brain from Bruisers the night before.

He was in bed—his bed, fully clothed—but he had no idea how he'd gotten there. Though the aftertaste of a night like last night was familiar, it still coiled his stomach. Still brought his body into a shadowy place he knew only time and dark quiet would ease him out of.

Somebody had drawn the blinds, God bless them. Whoever it was had also kept the place silent. Forcing himself up, he scrubbed the roughness of his face with both hands and let out a stale burp.

Faint rustling on the other side of his closed bedroom door hinted that Justin had been his designated driver last night. Justin didn't drink. For a second, Chance wished he didn't either. But he knew of no other way to rid himself, even if only temporarily, of what tore at him.

Stumbling to the shower, he peeled off his clothes as he went, dropping them along the hall with the carelessness of a child. He heard voices, looked, and saw Inessa, whose hands flew to her mouth as she whirled away from him with a shriek.

Realizing he was standing in the hall naked, his delayed reaction made him chuckle as he scratched at his chest and head. "Sorry, Nessa."

Justin suddenly appeared, dishrag in hand, a smile on his face. He shook his head. "Sorry, man. I should have given you a woman warning."

"It's your own fault now if she can't look at you after looking at me."

Justin sneered good-naturedly. "You wish. Get your rancid self cleaned up. I want to talk to you."

Though Chance shot him an indifferent jerk of his head, he sensed something serious in Justin's tone. He stood underneath the hot shower with his gut hollowing. What would he want to talk about?

Scrubbing the towel over his face, he looked in the fogged mirror, wiping a circle so he could see himself. Sooty smudges pressed under his eyes. He needed to shave or he could be classified as growing a beard.

He leaned on the sink. His eyes locked in the mirror, the dark gray of them swirling with the uncertainty of a ferocious storm. He sighed, dropping his head to his chest. He'd shave another day.

Pulling on a faded shirt and some old jeans, he headed out to the living room of the apartment he shared with Justin Wilde.

He had still to button the top button of his beaten jeans and when he did, he stopped, noticing how he could pull the waistband from his waist a good inch. When his thumbs dropped, so did his pants, settling lower than normal on his hips.

"You look scary, man," Justin said.

Chance looked up, tugged at his waist band and shook out damp hair. He'd never been good at taking criticism, his delicate defenses shooting up with the efficiency of porcupine quills. But he had spent the last year living with Justin and knew that he was one of the only people on earth who really cared about him, which made taking whatever he had to say a little easier.

"You're just jealous that Inessa's seen a real man." Chance glanced around for Inessa. "Where is she?"

"She had to go." Justin moved from the kitchen into the living room.

"Hey, I could have stayed in the back."

Justin shook his head and his blond waves settled around his face. "She had to." Crossing his arms, he leaned against the back of the couch and looked at him steadily. "You're a mess, man."

Friend or not, the hair on the back of Chance's neck prickled at the comment and he stood erect.

Justin saw the resistance. "Just hear me out."

It was respect that kept Chance's feet from moving. He'd learned that moving could prolong the inevitable. Itchy hands that would normally lash out in physical defense hid deep in his pockets. He waited in silence.

"You're—" Justin stopped himself, rubbing the back of his neck in a frustrated sigh.

It wasn't like Justin to mince words. He said what he felt, whether you liked it or not. That was part of why Chance was getting better at taking it. Watching him stumble over them now caused that hollow inside to deepen.

"You were so out of it last night I had to drag you in here, dude. Do you even remember that?"

Chance shifted uneasily. "You didn't have to." But inside, Chance was scrambling through his memory trying to recall what had happened.

"I couldn't leave you at that table." Justin stuck his hands in his pockets but Chance knew he was reaching out. "You okay?"

"Yeah, of course."

"Things settling down between you and Kurt?"

The muscle in Chance's jaw contracted but he kept his gaze level. "As settled as two rattlesnakes in a box."

Justin paused a moment that was long and tense. "If you need any help—"

"I don't," Chance broke him off with a bite. "Thanks."

It relaxed Chance when Justin's lip turned up on one side. "Yeah. Hey," he rubbed his hands back and forth. "I got a proposition for you."

With the serious talk over, Chance crossed to the kitchen in hopes of digging up something to eat. "What's that?"

"I made some waffles this morning, there's a few left on a plate."

Chance reached into the refrigerator and pulled them out. "Still warm." His fingertips lightly touched them as he took the plate to the microwave. "We got any sour cream and jam?"

Justin nodded. "A Wilde staple. Now, as you're between jobs, I was thinking you could take a short gig at the high school. Our art teacher's out on maternity leave."

"Yeah? That'd be cool."

"Figured you'd like that. There's one catch."

Chance pulled the waffles out of the microwave and began dousing them in sour cream. "What is it?"

"You gotta enroll in this ballroom class Nessa and I are taking."

"No way."

"It's one night a week."

"I can't dance, no way."

"It's a steal for your return, man."

"An impossibility. I can't dance."

"I couldn't either when I started, but the teacher's awesome."

With a firm shake of his head, Chance cut into his first waffle. "Nope."

"Consider it."

"No way."

"You mean you'd give up sharing your creative brain with all those squiggly kids because you aren't man enough to try a dance class?"

"That's cutting low."

"You know that's it," Justin taunted. "I saw you today man, you're nothing."

Chance laughed in spite of himself. His mouth was full so he shook his head. "You've forgotten that I know jiu-jitsu, dude."

"Only because I taught you."

"I can kick your butt anytime."

"I'd pulverize yours first."

Chance didn't doubt Justin would pulverize him in a one-on-one. The guy could take down a sumo wrestler in five seconds. That was why he'd been stealing lessons here and there so that he could learn how to finally finish someone.

It was a well-meaning bribe. There was nothing but real goodness in Justin. Silently Chance thanked God his friend had not kicked him out with all the crap and instability he'd put him through.

The life of an artist was anything but predictable.

Still, he had hopes of money on the horizon now that he'd been left his parents' earthly belongings—if Kurt didn't kill him first.

"Just come once, and I'll forget what happened last night." Justin grabbed his briefcase, glanced at his watch. "Tonight. Seven – at the studio."

"Good try but no-go." Chance took a mug from the shelf and filled it with tap water. "What did happen last night?"

"You really don't remember?"

Chance tried to be amused but the shadowing in Justin's eyes sobered him some. Setting the buttons on the microwave for one minute, Chance turned and faced him.

"Man, you—" The shadowing darkened before a mischievous grin broke out on Justin's face. "I'll tell you tonight—after class." Chance shook his head. Justin was half way out the door. "See ya tonight. Seven, at the studio."

"No way."

"See ya."

"Won't be there."

The front door shut and the microwave dinged, the hot water was ready.

And there he sat, tapping his thumbs on the steering wheel of his old VW. Chance's gaze darted around the parking lot, his neck and arm pits were sweating. Dancers of every imaginable kind threaded through the parked cars. Little pink ballerinas, teenage ballerinas, even male ballerinas.

He snickered. The guys looked ridiculous in their tights.

There were adults going into the building; couples as well as lone men and women. The sight did little to give him courage. He was here because he wanted to know what he'd done last night, in case he had to worry about damage control. He was here because he'd hit a dry run in his work, and was out of money, and hope.

And he wanted the stint at the high school.

Justin was so happy all the time. Chance doubted that dance or teaching had anything to do with it, but at this point, he was willing to try just about anything to have a little happiness of his own.

The tap on his window startled him. Justin's grin was huge. Behind him, Inessa peeked bashfully over his shoulder.

He got out and cursed under his breath. "I sure as hell hope this is worth it or your ass is mine tonight."

Justin threw his arm around his shoulder. "You'll dig it. I promise."

Chance nodded at Inessa with a playful grin. "Ness." She returned the greeting with her lashes lowered.

The studio was a hive of fast-moving dancers all anxious to get to class. Tiny ballerinas darted around their legs; kids laughed and shouted to each other. Instructors shepherded young dancers to and from the drinking fountain.

The room for the adult ballroom class was downstairs and in the back of the studio. They joined a half-dozen other adults who stood on the hard wood floor looking at themselves in the wall of mirrors.

"I can't believe I'm doing this," Chance said, nervously glancing around. "Everybody has a partner. Who am I gonna dance with? Myself?" He reached out and grabbed Justin, squeezing his neck. "What have you gotten me into?"

Deftly, Justin ducked out of the hold, snagging Chance's right hand and twisting his fingers in a harsh finger-hold that brought Chance to his knees in a buckle and a groan.

The door of the studio swung open and everyone turned.

Chance, still in Justin's vise grip, let out a, "Jeez" that echoed through the cavernous room. Justin pulled him up. It was then that Chance turned toward the door and saw the teacher staring right at him. His eyes widened and his heart tanked. It was the woman he'd danced with at Bruiser's – Michelangelo's Avery.

For a moment she studied him and only him. Then she clasped her hands at her chest as if in prayer, and her intense study of him was broken as she floated across the front of the room.

"Good evening everyone."

Every voice echoed her back with, "Good evening Ms.Glenn."

She wore black from head to toe: tight slacks and a long-sleeved shirt that looked made for her, with a fit that knew where to hug, where to lightly caress, where to flirt. Her long, creamy curls were up in a ponytail that hung like a pom-pom down her back. A back, he thought, that was beautifully erect in a posture so sure that he'd only seen such perfection carved in marble.

His tongue brushed his lips.

She was doing something with the music, so her back faced the class, and Chance's study of her swept her rounded bottom, tight and feminine above two long legs. As a painter of women, he was particularly in tune with every aspect of the female body and could easily imagine this woman's underneath her clothing. His brain suddenly filled with images of her as he would draw or paint her. Lying on a modern couch of simple lines with little or no color with the exception of her alabaster skin, and a sheer scarf in lavender – no, red – draped across the intimate parts of her body. Her legs, her arms, comfortably extended as if she were the only life, the only light, in the dullness of the room.

After putting on some soft music, she faced the class. Chance stood as erect as he could, noticing the extreme posture of everyone in the room.

"Ladies and gentlemen, we have a new class member," she said, looking right at him again. She wore a congenial smile. Chance knew it was not sincere, but it didn't bother him. He'd been an idiot last night; he figured he was lucky to be getting even that.

"Would you introduce yourself, sir?" she asked, moving through her students and straight for him like a feline in the grass.

Chance cleared his throat. "We met last night. You don't remember?"

Her head tilted, but her slow, calculated stride didn't break. "Did we?"

That stung. Chance's eyes narrowed over a thin grin. "Chance Savage. And you're Michelangelo's Avery."

She stopped, a small smile creasing her lips. "Avery Glenn." She extended her hand. "Welcome to class, Chance."

He shook it and she continued back to the front of the room.

Chance leaned to Justin. "Please tell me whatever I did last night had nothing to do with her."

Justin's teasing grin was short-lived. She began to speak and all eyes were intently on her.

"Partner up. We'll be working on Waltz today. Remember, the Waltz only has four steps. Front together, side together, side together, back together." She demonstrated the open-box formation of the dance in one seamless movement holding a phantom partner.

As the couples stood together, Chance found himself alone.

Avery extended her right hand. He felt a ridiculous tremor as he looked at her beckoning to him. *She's a teacher for crying out loud, she has to dance with you.*

His approach was slow and steady, until he slipped his hand in hers and she drew him close. The slightly aggressive move, though completely necessary, pulled the tremor inside of him taut.

Her eyes locked with his. "It seems you will get your wish, Chance."

"And what wish is that?"

"I will teach you something after all."

He couldn't help the breath that escaped his chest. To be close to her again was not something he ever thought he'd find himself doing. But here he was, inches away from a face that he couldn't stop admiring, illuminated with something that drew him to her in spite of the way her bones were sculpted.

Though she was in his arms, she turned her head toward the class. "Begin please. And one two three, two to three..." Then she looked at him.

"I can't—" he pulled away from her in protest but she cut him off, bringing him back with a firm tug.

"You're not quitting, are you?"

There was challenge in her eyes. He met it with his own. "Not a chance." But he knew playful conversation would not hold up once she saw how he possessed two left feet.

Her calm yet studying gaze never left his face. "Waltz is about perfect form," she told him. "But it is not to look stiff, though the body is held quite erect. The arms are tirelessly held up and out. Your hand is never to sag, but to hold mine as if the most delicate Faberge egg from the collection of Marie Antoinette lay in your palm and you have been entrusted with it. Up with your chin, Chance. Strong lines, defined movement."

As he looked into her eyes, the blue was as clear and endless as the sky at mid-day, and hope lit him inside. Maybe he could do it.

"Now." She urged him gently forward. "Take one step toward me, dipping slightly as you step, coming onto the balls of your feet before the next step."

It seemed there were four sets of feet down below rather than two and Chance had to keep checking to make sure he was doing just as she told him. His hands gripped hers like he was holding on for life.

"Gently, Chance." She gestured with a soft nod of her head toward their hands and he immediately loosened his grip.

"I crushed the Faberge egg," he said. She merely smiled.

Self-conscious but determined, he continued to try, finally getting the rhythm of the steps, only to find that his neck and arms were tiring from the erect position. Suddenly the ease with which she carried herself put him in awe of her.

"You make it look so easy," he told her.

She was taking a moment to watch her class, but she answered him. "I've been doing this a lot longer than ten minutes. Don't be hard on yourself."

The hour passed and he had to double check his watch,

sure the clock over the door was wrong. It seemed they had just started and he'd completely lost himself in the lesson, enjoying it more than he expected.

After class officially ended, Avery left to turn off the music and was snagged by questioning students. Chance stood casually nearby, not ready to leave yet.

"You did good," Justin told him. "You like it?"

Chance lifted a shoulder. "It was okay."

"The waltz can be hard to get. And you were dancing with a pro." Noting the way Chance kept glancing at Avery, Justin took Inessa's hand, readying to leave. "So you'll come back."

Again Chance shrugged. "I don't have anyone to dance with."

"You can dance with her." Justin tilted his head Avery's direction.

"What about her partner?"

"He only dances with her when they compete." Justin patted Chance's shoulder. "See you at home."

"Yeah." There was that detail about what had happened last night and there was the deal with school, but Chance's gaze was fixed on Avery, now alone as she packed up her music. The rest could wait until later.

The door closed behind the last couple and he slowly crossed to her. She didn't turn to look at him, as if she didn't care, or expected stragglers to stay behind and chat. He wondered if she knew it was he that had stayed to straggle.

He came up right behind her and stood just a foot away. They'd been inches apart when they'd danced, and he could smell her perfume again, light and floral.

Without looking over her shoulder she said, "And how did you like your first lesson, Chance?"

It brought a grin to his face. "I liked it fine. How did I do?"

She was about putting away her CD's, marking roll. "You

did very well." Then she turned and they were face to face. He hoped to see a spark of interest in her eye. They'd been so close dancing; he half expected a morning-after thank you. But he could find nothing in reference to their intimacy in her eyes and it bothered him.

He couldn't help that he didn't want to leave. It had been the first tender contact he'd had with a woman in so long he felt the strange stirrings of commitment after being in her arms.

Tucking the attendance roll against her chest, she looked up at him. He found he didn't know what to say.

He looked away for a moment before meeting her gaze again. "I'm sorry about last night," he said. Apologizing had never been easy for him, having been bullied into submission most of his life. Something about her made him feel safe. Like she'd not take the apology and shove it back. She'd carefully consider it, like one of those fancy eggs she talked about.

"I accept your apology." She didn't say anything more about it, but he saw the way she was carefully looking at him. Chance's chest tightened suddenly with sentiment. Emotion was something he wasn't comfortable with.

He stepped back from her.

Her brows knit with concern. "Will you be continuing with the class?" she asked.

"Is there room for me?"

"Yes, of course."

The relief he felt almost shamed him, it lightened his mood so. "I will then."

She passed him, heading to the door and he followed, feeling better than he had in weeks. He marveled at her fluid walk. The way her body moved like honey pouring from a jar.

He'd paint her back, he decided. She'd be standing by an open window, looking out. Wearing nothing or something draped, but fitted snugly around those hips. He'd pose her himself, draping her naked form with the bright fabric placed just where he wanted it. As he smoothed and tucked, he'd let his lips wander.

When the door opened and her partner entered, Chance slowed, the tempting image vanishing.

"Scott, I'll be right back, I'm just going to take the roll to the office." Avery stopped when she saw the way Scott's eyes hardened on Chance, that he dropped his duffle bag to the floor and was ready to lunge. She slapped a palm on his chest. "Scott, don't."

"It's that guy from last night."

Chance's stomach clenched. He stood ready to defend himself.

"He's apologized." Avery still held Scott firmly in place.

Chance could see that didn't pacify the light-haired man whose face was bleeding red with anger.

"He deserves a kick in the head." Scott advanced regardless of Avery's hand.

It was too ingrained in Chance not to take a fighting step, and when he did, Scott shoved him back. Chance snapped a hard fist across Scott's jaw, sending him stumbling. Blood shot out in a spray, covering the front of Scott's shirt, Avery's left arm.

"Stop it, please." Avery's voice boomed with authority that caused both men to freeze and take a breath. She moved in between the two of them, first looking at Scott. When she reached out and touched his face with fingers both gentle and caring, Chance felt an unexpected twinge of jealousy.

"You'll be all right." She turned his head with her fingertips, produced a tissue from somewhere. Lightly, she dabbed at Scott's nose. Chance watched with the childish wish that it was he that had gotten hurt.

"Go to the bathroom and wash up," Avery instructed. "I'll meet you back here in a minute for practice."

"I don't want to leave you alone with this goon," Scott snarled, holding the bloodied tissue to his nose.

She kept her back to Chance as she spoke soothingly. "I'll be all right. Chance is not going to repeat what happened last night, are you?" Her head barely turned over her shoulder.

What had he done? He'd given her a rather mean brush-off on the dance floor—that much he remembered. Since he couldn't remember anything more, the uncertainty skipping through his system made him itchy to get out of there.

"I should be going." Chance shouldered past her but she tagged his arm.

"Not so fast," Avery said, then gently nudged Scott out.

After Scott had left, Avery shut the door, turned and looked at him. "He was very angry about last night. I'm sorry if he hurt you." Her caring eyes examined him and even though she didn't touch him, Chance found the gesture deeply comforting.

He'd never had anyone apologize for a threat. Not even his parents, who had not intervened in his and Kurt's battles. Chance had grown up thinking that fights were part of life—part of his day, like eating breakfast or showering.

Embarrassed she had seen him strike out so easily, even more mortified that he'd done something last night he'd forgotten about, he thought she probably would not want him to come back to class.

"I'm sorry," he said again, and the raw tone of his voice made him defensive. He tried to pass her. "I think I should go now."

But she held him back with a light tug of his sleeve. "Tell me," she eyed him curiously. "That punch was instinctual. Professional?"

He snickered and reached for the knob. He might as well have been, only he'd been fighting for survival for so long, he'd never taken the time to learn the art of it.

Her eyes wandered his face with care. Without warning, emotion tightened like a band around his heart. "Look, I'm sorry that happened," he said. "And for whatever else I did." Afraid she'd seen too much, too soon, he opened the door and went out.

THREE

Avery shut the door of the rehearsal hall. The faint thudding of music seeped through the walls where next door a funk class was just beginning.

He was an interesting, if not puzzling man, Chance Savage. Her heart had nearly lodged in her throat from surprise when she'd walked into class and saw him. He was hard to miss. Like a storm on the horizon with clouds and sky so dark and fierce, your eyes were drawn to the frightening beauty just to see what it would do.

As she crossed the floor to the sound system, she thought of last night. He'd been lurking at the bar when she and Scott first entered Bruisers, his mysterious form a standout among the artfully dressed patrons there to dance.

That she'd found her gaze drifting back to him more than once, had bemused her. He had danger written all over him, and she'd never been a risk taker. One look at Chance as he'd cut into her dance with Scott, and a delicious thread now dangled inside of her she had never felt before.

Last night, as she and Scott, Justin, and Inessa had enjoyed drinks at a corner table, Chance had sauntered over. It was easy to see he was completely smashed: he practically tripped and fell onto the table. He slurred and laughed, but the undeniable hurt in his eyes was not easily masked by the giddiness brought on by being drunk. The scene had captivated her, as if she was watching some sort of tragic movie unfold.

"Here's the party," Chance said, leaning on the table,

nearly causing it to tip.

Justin and Scott clamped down, holding the table in place. Chance's stormy eyes flicked over every face at the table, finally singling her out. She met his penetrating gaze equally.

Avery had learned that to really look at someone, even to the point that they squirmed from the pressure of it, opened a person up like unwrapping a gift. She could thank her brothers for that. A man that could take her gaze like Chance had either nothing to hide, or something deep inside he desperately wanted found.

"How'd you rate," Chance started, addressing everyone but keeping his taunting eyes on her, "having miss-holier-than-thou in your company?"

"Have a seat." Justin tugged on Chance's sleeve but Chance jerked free, stumbled back and cursed. The bottle he held swung hazardously from his finger tips.

"No thanks. Don't wanna interrupt." He lifted the bottle to his lips and drank, swiping his mouth with the back of his hand. Then he brought the bottle down on the table with a crash that startled everyone.

Scott jumped up. "Should I get security?"

"Simmer down, simmer down mister nice guy." Chance reached out to pat Scott's shoulder but Scott jerked out of reach. "Bet you're as nice as a boy scout."

"Why don't you join us, Chance?" Avery asked pointedly. One thing she'd learned from having bossy brothers was to speak up, no matter how uncomfortable it made things.

Chance looked right at her and swayed. Then he leaned toward her over the length of the table, licking his lips into a grin. "I got a better idea. Why don't you and I go back to my apartment? Ditch mister nice guy here and we can do some dancing in the sheets."

"That's enough." Scott stood again.

Ignoring him, Chance blinked heavily at her. "Yeah. I'll teach you some moves that will rock that beautiful body of yours."

Scott edged closer, his hands snatching the fabric of Chance's shirt.

"He's not serious." The shudder of pleasure that rammed Avery's system shamed her. Calmly, she put a restraining hand on Scott's arm to pull him back down into the seat "It's clear that Chance is not himself tonight."

"Oh, I'm all here, missy. I'm all here. This is me—Chance Savage. You either like him or you don't and I don't really give a hill of—" Chance fell flat on the table, his arms straight out to his sides. The bottle crashed to the ground.

His face was right in front of her, and Avery looked at him as Scott rambled angrily and Justin decided what to do. A few nosey patrons nearby paused for a look and for some reason, it bothered her.

As Justin and Scott stood to gather him up, she gently pushed the hair off of his face. Even out cold he looked troubled, his handsome features crimped and twisted. She and Inessa helped drag him out to Justin's car where he lay like a discarded doll in the back seat.

Avery couldn't take her eyes off the vehicle as it disappeared into the night, and she hadn't stopped thinking about him since.

Reflecting on the incident, she went about readying the studio for her private rehearsal with Scott. Her life had been fairly constrained, she knew that. She was a girl who taught ballroom dance, a girl whose parents had introduced her to the finer things early in life and she gravitated to them by choice. Her older brothers and parents still liked to screen the men in her life.

She doubted Chance Savage had anyone screening the females in his life. Everything about him spoke of roots contradictory to the sort she had blossomed from.

Avery liked to know what she was doing today and what she would be doing tomorrow. Certainties were a must. Spontaneity and diversion were things she considered carefully before engaging in.

The music she had played that night in class trickled in her head. To find Chance a new student in her adult ballroom class disrupted the smooth and predictable world she had created for herself.

It wasn't that she couldn't deal with the occasional disruption. As a teacher, it was a given to expect a certain amount each day. But she avoided any distraction that she could help.

She was sure Chance would present a distraction.

Still, she felt a sense of relief that he had been in class. Why she cared, fascinated her. She didn't know him at all. He was a man, and he could take care of himself. But there was something achingly vulnerable underneath the layers of anger he cloaked himself with.

What she couldn't figure was why he was taking a ballroom dance class. She'd been teaching long enough to know the type—eager perfectionists with an eye out to socialize—Chance Savage definitely did not fit the profile.

To nourish her thoughts of him, she put back on the Johnny Mathis CD she often used for teaching and let it fill her head as she plucked stray water bottles and waited for Scott to return. Chance had picked up the steps fairly well for a man claiming never to have danced before.

He'd also slugged Scott with the ease of a cough. She wondered what he did for a living. At one glance, he might be a ski or beach bum.

But his clothes were too nice for a bum. She'd noticed that when she'd laid her left hand on his shoulder and felt the softness of raw silk. He'd been dressed in dark plum tonight. So dark, if she'd not been close enough, she'd have guessed the color to be black. And he'd worn decent shoes. Yet Chance's dark hair dared to be tamed, his scruffy jaw had not been shaved.

"Huh," she said aloud, stopping at the trash. She dumped an armload of cans, bottles and empty snack bags into the bin then grabbed the floor duster.

Beginning the long back and forth trek across the length of the floor, she continued to challenge herself with this game of figuring out who he was. Avery decided Chance must be in some field of the creative arts. Nowhere else would you find someone so bohemian.

Though he'd apologized for what had happened at Bruisers, she had not forgotten his words, and another shudder raced through her recalling them even now. She could appreciate a man who wouldn't cave under pressure and say anything, do anything he wanted. But he'd been intoxicated, she reminded herself. Perhaps he hadn't known what he'd said.

But what was she doing, dissecting last night. *You know better.* She propped the broom in the corner of the room and crossed brusquely to turn off the music. Dance had taught her many things, not the least of which was self-discipline. She could keep arms-length between her and Chance Savage. He was her student, that was all. It would be easy.

Chance hadn't worn a tie in years, with the exception of his parents' funeral a month ago. As he walked through the halls of Pleasant Grove High School behind Justin, he tugged at it. The accessory felt like a collar, and reminded him just why his rebellious spirit had chosen to be an artist – never to wear a leash.

The place was a mad house. He didn't remember school

being so loud. Everywhere kids talked and laughed, walking, shoving—swearing. *Things have changed,* he thought wryly. He'd been thrown in detention for swearing.

Justin knew everybody, and was well-liked. That didn't surprise Chance, who tried to look as comfortable as his friend as they made their way through the stifling crowd.

"How long is maternity leave, anyway?" he asked Justin.

"Two months. Hey, how ya doing?" Justin waved at students, greeting them with his usual cheer. Chance was ridiculously nervous—butterflies in the gut, sweaty-palm nervous.

The room he was to occupy was bright and cluttered with supplies. Six long tables faced the teacher's table at the front of the room. Everything from easels to pottery wheels to ceramic ovens to plaster statues stood ready along the walls. Paint pots were piled in green plastic tubs. Oil tubes, paint brushes and watercolors filled red and white boxes like colorful toys. Canvases were stacked in a corner near a small stage where live models could pose.

"Here's the place." Justin took him to the desk centered against the front wall. It was the only clean surface in the room. Chance set down his portfolio and personal supplies, taking another look around the room as he tugged at his tie again. Then the first teenager entered.

"Hey Mr. Wilde." The girl smiled coquettishly.

"Chrissy."

"You subbing for Mrs. Allman?"

"No, my best friend is. You be nice to him, 'kay?"

Chrissy looked Chance over, then smiled.

"See you at lunch, dude." Justin headed for the door. "In the teacher's lounge. Have one of the kids point it out."

Chance nodded. The steady hands he relied on for his craft shook embarrassingly. He stood at the desk and watched the talking, laughing kids file in. Twenty-six in all, he counted.

More comfortable behind a canvas than in front of an

audience, he cursed his foolishness for making the deal with Justin to begin with. Since he'd been given the teacher's outline a few days earlier, he was familiar with the lesson plans. He didn't feel inadequate, just nervous.

Once the bell rang, his knees stiffened. Every eye in the classroom was on him and a hush filled the air.

"Okay," he began, "I'm Chance Savage. I'll be substituting for your teacher the next few weeks."

Almost instantly, the students began to whisper and chat. Not sure if he should bowl on or try to get their attention, Chance grabbed his portfolio, hoping his credentials would at least buy him some interest. "I'm an artist, not a teacher, so bear with me here."

"What kind of artist?" Somebody called out.

"I paint women."

That silenced the group. A few boys snickered. The girls' faces broke into intrigued smiles.

Chance opened his portfolio and the silence crisped. The class's focus was drawn to his sketches. Though he had some nudes in the book, he skipped those as he showed each sketch, discussing why he chose the subject, the setting. Why he settled on the angle, what to emphasize, how to decide what colors to use.

Half-way during the display, he got a full discussion going and by the end of class, he relaxed. A few curious students loitered behind as he readied for the next class. Unaccustomed to idle teenage chatter, he merely smiled at them and straightened the desk top. With a glance at the clock he took in a breath.

Only six more hours to go.

Most of the staff brought lunches, ordered take-out, or

took off, Chance noted as Justin handed him a sack lunch he'd grabbed from the ala carte section of the cafeteria. They headed toward on an old, green couch situated by a window where they could look out over the empty football field. Loosening his tie, Chance fell into the couch with a sigh.

"You gonna make it?" Justin pulled out a sandwich.

Chance dug into his bag. "It wasn't that bad."

"The kids are pretty good, if you can relate to them instead of just being a holier-than-thou teacher."

Chance's gut squirmed at the mention of the phrase. Justin told him what had happened the night he'd made a fool of himself in front of the beautiful ballroom teacher, and he'd sworn he'd never go back to her class.

"Hey." Justin smiled just over Chance's shoulder and rose from the couch.

In the middle of chewing a potato chip, Chance glanced around to see who Justin was addressing. The chip lodged in his throat. Avery stood with a pleasant smile on her face and a salad in her hand. She wore a soft ivory blouse and cream-colored slacks, creating an angelic vision.

Chance shot up, clearing the chip with a thick swallow. Amusement lit her blue eyes and he had the sinking feeling it was aimed right at him.

"Want to join us?" Justin asked, pulling a chair over for her.

She nodded. "I'd like that very much."

"This can't be real," Chance muttered.

As they sat down, Chance reached for his bottled juice and opened it. The sweat that had finally calmed down at the end of his last class was back in full bloom.

"It's nice to see you again, Chance," she said.

How could he look her in the eye when he'd been so insulting? It was chokingly humiliating, and to his horror he could see that his hands were shaking as he set down the juice bottle. "You can't be serious," he said on a self-depreciating laugh.

"But I am." Primly she held her fork, ready to spear a leaf of lettuce.

His appetite had vanished. He glared at Justin. "Justin didn't tell me you worked here."

"I imagine he didn't. I teach ballroom," she began as Justin grinned. "The school has a very advanced competitive program."

"No kidding." Chance shot a look around the lounge. "You and your partner?"

She laughed. "Yes, as a matter of fact."

"Great."

"He rarely eats in here, no need to worry. You're taking Maria's class while she's on leave?"

Chance nodded, still avoiding looking at her. The knots in his stomach would not go away until she left. He sat back, uninterested in finishing his meal, only in getting out of there.

The taunting grin Justin wore caused Chance's fingers to flex. He'd ring Justin's neck before the day was over. "Well." Crushing his bag in both hands Chance stood. "I'm out of here."

"So you're an artist." Avery asked. Challenge was in her blue eyes and he tried to ignore what it did inside of him.

Chance looked down at her. She shouldn't be giving him the time of day. Was she enjoying that he'd been an idiot, now rubbing his nose in it?

"What is your forte, Chance?" As she chewed, her rosy lips formed a pouting heart. Her gaze pointedly held him, without the least indication that she was going to let him go.

Chance didn't give her an answer, just stared into her eyes. If she was trying to make a fool out of him he'd not stick around and let her. If she was trying to make him feel like she really was better than he was, well, it was too late for that.

"Dude, sit down," Justin said.

Without shifting his gaze to Justin, Chance said, "I'm finished here." Then he strode from the teacher's lounge without looking back. The last face he wanted to see was a face he was now going to find in his life every day for the next two months.

FOUR

All he could think was that he needed a drink. With the first day of teaching finally under his belt, Chance's adrenaline drained as if he were a popped water balloon. After the last group of laughing teens filed from the room, he almost sunk to the floor behind the desk.

Instead, he erased the black board of his example sketches showing how the angle of a solitary object could change the mood of a piece. His shirt was hopelessly wet and he stunk. He was sure he couldn't continue in such a frazzled state for the next three months.

A noise at the door had him turning. Avery was there with that same smile she'd had on her face when he'd left her in the lounge. Her expression wasn't quite as amused, veiled as it was with something he couldn't put a finger on.

Slapping the eraser in the metal lip of the chalkboard, he wiped his chalky hands together. "What do you want?"

She clasped her hands before taking slow, elegant steps toward him. "Have I said something to offend you?"

He wanted to laugh and would have had her tone, the look in her eyes, not been completely sincere. Planting both fists on the top of the desk, he leaned toward her. "Why are you talking to me?"

"Should I not?"

For a moment he ground his fists, felt tension in his jaw. She was good at playing the sophisticated innocent. "I insulted you at Bruisers and you pretend like I didn't."

"You apologized. I accepted. As far as I see it, it's over."

She stopped in front of the desk.

He narrowed his eyes. "What do you want?"

"You're still angry about something."

"I'm just wondering why you'd want anything from a guy who—"

"And I just told you, that's over. I've forgotten it, perhaps you should as well. Tell me about your work."

"I paint. I draw." He gestured to the room. "And right now, I teach."

"I'd like to see some of your pieces." He shook his head. "But you're an artist. Isn't that what you do? Show your work?"

"When I have someone interested in buying, maybe. Even then, I'm selective."

She tilted her head at him. "I see. How lucky for you. I had no idea artists could pick and choose."

"You thought we were all starving gypsies?" He snickered, breaking his taut pose to gather his things. "I'd expect as much from—" He stopped himself.

"No, please go on," she said, her tone carrying intrigue.

Lifting his portfolio and his supplies, he moved out from behind the desk but she blocked him. For a moment they stood looking at each other. He smelled her perfume again. Suddenly he saw her dressed in all white in a field of colorful flowers. The flowers would be in her arms, tucked in her hair in an inviting gesture of innocence. The sky behind her would be wild blue.

As his eyes stayed with hers, her hand lifted. A fantasy flashed through his mind of her touching him – anywhere, everywhere – and his heart pounded dreaming of it. But her fingers gently took his portfolio and it slipped from his grasp. He didn't stop her, was helpless to, caught in the captivating aura of her. She didn't step back when she opened it, rather she turned in such a way that her side now brushed his chest.

A bolt of heat jagged through him. Slowly, she turned each page.

She took her time looking at the drawings. She paused at the nudes, without showing any change in her expression or her body language. After she had gone through the entire book, she closed it with reverence and her eyes lifted to his.

"They're beautiful."

He tried to read her. Her expression was as blank as an empty canvas and he reached for the portfolio and tugged. She held it still.

"There are only women in your book," she said.

"Because that's all I do."

Her brow lifted slightly and a glimmer of a smile lit her lips. He tugged again and found her unyielding.

"Why?" she asked.

"My drawings."

"Why only women?"

It was something that had plagued him since his youth, something even he couldn't completely understand, this need he had to paint women – to understand why they did what they did to him. He shifted, finally putting some space between them as he took a step back on a sigh. "Fine. Keep them." He turned to go but she spoke.

"I'd like that very much."

"Why?"

"Because I don't know any artists."

"You don't know me."

"I know part of you—your name. I know you take ballroom dance one night a week and that you deliver a hard punch."

He snickered, rubbing his jaw. "That's nothing."

"You draw exquisitely. And you draw women, a fact I find very interesting."

"It's just something I do."

It's much more than that, Avery thought as she took a step closer to him. She liked that the move stole the fire from his eyes. That it took the angry words from his mouth and his emotions stumbled close to the surface.

"It's something you do brilliantly. May I take this home with me?"

His stormy eyes stilled with suspicion and flattery. Clutching the portfolio to her breast tightly, she meant for him to see that she would not give them back until she was ready to.

"Whatever," he said and strode for the door.

"I'll give them to you at dance class," she told him. His furious stride froze and a quiet smile lifted her lips. He didn't turn back around.

Chance almost drove to a bar right from the high school, so flooded with discomfort he thought he'd die if he didn't get some relief, fast. But Justin had very subtly warned him that he couldn't drink during his substituting gig. In fact, he'd told him he'd have to watch his steps and clean up his act, which Chance had unwisely agreed to. Now, he was itching inside.

Jamming his hands through his hair, he paced the kitchen of the apartment like a caged wildcat. There was a six-pack in the fridge screaming to him. Justin was gone, and his bones yearned for calm.

Limiting himself to just one would be futile. Still, he hung on the refrigerator door and stared at the bottles with his mouth watering. Rubbing the back of his hand across his lips, he could practically taste the stuff as the antsiness in him intensified.

Pathetic, he thought, drooling over the amber liquid in the bottles. He slammed the door, hating that he'd given Justin his word. He hated more that he'd decided it was time he showed his friends, himself, that he could get through a day without drowning in a few bottles.

He strode through the apartment, twitchy as a dog with fleas. His mouth hadn't stopped watering and with the vision of the six-pack fresh in his mind, wasn't going to. He'd have to get his mind on something else fast.

Taking his supplies back to his room, he set a blank canvas on an easel and stared at it. Closing his eyes, he took in a deep breath. He could see her – Avery - on the cold lines of an empty couch. She was relaxed, confident and sure lying across it, looking right at him. The stark contrast of her ivory skin against dull grey came at him first. But her soft, rounded, female form came into his mind next. Her softness would only be emphasized against the unforgiving harshness of the settee—a sculpted calf, the long line of leg pulled up with invitation. The only color would be the slight blush on her skin. Blush that came not from being the focus of his eye – but knowing she was the desire of it. One sheer scarf would be draped over her, only hinting at mysteries and secrets her body held.

His blood coursed through his veins. He pulled out his brush and began organizing the lines of where she would lie.

Why hadn't she left him alone today? She had deliberately sought him out more than once. That confused and intrigued him, especially after he'd been crass and rude. He'd never thought a woman like her would take a second look at a man like him.

She had his drawings. Most women found them exciting for their own purposes. More often than he could remember women begged him to sketch them. His hands, his brushes, his smile, were all tools he'd used more than once to seduce his subjects.

Michelangelo's Avery wouldn't be easily seduced, and he

didn't want to seduce her. Oh, his body could easily take her, enjoying her luscious beauty as a traveler enjoys a tempting dessert in another land, knowing he'll never savor it again. But in his mind he couldn't. It was always that way with something he considered too pure to touch. He and Avery were poles apart, and he knew better than to try for something out of reach.

The thought brought the familiar ache of injustice to him, her purity...his imperfections.

But she was a perfect subject to study. To draw and paint. Immortalizing perfection without the need to take creative license would be something he'd rarely done before.

With the lines of the settee in place, he stood back and let out a breath. In his mind he could all but see her there and the frustration was bittersweet.

She was being too nice to him. Had she any idea how hard it was for a guy like him to be faced with something that tormented him? And women tormented him. It seemed calculated, cruel, her overtures. They had to be premeditated. Experience had taught him that most of what people dealt you was meant to exploit you for gain.

He felt the rushing need for a drink.

Setting down his tools, he ran his hands over his face as the disgusting feeling of dread seeped into him. There was no other explanation for her interest. She had to want something.

He started from a heavy knock on the front door. Not expecting anyone, he hesitated answering but the pounding grew insistent. Then he recognized the vehemence with which it was delivered.

He took himself to the door even though his body pulled him toward the refrigerator – toward those bottles.

Pulling open the door, he stood firm, staring into his brother's eyes.

It had been weeks since Chance had seen Kurt, their

parents' funeral their last meeting. That day they'd sat on opposite sides of the chapel, consoling different sets of relatives, and stayed far away from each other.

Chance knew this day, and many more like it, were inevitable. His brother wanted something, and Kurt always got what he wanted.

"We need to talk." Kurt looked him up and down and took a step through the frame, butting purposefully into Chance's chest. Ever since Chance could remember, Kurt had taken every opportunity to ignite a fight. Chance let the obvious affront pass and shut the door.

"Say whatever you came to say and get out."

"You thought about what I said?"

"Why would I think about it? I told you, no."

"I've talked to Frank. We can do whatever we want."

As his parents' long-time friend, Frank Nesbitt was loyal. But as their lawyer, he was as flaky as sand. He would take sides with Kurt, Chance figured that. Kurt was the good boy. Chance was the prodigal son.

"It's not about what we want," Chance said. "That's why I'm not changing my position."

Kurt looked around, hands casually hanging at his sides. Chance watched him carefully, waiting for the first sign of a fight. It was hard to believe they were related. Except for their height, there was no familial resemblance.

When Chance had been a kid, he'd been so terrified of his white-haired, icy-blue eyed brother, he'd thought all blondes were monsters. Time and maturity had taught him that monsters came in many forms, but blood monsters could be the most vicious.

"Then I haven't convinced you." Kurt moved around the small living room carelessly picking up whatever he pleased, looking at it and just as carelessly putting it back.

"And you won't."

"You're holding out – on purpose."

"Even if I was, and I'm not, you deserve it."

"I deserve everything!" Kurt exclaimed, his body tensing. "You're such a loser." They stared at each other then, the air around them swarming as if laden with deadly bees. "What do you want with the house, anyway?" Kurt's voice was near a growl.

"They left me the house, you the money. That's the way they wanted it."

"Since when did you care about what they wanted?"

"I could ask you the same question."

Kurt advanced and was in Chance's face, breathing hard. "I should be getting it all."

"But you're not," Chance spit back. "Get over it."

Kurt was boiling; Chance recognized the signs. They stood facing each other like snarling lions. Chance's heart raced with his breath, the tendons and muscles in his arms twitching. When Kurt's hand shot out and a sharp finger pointed at him he automatically whipped up his fists.

Kurt's quick glance at Chance's ready fists curled his lip. Without a word, he started bouncing on the balls of his feet, his mouth twisting into a snarl. "It's been a long time."

The last thing Chance wanted to do was fight. He'd only been reacting, like he had with Scott. Now the pump of adrenaline fired through his blood with the familiarity of a nasty fever.

Taking the first shot, he caught Kurt across the jaw, just like he had Scott. And, like Scott, he grazed the thick blood vessel in Kurt's nose and it spouted off like a geyser. Stunned, Kurt stopped a moment, his fingers touching the wet ooze of red. Hard as rock, his eyes shifted to Chance.

Nimbly Chance bounced, waiting. Kurt lunged but Chance dodged out of his way. With aggravation Kurt swung around, capturing Chance's neck in his forearm, bringing his head down, squeezed against his hip. Then he proceeded to slam punches into his face.

Within seconds, Chance had Kurt's upper thigh in a hold with one arm, while his fist rammed into Kurt's genitals. Buckling over, Kurt fell to the floor just as the front door opened and Justin walked in.

Justin lunged toward the two of them then abruptly stopped in his tracks. He looked at a crumpled Kurt, then at Chance whose face was bloodied.

"You all right?" he asked.

Chance wiped at his mouth, looked at the blood smeared on the back of his hand and nodded, his eyes on Kurt.

Kurt groaned as he pulled himself up, his hands cupping his crotch. He glared at Justin, shot one more piercing glare at Chance and hobbled through the door and left.

Blowing out a breath, Chance leaned over, hands on his knees, head bowed. Justin shut the door. "Dude - your face."

Chance nodded without even seeing the damage and went to the bathroom with Justin behind him. It wasn't that bad, he thought, looking in the mirror. He'd have some nice bruises, a minor scrape under his right eye where Kurt's class ring had grazed him but as injuries went, it was mild.

He'd had a lot worse.

Justin stayed in the doorway. "I thought you two were civil."

Searching for a washcloth, Chance let out a sneer.

"Did you know he was coming?"

Chance shook his head. It was his brother's normal mode of operation: the element of surprise. Dabbing at the bloodied spots, he avoided his own eyes in the reflection.

"You gotta show me something I can use," he told Justin.

"Didn't look like you needed my stuff."

"Anybody can hit the balls. I want something that will get him off my back permanently."

Justin shifted in the door. It amazed him that Chance didn't even wince as he cleaned himself up. Amazed him even more the tone of acceptance in Chance's voice. "Man, Jamie and I outgrew that stuff a long time ago." Chance laughed but Justin caught the bitterness in it. "Your parents, they never stopped you?"

"Mom hated it. She'd beg us to stop." Only the slightest hesitation in the way Chance folded the washcloth before applying it to his face again hinted at any emotion. "Kurt would just take her outside and lock the sliding glass door." Finished, Chance set aside the washcloth, looking himself over. "Dad said it would toughen us up - make us men."

Justin couldn't help the sadness he felt. Hopelessness, dark and final, set in Chance's eyes. He'd put up with his friend's lack of employment, drinking and partying, hoping friendship would be the branch Chance could use to pull himself out of the river he was drowning in. Having a decent relationship with his own older brother made it hard to stomach what he saw between Chance and Kurt. "Let me show you a few things before class," Justin said.

Chance's eyes widened. "I'm not going to class."

"Then I guess you'll keep hitting balls, bro." Justin turned, leaving the bathroom.

After a groan, Chance followed him into the living room. "What is it with you and this dancing thing? I'm never going to be Michael Jackson, Fred Astair - whatever."

"Neither am I. But if you want to know the secrets of taking guys like your brother down, you'll keep coming to class. In fact, for every class you go to, I'll spend that much time showing you take-downs. Deal?"

With a nod of his head, Chance set his hands out and ready for Justin with a weary smile. "What are you doing? Trying to keep me busy every hour of every day?"

Justin shrugged with a grin before he lightly jabbed at

Chance. That was exactly what he wanted to do.

FIVE

Chance hung behind the rest of the couples, knowing his face would raise eyebrows. The seclusion didn't bother him; he'd always been a loner. He answered suspicious looks with well aimed glares meant to silence.

He stood with his back against the wall, watching the other couples practice steps. He wasn't going to commit to dancing, so what was the point in participating in idle talk and useless practice.

There were two reasons he was there. He needed the skills Justin could share with him to finally put an end to this physical battle he had with Kurt. And he was intrigued by Avery Glenn.

When she entered, her gaze swept the class as if she was looking for something. He would only let himself fantasize for a moment that it was him. The fantasy caused him to keep himself hidden from her view as long as he could, slowly moving himself along the back wall, just to see what her eyes did.

Finally, they lit on him. She stared for a moment, a moment that heated his skin when he saw the flash of concern on her face.

Immediately she crossed to the music system. She wore all black again. Chance figured it must be because she knew she looked great in the color. Or it was simply what she wore when she taught.

The tempo of the music was slow and she turned, facing the group. "Good evening ladies and gentlemen. What dance will we be doing to this?" she asked.

"Waltz," somebody answered.

The answer made her smile and Chance was glad. Her smile was soothing. He couldn't help that it made him take in a deep breath. Something drew him to her. He was fighting the pull, and it would be more difficult now, being bribed into coming to the classes.

He listened to her explain the finer points of waltz, and his minds eye conjured up an image of her in an ivory gown, form-fitting around the bodice, flowing to her feet in a whirl of glittering sparkles. He saw her dancing around the floor of a gilded ballroom. Though he only saw her image clearly, a man's dark form held her. Knowing he could never complete a picture so exquisitely, he closed his eyes, pushing the image from his mind as well as the distaste of impossibility.

He would have to paint the vision.

"Chance?"

Her call brought him out of his daze. Everyone was looking at him.

"We're ready to start. Will you dance with me?" She was extending her hand to him and again, somewhere inside of him he enjoyed the gesture.

The light melody was pretty, not like anything he chose to listen to. Instantly he thought if he could put her face, her body and spirit to music, it would sound like this; angelic hope, infinite loveliness. A melody of Heaven.

The other couples had started dancing. She held her arms out, looking into his face as he approached. "What happened?"

"I ran into a wall."

Urging him forward with the gentle pressure of her hands, she studied his injuries with intense interest. The concern he'd seen fleetingly on her face when she had first laid eyes on him was there again, though with their close proximity, she veiled it some. After a few moments, he felt the weight of her gaze shift as she looked out over the class, correcting individuals who needed help.

"Excellent," she told one couple.

Chance liked that he was an accessory in her arms. For a fleeting second, his life had purpose.

He caught the scent of her as they turned, sweet and floral, like she'd been sitting in that field of flowers he'd envisioned. Her ivory skin was beginning to show a glint of sweat. He liked that it didn't bother her.

When her head turned and her eyes met his, his stomach fluttered. "You're doing very well tonight."

"Thanks to you."

When they moved on to fox trot, she left him standing at the front of the class as she demonstrated the basic step. He tried to follow along, finding it easier than he had thought.

It was his intention to make a quick exit when class was over but she stopped him.

"Chance, would you mind staying for a moment?"

"Is your partner coming?"

She smiled at his obvious discomfort. "Actually, he's not. He's away for a few days."

Chance's nerves uncoiled. One confrontation was enough for the day. He stood by the door as she finished chatting with loitering students before they were finally alone. Without saying anything to him, she crossed to the music. Her black dance pants hugged the long lines of her legs, hinting at the hard, rounded hamstrings along the back of her thighs. Her black blouse was fitted and unbuttoned to the center of her chest, where a lacy black undergarment peeked through.

Again she put on soft, delicate music. With the melody sweetly filling the silence of the large room, she turned to him, her hands clasped as she slowly walked toward him. "I was hoping you would practice with me."

"Me?" His heart began to pound. "I can't dance like your

partner."

"That's not what I'm after." She looked up into his face with a gentle smile.

"What are you after?" he asked. Her lips had just a hint of color, but it was enough for him to take a long, second look at them.

"I've had a rough day," she said. "The waltz relaxes me."

"But, I don't dance."

"But you do." She held up her arms.

"Waltz is so rigid."

"Not really. When I hold my body in form, the rest of me - my mind, my soul, can then be free to think, to feel, to understand what is bothering me. I know it sounds contradictory but it helps. Do you mind?"

He felt ridiculous. He'd step on her feet, ruin her oasis of relaxation and she'd be sorry she'd ever thought about her respite dance being with him.

He hemmed a moment but finally nodded. With a pleased smile she slid her hand into his and urged him to the center of the room. An involuntary breath shuddered from his system. Rather than look over his shoulder, as she had told him was the standard expression for the waltz, she kept her penetrating blue eyes on him.

They floated in the open box pattern of the dance and for the first few moments it was all he could do not to trip. "Keep your chin up, Chance," she said, "and your eyes on me."

"I thought I was supposed to grin insipidly out at the audience."

She smiled. "Not tonight."

He did as she told him, locking eyes with her. They didn't speak. The soft heavenly melody filled his insides, and he barely noticed that his palms weren't sweaty any more. That his heart had slowed and he hadn't made any mistakes.

"You're doing wonderfully," she said softly. Her head

tilted. "You've picked up so quickly, I can only assume artists and dancers think from the same side of the brain."

"I wouldn't know."

"What kind of music do you like?"

"Depends on my mood." He urged her along with his body.

"Ever work to music?"

"All the time."

"Rock?"

"Hard."

"I would believe that about you."

Chance pulled her closer. "Scary, aren't I?"

"I grew up with three older brothers. Men rarely scare me."

"I could have figured as much," Chance said. She was light and easy in his arms. The steps were coming naturally and he wasn't thinking about them at all as she led him around the room.

"You talk to men like you know them."

"Once you understand something, there's no reason to fear it. I find you interesting. And I most definitely don't understand you."

"So you're afraid of me?"

She'd not tell him that her insides quivered just looking at him, or that she couldn't stop thinking about him, yes, that made her very afraid of him. "I'm looking to get to know you." Avery had decided to face this fear head-on, sure once she knew him, she could move on.

She slowed them down, easing back from him, but still holding him in position.

Chance wondered why she wanted to get to know him when it would be such an obvious step down for her. Most women wanted something from him; intimacy, which he would never give. Oh, he could easily give a woman sex, but nothing more. His heart he held guarded inside, and would not allow anyone access to.

To model for him, be a one-nighter—that he could do and that he had done. Avery wrapped whatever she wanted up in a classy package, doing fancy steps to get to the point, whatever it was. But he'd figure it out soon enough. She'd probably use him and dump him. That was the pattern he was accustomed to.

He eyed her. He didn't have to let her. He could give in turn whatever she gave and if they hurt each other, disappointed each other, dumped each other - well, he'd figure they both got what they deserved.

"Do you mind that I want to get to know you?" she asked after his silence.

Habit had him forcing her to wait for his response. "I can live with that," he said finally.

Though she didn't let go of his hands, she did smile and nod. "Good. I have something for you." Her hands slipped from his and the emptiness left behind caused him to rub them together as he watched her cross the floor.

She opened the cabinet, pulling out his portfolio.

"These are wonderful." Again she thumbed through them. "I particularly like the one of the mother and daughter, and the woman at the window. Was it done in Paris?"

"You've been there?" He took the book, opening it to the drawing she was discussing.

"Yes. You captured the city beautifully in just the small space of the open window. The woman looks contemplative. You can see it even in her profile—very well done."

"Thank you."

"How do you do it? Capture life and hold it still like this?"

He lifted a shoulder. "When I see it in my head, it's alive. I try to bring that energy to the canvas. Techniques help, whites, glossy sheens and black for depth."

"Remarkable. Your parents must be very proud."

"They never said."

"Said?"

"They were killed in a plane crash a few months ago."

Her brows knit fast and hard. "I'm sorry."

Shrugging, he supposed he looked like he didn't care because he was trying so hard not to. "It was stormy. Visibility was bad. Dad flew the plane into the mountain."

"Yes, I remember hearing about that in the news. Do you have siblings?"

"A brother."

"How nice that you still have each other."

He snickered and turned, heading to the door. "I gotta head out. We both have class tomorrow. I don't know about you but I could use a little time to regroup."

As they approached the door, she said, "That was what tonight was for." She reached out and pulled on the knob for him. "Thank you. It was just what I needed."

His eyes skimmed her face and he realized that all of him felt relaxed as well. Her little exercise had worked. "See you tomorrow."

He went through the door not sure if he should be happy or worried that he was feeling better. She'd reached in fast. The familiar discomfort of a female hand groping for something inside of him was what kept him from taking another look at her before he got in his car.

Avery couldn't stop thinking about him. Here she was at school, finishing another ballroom class, and her mind was drifting again.

He was a reluctant man; a man hiding, protecting. Running away. Each day Avery had been careful to be friendly, and not too inquisitive – a trait she fell naturally into. Though she had not been able to get anything more than just general chit-chat from him since the night he'd come to dance class with his face battered, she was not discouraged. It didn't matter how long it took for her open the package. Along the way, each exposed lining was more interesting than the last.

He'd explained how he chose subjects to paint and she'd found that telling. He could be anywhere, see a woman doing something as mundane as choosing a can from a grocery store shelf to playing with a small child and a vision would come into his mind.

She was fascinated with the process, that something so intro-spective and comprehensive could come from one idea. Her first impression had been that most of his inspirations had to come from a sexual motive. His nudes had been tasteful, but highly sensual. It was easy to picture a woman naked, vulnerable, alone with a man like Chance, his dark, brooding eyes roving every inch of her as he painted. The very idea of it pleasantly teased her.

It was wrong of her to think like that. She'd not grown up a prude, but she considered herself a traditionalist. That was part of why she'd decided long before she'd started to date that she would be married before she gave herself to a man. It had been her mother's way, and the way Avery saw it, it was the smoothest way to avoid unnecessary entanglements that could choke a relationship if things didn't work out. But more than that, she valued the giver as much as the gift.

The men she had dated, though select they had been, had respected her way of thinking. Judging by Chance's lifestyle, or what she had seen of it, he might think her a prude. But Avery didn't care. She wanted to be able to live with herself when she put her head on her pillow every night, and she wasn't really looking at Chance as anything more than an interesting friend.

She wondered if he involved himself with the women he drew and painted. That was something she definitely would find out. But after watching the way his eyes lit with something both innocent and childlike as he described his work process, she knew sex had very little to do with his art.

One thing was obvious to her—that his need to express a vision that inspired him was just as great as her need was to dance when she heard music.

Maybe it was that she'd had a good life, that she was a dreamer and an optimist. She had the feeling Chance lacked that conviction. The more she observed him, the cocky way he first appeared seemed only a front for someone lost, still seeking fundamental reasons for being.

She was analyzing their relationship far too much, thinking about him more often than was safe. If she was at school, like she was today, she found herself watching for him in the halls.

Her curiosity wouldn't be over just because it was time for lunch.

Having grown accustomed to eating with him and Justin, her eyes sought them both out. She commanded her heart to calm. Chance's reckless smile broke right through her determination to keep him at arm's length and she found herself heading in the direction of where he sat with Justin.

She couldn't tell what his physique might look like, though her mind had conjured something lean and sculpted. In tune with color, texture, it didn't surprise her that he wore dark colors, like he had on today – deep muted tones with enough black to make him look like he was either moody or ominous. Or both.

She'd never met a man whose face was both masculine and boyish at the same time. She figured it was the angled lines in his jaw adorably softened by those deep dimples. Most certainly it was his round grey eyes that made her heart skip both with the instinct to nurture and the craving to love. His dark, unruly hair fell in soft curls and waves around his face. If the moody artist image was what he was after, she thought he'd achieved it quite nicely.

She sat in the chair opposite him and felt that stormy gaze hovering across the table at her. "Gentlemen," she said.

"Hey." Justin leaned over and peeked at her salad. "That looks good today. Think I'll go grab one."

Chance's mouth, wide, full and just a little mischievous, was turned up into a grin that heated her cheeks. "Good afternoon, Chance," she said, taking up her fork.

"You're always so formal."

"My parents are rather formal people."

"I like it."

A delightful tremor snaked to her belly and she pierced a bunch of field greens. "It's said that without the refinements of life, the monotony of day to day would be unbearable."

He pulled a sandwich out of his brown bag and looked at it curiously. "I don't think anybody in the cafeteria got that memo."

Avery laughed. "You have a sense of humor. I didn't think serious artist-types had them."

"We have to. Nobody takes us seriously. If we laugh at ourselves, then the days are bearable – with or without refinements."

Avery noticed a goggle of single women teachers making their way over to the empty table next to theirs. Their eyes were all on Chance. Dru Kinskie, tall, violin- shaped, redheaded and legendary for being aggressive with the single men, chose the seat nearest Chance's back. Avery stiffened a little.

The women settled in their chairs with their lunches, their conversation quieting as they kept their glances regularly aimed at Chance. Finally, Avery sent them a smile.

Dru got up and stood in front of Chance with her hand

extended. Her acrylic nails were painted gold. "You're subbing for Maria, right?"

Chance swallowed his bite and stood hospitably. He shook Dru's hand. "I am. Chance Savage."

"The artist." Dru slid back into her seat, twisting so that she faced him as he sat. "I'm Dru. I've seen your work."

"Oh, yeah?"

"A girlfriend of mine owns one. A nude I believe." With that, Dru crossed one bare leg over the other, her short skirt riding high enough to tease with the peek of firm thigh. "It's outstanding."

Chance glanced at the skin she'd bared for him. "Thanks."

With a salad in hand and a grin on his face, Justin sat back at the table, amused at the group of women leaning on their elbows anxiously.

"You really paint only women?" Becky Fairchild asked, pushing her black glasses up her stub nose.

Torn between the necessity to eat and the need to appear friendly, Chance shifted from facing his meal to facing the women. "Yeah, I do."

Dru's brow shot up. She and the other women exchanged looks of intrigue. The doughy woman chuckled and lifted her hand. "Where do we sign up?"

Chance forced an even smile, the one he used whenever he had a show, or met prospective clients. Inside, his nerves itched.

Avery poked her fork into her salad. Alarmingly, she found herself annoyed at the women's open flirtations. Chance only slightly blushed, she noticed. It made him even more adorable when those deep dimples squealed from the sides of his mouth.

"Nice to have met you." Chance turned back and took a bite from his sandwich.

"You too," Dru purred even though he was no longer looking. "We'll talk later."

No doubt this kind of googly-eyed admiration was common for him, Avery thought. What woman wouldn't want to be the focus of a man who immortalized women? But the twinge of jealousy in her stomach bothered her. She had never been the jealous type, secure in who she was and what she could offer in any relationship of her choosing.

"The word is out," Justin took his first bite.

"And it's only been a few days," Avery added, looking directly at Chance. "You did that well. I imagine a result of practice."

Chance's eyes flickered. Instantaneously she regretted the comment but she held his gaze. He didn't reply. She wanted to apologize, but the female in her felt ridiculously threatened with the table of women still eyeing him greedily.

Without responding to her quip, he continued to eat. Justin filled the uncomfortable quiet by rambling about how students couldn't identify an adjective over and adverb in his English classes.

When Chance finally finished and stood, Avery felt a rush to stop him and clear the air but Dru had already bolted up out of her seat.

"Mind if I walk back to class with you?" Dru asked, purposefully brushing into his side. "I've finished my lunch."

Chance's gaze swept over her. He crushed his brown bag in both hands. "Sure."

Avery sat back on a frustrated sigh and watched Dru's bare legs suggestively cross in a walk that looked like it belonged on a runway instead of down a high school hall.

Justin was grinning. She frowned. "Dru's fast," he said.

"Maybe he likes that." Avery gathered her things, uninterested in finishing the remainder of her salad. She wasn't going to ask if Justin knew what Chance liked. She was a woman who never sought information outside of the source. If Chance liked easy, fast women, she'd find that out for herself.

Walking back to the gym, she purposefully avoided his classroom.

Frank Sinatra was singing. The lonely tones, the haunting words of love had never bothered Avery before but the piercing message might as well have been an arrow lodged in her heart. The disappointment she had felt earlier that day was still inside somewhere and when dance class started and Chance wasn't there, she had to force herself not to think of wildly foolish alternatives – that Dru had talked him into letting her pose and then seduced him.

The ridiculousness of the situation shifted her into a laugh. They were just getting to know each other. He could and would do what he wanted. If what he wanted was to fall prey to a woman like Dru, then why should she care?

Besides, Chance wasn't her type. The danger factor, she kept reminding herself, was far too great.

Padding her ego with a shrug of common sense only worked until she saw him. She hadn't heard the studio door open. She was busy roaming in and out of couples, checking their form, making suggestions to see that Chance had entered, ten minutes late.

But suddenly he was there, leaning against the far wall of the studio, a mystic, shadowy form with predatory eyes. An indescribable tremor crept through her every limb. When that appealingly dimpled grin of his hit her from across the room, any thoughts of Dru, or of Chance's danger to her, vanished.

She took her time weaving through the waltzing couples, feeling the build of excitement in her veins as she neared him. He was watching her. Watching her unlike any man had ever watched her – as if he was memorizing every detail. She felt naked, and didn't care that she did. She stopped in front of him with her hands clasped casually behind her back. "You decided to join us."

"I decided that weeks ago." He brought his body away from the wall and stood close. "Am I too late?" His eyes searched hers.

She shook her head and put her hand out for him. The simple question carried a deeper meaning; she read that in his eyes, now waiting for her approval or dismissal. Her hand burned at his touch and that burn raced through the rest of her as she led him to an empty spot on the floor. *Where is your resolve, your strength?* she reminded herself.

"By the way," she looked right at him so that he would know that she was sincere, "I'm sorry for that comment I made at lunch today. It was uncalled for."

"What comment?"

It was nice of him to overlook it, and she smiled as she urged him into a waltz turn while the other couples followed suit. "We're working on a routine for a show."

"A show?"

"Yes." She moved them both out of the way of dancing couples. "The studio does shows occasionally. This one's kind of like a recital."

"But recitals are for kids."

"Not true."

"I'm not going to dance in front of people."

"The class will be dancing as a group. It's a chance for family and friends to come support their loved ones."

His snicker came from the depths of bitterness and neglect. "There's nobody I would invite to something like that."

"What about your brother?" His hands quickly tightened around hers before easing up again. He looked off over her shoulder, his face hard and blank. "You have friends and other family perhaps?"

He turned his face sharply to hers, the grey in his eyes chilled her. "There isn't anybody I'd invite," his tone was cold.

"But you'll participate," she told him.

He didn't respond and she waited, watching the mood on his face shift as if he was deciding. "We'll be dancing in formation," she added quickly. "If you don't come, there will be a hole."

His eyes narrowed as they darted along her face, finally falling on her mouth. The grey was stormy, intense. "Will I be dancing with you?" he asked, a boyish hope lined his tone and her heart skipped.

"If you'd like."

"It's the only way you'll get me on the floor."

"Well then," she said. "You have a partner."

She took them around the dance floor one last time in the waltz. It pleased her that he was beginning to relax more. His body had more give - that meant he was willing. It would be some time before he could lead sufficiently, but it would come. There was nothing more exciting to a woman than a man who knew how to lead a woman on the dance floor.

She liked that he remained after class. Casually leaning against the wall, he looked enticing, stirring her mind into a blur of wonder at why he had chosen to stay.

"You mind if I watch some real dancing?" he asked.

"Not at all."

When Scott came in, he shot a wary glance Chance's direction to which Chance gave a friendly nod.

Avery had danced for hard-to-please judges but this man made her more nervous than any of those. She went through her standard routines dismissing the dark vision of Chance poised against the wall. To her relief, she and Scott were quickly lost in the session, discussing weak spots they wanted to improve, new moves they wanted to try.

Chance shifted. Admiration pulsed through his limbs as he watched. The romantic lyrics of Johnny Mathis singing about that feeling stirred his heartbeat to a soft rhythm he had never felt before.

She was magical. He felt like a boy watching a prince dance with a princess. The two of them were perfectly balanced; their feet barely skimmed the floor. He found himself both enjoying the rehearsal and itching to dance with her again. Knowing he'd never dance with her and look like that, he felt a familiar dig at his inabilities and envy at Scott's.

Chance had never experienced jealousy where women were concerned – they had always come easily to him. The tiny threads now creeping into his system he found amusing and interesting. Maybe it was because she was so different than any woman he'd found himself attracted to.

He'd known both beautiful and unassuming women. But none possessed what he saw in Avery, a carefree, compassionate manner that promised unconditional friendship, or, he dared think – love. It was not something he'd come across in the many places his life had taken him.

Though he knew for certain that Scott was her dance partner and nothing more, to watch them create romantic illusions so believable created a knot of uncertainty inside he wasn't comfortable with. It shouldn't matter to him. They were just getting acquainted; she'd as much as told him that. It would be his responsibility to keep the friendship within the boundaries their respective lives demanded.

He'd never had to hold back from a woman before. If he'd seen one that stirred his interest, and he felt inclined, he pursued. This would be different. Avery was so far out of reach, he knew contentment would have to be complete with just a look – with paint and canvas. A sigh of resignation left him then.

After she and Scott finished, Chance was amazingly relieved. He felt even better when Scott left for the evening and they were alone again.

He crossed to her as she pulled her mass of curls up into a pony tail at the crown of her head. Her face was rosy, her skin glistening.

"You two are really good," he said, the awe fresh in his voice.

"Thank you. It takes a lot of hard work."

"It shows."

"No more than what you do, I'm sure."

He shrugged. He wondered if it would be within acceptable parameters to invite her over. "You busy now?"

"No." She tilted her head. "But I need to shower and clean up."

"I have a shower at my place," he suggested with a smile meant to tease.

Her smile mirrored his. "Lucky for me I brought a change of clothes."

"I promise to be good and stay in the living room."

"And then what?" she asked, collecting her black CD case. They headed to the door and she turned off the lights.

"I don't know. We could eat."

She opened the door and the light from outside cast an angelic glow on one side of her face. "How about you show me some of your paintings? Maybe let me try to paint?"

"Me teach you?"

"I'm teaching you."

"Then I guess that'd be fair," he said, opening the door for her.

SIX

His bathroom was white and plain, and as empty as an eggshell. The only sign that two men occupied the place was two navy towels that hung on the rod and a shaver propped to dry on the sink lip.

She dressed, hearing a far off clatter in the kitchen. Again she glanced at the door knob, verifying that it was locked. Her wide-eyed reflection peered back at her in the glass of a small medicine cabinet. She wiped the condensation away.

"What are you doing?" she asked herself. She'd never been so bold with a man. Taking a shower in his apartment? Her hands flew to her cheeks. *Get over it, Avery. This man invited you over for...*for what she wasn't exactly sure but she'd taken the bait so easily, it was almost frightening.

But women do this day in day out, what's the big deal?

She leaned on the sink, got closer to her face in the mirror. "The big deal is," she whispered to herself, "you're not like every other woman, you never have been. You've always wanted something more, something better. Something special."

I'm not compromising, she told herself. *I'm still the same Avery that I was an hour ago. I just showered in a different shower.*

She gathered her things with the resolve not to analyze but enjoy the moment, whatever it might bring. There was always the front door and she had two legs. She could walk out any time with her integrity intact.

But this wasn't about tempting integrity was it? She

stared in the mirror again. In the weeks she had gotten to know Chance casually at school, in ballroom class, he'd not struck her as all that dangerous, really.

Or am I justifying sudden weakness?

What if he came on to her, challenged more than her integrity? She was enveloped by a sudden shudder as the wonder of his lips against hers streamed through her head. Would she be able to stop at just a kiss under the hands of a man like him?

After a sigh, she reached for the door. She was Avery Glenn and Glenns don't let people, places or things change who they are inside. She'd lived that way for twenty- seven years. A man was not going to change that.

As Avery showered, Chance tried to keep from thinking about her all slick and shimmery under the water by whipping up some dinner, but it was useless. His mind flashed her image anyway.

He stuck his head in the cold of the refrigerator, hoping to cool the heat he felt building. It was predictably bare. Two bachelors that didn't spend a lot of time at home, neither with a great deal of money, never had more than the basics. There was eggs, bread, milk and what Justin called the Wilde staples for breakfast, so Chance made French toast and put out Justin's sour cream and jam.

He'd gone out on a twig asking Avery to come home with him, and had all but expected that twig to snap with her refusal. Michelangelo's Avery was in his apartment, in his shower even. It seemed unreal, and yet the water humming through the pipes confirmed that the beautiful creature was indeed under his roof.

For a moment he fantasized about that – possessing a

woman like Avery. If she were his, he would place her on a pedestal and just admire her, not even touch her, and that would be enough.

The strumming in his nerves had him laughing at the idea. That would last until he couldn't bear just looking any more. Until every part of him was so swollen with need for her, he'd detonate with a glance.

She came around the corner dressed in jeans and a red-knit top that followed every curve. She had text-book arms: well defined, long and elegant, and small breasts that he was sure were another perfect study. Though he'd seen plenty of women naked, both in the name of art as well as pleasure, he found a tastefully dressed woman even more stirring than a woman without clothing. Her hair was slightly damp, cascading everywhere, and he had the sudden urge to tangle his fingers in the blonde waves.

"Smells like breakfast," she said, joining him in the kitchen.

"French toast." He turned the first two pieces in the frying pan. Butterflies launched everywhere inside of him. He could smell his zesty soap on her. "It's all we had. That okay?"

Pushing up the sleeves of her shirt, she nodded. "So you cook and paint."

"And dance," he added. She smiled and he thought he would melt.

"You really are doing well with it, you know."

"I watch you and Scott and I...I think I'll never be able to do it that well."

Leaning her back against the counter there next to him, she looked up at him as he worked. "Don't think about it from the standpoint of competing. Are you enjoying it?"

The French toast sizzled. "I am."

She looked at him intently. There was that little boy in his face now, a little boy on the verge of a wonderful discovery.

The sight drew her heart into a fervent beat. Something about his head cast down as he focused on his task made her yearn to touch the side of his face.

"Let me set the table." She started opening drawers. "Where are your linens and silverware?"

"Linens?" he chuckled. "If you call paper napkins linens, they're in that pantry."

She opened the pantry and pulled out the only placemats there were: red straw, and set them on the table. Then she searched for the silverware.

"Third drawer down," he told her, setting the French toast on a plate.

By the time he'd finished cooking, she had red placemats, white napkins and had found matching red plastic cups he didn't even know they had. Her woman's touch made him smile as he set their plates down. She was eyeing the sour cream and jam with a quirked smile.

He pulled out her chair. "Try it."

"I thought our family was the only family that ate sour cream and jam on pancakes and waffles," she told him as she sat.

"It's Justin's family's thing."

Primly, she set her napkin on her lap. "And what about yours?"

He shrugged without looking at her. "We were a dull syrup family."

"Tell me about your dull syrup family." She spread the sour cream.

"I'd rather hear about yours."

She sensed he wasn't ready to talk about his family yet. That was fine, for now. "My brothers are all married and have children."

"They live around here too?"

"All of us Glenns are here."

"You close?"

She nodded, took a bite and let out a little hum of pleasure, realizing just how hungry she had gotten. When she opened her eyes, he was looking at her with the faintest curve to his lips. For a moment, she stared at his mouth. It broadened when he smiled, those full lips pulling back enough to tantalize. Compliments had always been easy for her to give, having been showered with them most of her life from her family. "You have a beautiful mouth."

She expected him to be pleased. A man as attractive as he surely had features pointed out and admired. The dark flash of something unsettling in his eyes was a shock to her. "I'm sorry, did I say something to offend you?"

He wiped at his mouth with his napkin. "No. French toast okay?"

But it lingered inside of her, the strangeness of that moment. She nodded, masking it with a smile. "You're good with bread."

He let out a deep laugh, settling back in his chair. "I thought you might be too formal to have a sense of humor." He resumed eating but looked at her with smiling eyes. It eased the troubled feeling away from her.

"I couldn't have grown up with three brothers and not had a sense of humor."

"Were they nice to you?" he asked. There it was again; in a blink Avery saw dark melancholy in his eyes. She set down her fork and propped her chin in her fingers as she studied him.

"Mostly. I want to talk about you," she said. She watched him swallow. His body was tense underneath his loose-fitting clothing but he held her gaze steadily.

"Where did you grow up?" she asked.

"Springville." His flat tone cautioned her, but she ignored it.

"Lots of beautiful scenes out there to paint."

He shrugged. "I hardly ever painted landscapes." There was an attempt to hide the struggle going on within him to share this information, Avery could see that. But she wanted to know more than she wanted to grant him freedom from the discomfort of talking about it.

"When did you decide women were going to be your focus?"

"Sometime in junior high." The dusk of something she didn't understand appeared on his face.

"Did you always like to draw?"

"Doodling was something I did when I was bored or ignored. My teacher saw that I had a talent for sketching faces and hands. She suggested I take it seriously."

Avery could imagine a dedicated teacher making a find in a young student, wanting him to run with his gift. She'd done it over and over with her dance students. "So what then? Your parents enrolled you in every art class they could find, thinking you were the next John Singer Sergeant?"

He snickered. "I started doing sketches – friends, you know."

"Girlfriends?"

He looked at her. "Before I knew it, I took a painting class, enrolled in all the art classes the high school provided and then it became what I did every moment of my free time."

He wasn't comfortable. She wasn't sure why she felt compelled to put him on the spot. That a man as mysterious and obviously free-spirited as he was could somehow be lassoed into painting a woman, concentrating on her in such a condensed way, drew her to him inexplicably.

"May I see where you work?"

"I don't have a studio right now. I work in my bedroom."

The idea of seeing his bedroom interested her. She stayed close behind him as he led her down the short hall to the last door on the left. It didn't surprise her that the room was disheveled. The bed wasn't made, clothes were strewn about. Instantly she smelled his scent and it tickled her senses.

He bent to pick up a discarded pair of jeans. "I'm not much of a housekeeper."

She walked to his easel, glad he'd tossed the jeans onto his bed and stopped trying to impress her by doing something he clearly had no inclination to do. He came up behind her right shoulder and she felt the heat of him.

"That's my current project," he said.

"May I?" she asked, her fingers taking a corner of the covering. He nodded.

Pulling back the cloth, she saw plain lines of a settee and an empty spot in the form of a figure.

"What's it going to be?"

He wasn't ready to tell her the subject was her. He'd had a few women freak when they discovered they were the focus of his work.

"A woman on a settee."

Avery looked around the room for the couch. "I don't see the settee."

"It's in here," he tapped his temple. "Not all my work comes from live sittings, though I wouldn't mind having this woman model for me when I'm ready."

Her eyes lifted to his, round with curiosity. "So you have someone in mind?"

"Yeah."

Avery looked at the canvas. Folding her arms thoughtfully she said, "Describe it to me."

"Well..." He set nervous hands on his hips. "She's lying on it. Not like she's ready to sleep, more like she's taken a moment to consider herself." Unconsciously he moved closer to her, his chest brushed her arm as his fingers lightly coursed the canvas.

"There's soft music playing and she's thinking about the man in her life. It's in her eyes. Need, longing, desire – all of that's building inside of her. She wants him. She knows he's looking at her, wanting her. It's that look, that feeling I want from her. The only thing covering her is a sheer fabric of some kind, a scarf or something she has grabbed and covered herself with, knowing he's going to see her and want her."

"She's seducing him?"

"Not really." He moved closer to the canvas, staring at it intently as she stared up at him. The firmness of him now pressed into her side. His hand skimmed the empty spot where his subject would be and watching the long, gentle stroke of his fingers sent a shiver through her.

"She knows her power," he continued, almost in a daze. "She knows he wants her but he can only have her when she wants him." He shifted his intense gaze to her, heating that shiver to a flame. "If she wants him."

"Sounds…very interesting." Her voice was lower than she liked. Her gaze slid to his mouth again, wondering what it would feel like if those lips kissed her.

"It's called *Hope*," he said.

"Do you title all of your work?"

"Yes."

"May I see more?"

The tight line between them broke when he turned and opened a closet filled with various sized canvases. One by one, he pulled them out.

The pieces were astounding. His attention to realism and color had Avery feeling as if she'd stepped into the picture and was just a few feet away from each subject. The women weren't all beautiful, most were average, caught in every day settings. But all of them radiated the life that he'd captured with light and energy in their faces that made you think you could reach out and feel warm skin, sense joy or share sadness.

One portrait in particular caught her eye, a woman looking mournfully off from a kitchen table as she arranged colorful flowers in a vase. The older woman with dark hair and sad eyes was in neutral colors of grey and off-white, the only bright spot the flowers she had in her hands.

"What was she looking at?" Avery asked absently.

He shrugged. "I don't know. It's my mother. That's just how I always saw her. Melancholy." He slid the painting back into the closet, but left the others out for her to look at.

A darkness shadowed his face. Avery wasn't sure what to say next. "She liked flowers?"

"She was usually unhappy."

Avery felt her brows knit tight. Again the efficient dismissal of something he didn't want to discuss left his face. "And what is that painting titled?"

"*Chance*."

He replaced the painting of his mother on the right of the closet, with a half-dozen other large canvases she noticed he had not brought out. Without thinking, she stepped over and reached for one.

In a flash, his hand wrapped around her wrist and he stopped her. His eyes were sharp. "Those are private."

She blinked hard before looking at the mysterious paintings, then at him. He released her, and took a step back, as he shifted the canvases.

"Your work is exceptional. Really. Your parents must have been terribly proud." She refused to believe that painting of his mother with its sad grays and lonely whites was accurate.

"They hated that I painted," he said flatly.

"But you're—"

"They hated it."

The ice in his eyes chilled the room but she wasn't going to let it come between them. She kept her eyes level with his.

Something was secreted deeply beneath the colors, brushes, and canvases hidden in that closet. It was just as deeply hidden in the man. The urge to reach deep and find it pulsed hard inside her, even with the cold surrounding him. His jaw hardened for a moment, his granite eyes narrowed. She resisted reaching out to comfort him, judging it would be ineffective.

She thought again about his work. She imagined he was used to having his way with women, reading their intentions clearly. He'd have to, to be able to see beyond the flesh and bring life to his work the way he did.

At that moment she realized, by the wary look on his face, that he had no idea what her intentions were with him.

"I want you to draw me," she said suddenly. She hadn't really thought seriously about it. She just knew that she wanted to be the object of his concentration. It would be exciting to see what he saw in her, what he could do with her, as he created her on a canvas. It would be dangerous. *Time to step out of your safety zone, Avery*, she told herself as she waited for his answer.

She watched his tongue run along his lips. He let out slow breath. She expected his grey eyes to warm at the suggestion; he'd been flirting with her these past few weeks; she'd read interest there.

"Why would I?"

"Why wouldn't you?"

He moved away from her, covering the canvas on the easel with the cloth. "I think you should go now."

His reply was worse than a slap and for a moment she stood without words, digesting what had just happened. She had never been invited to leave. "You're asking me to go?"

He smoothed the covering without the courtesy of looking at her again. "I'm telling you."

Her mouth opened but nothing came. She watched, stunned speechless, as he took the canvases he had brought out for her and slid them back in his closet.

"I don't understand," she muttered. "Did I say something wrong? Tell me how asking you to paint me made you angry. Isn't that what you do? Paint women?"

He turned and she could see how tight the muscles were in his back and shoulders. "Forget it."

Angry now, she defiantly approached him. "Is it about money? Did you think I wanted it for free?"

"It's not about the money," he said, his eyes fiery. "I don't care about that."

Chance knew she could never understand how torn up he was inside. How could he tell her his feelings for her would be mercilessly challenged if she were to sit for him? What would she think if he told her he wanted—no needed—for her to be different than any other woman?

"It's getting late," he said with finality. He wanted her to go, so she'd remain in his fantasy, safely tucked away. The flickering of pride in her eyes tried to worm into his conscience. He watched her leave the room with the dignity he knew she held intact. Standing in the doorway, he watched her gather her things from his bathroom and walk out the front door without looking at him again.

Chance closed his eyes, gripping the doorjamb with his fingers. He'd paint her—but from memory.

SEVEN

Avery went out of her way to make sure they didn't pass each other in the hall at the school. She ate with Scott like she had before Chance had taken the substituting job, teasing her heart in foolish directions.

When she saw Dru and the pack of single women surround him one day and insist that he eat with them, she made sure her back was turned and she ate alone.

But her ears had strained to listen.

During dance class she was cordial, as if nothing had happened. And nothing had happened, really. She kept reminding herself that he'd invited her to his apartment on a friendly whim. It had been she who'd asked if he would paint her. Something about that had bothered him. What, she still couldn't fathom.

Having three older brothers, she knew men dealt with women differently. Alex always tried to fix things, going out of his way to set things right if they weren't. Matt floated through relationships figuring things would work themselves out. Dan's heart had belonged to one girl since high school.

It was Alex she called from school one day. "Can you do me a little favor?"

He always sounded distracted when she called him at work, but then the stress of writing daily copy for the city newspaper was demanding. "I'm on deadline, Avery."

"I know, I know. I'm sorry. Could you look in your archives for anything on that plane crash three months ago – the one that killed that couple? Their last name was Savage."

"And what, email it to you?"

"That'd be great."

"If I can squeeze it in."

Alex demanded the best of himself and sometimes in doing so, he came off abrasive, like now when he hung up without saying goodbye because there was no time for it. But Avery knew he'd send her the information.

She taught ballroom with Scott and after class, checked her email. It didn't surprise her that she was still curious about Chance, even with his rejection. It was her nature to want to know everything about anything she was interested in, be it cooking or traveling, languages or men. Rejection or not, she was still intrigued with Chance.

Clicking the note from Alex open, she read:

This what you're looking for?

Darrell and Marva Savage were killed instantly when their small, private aircraft flew into the side of Nebo Mountain late Thursday night. A preliminary investigation shows that even though Darrell Savage was a seasoned pilot, he lost his bearings. Darrell and Marva Savage were owners of Savage International, one of the most successful importing and exporting businesses in the country.

Alex also sent along their obituary. The article was a quarter of a page, with a picture of the late Mr. and Mrs. Savage. Both were attractive, tailored-looking people with an aristocratic glimmer in their eyes and pride in their erect shoulders. Chance favored his mother—she had two Shirley Temple dimples in her smile. His father was severe-looking, wearing a stern look that hadn't broken into a smile even for the sake of the photo.

Much of the obituary was business related, citing their generosity to charity, their entrepreneurial business history and their successful business, Savage International. Marva had enjoyed cooking and traveling. She regularly donated money to the Springville Art museum, one of the most prestigious art museums in the state. Darrell loved hunting, golf and fishing.

No mention was made of their two sons except that they were survived by Kurt, 30, and Chance, 28.

A knock at her door startled her and Avery closed the window of her email before saying, "Come in."

Dru stood in the door with a smile meant to be friendly but to Avery, the transparency was clear. Her red waves fell to her shoulders. She wore a short skirt in tartan plaid with a tight green sweater that reminded Avery of a sexy poster girl rather than a math teacher. Her emerald eyes glittered with mischief.

"Dru."

"Avery."

"Do you by any chance," Dru smiled at the play on words, "have Chance Savage's phone number?"

He still hadn't given the woman his phone number. Avery hid a smile of pleasure, but at the same time realized how out of bounds she was letting her feelings for him roam to elicit even that reaction. "I don't know his phone number, no." Casually, she turned back to her computer and opened her class ledgers.

Dru entered the small space and Avery smelled the strong scent of musky perfume.

"Do you know where he lives?"

"I do, yes."

Dru moved to the side of Avery's desk, a smile that lay halfway between intrigued and annoyed played on her lips. "I don't suppose you'd share that with me"

Avery's gaze returned to the screen, and she continued to scroll down her list of students. "I imagine if he wanted you to know that, then he would tell you."

"He's asked me to pose for him." Dru crossed one long, bare leg over the other. "But he neglected to give me his address when he was…asking."

The hair on the back of Avery's neck prickled. "I'm his friend, not his social director." Avery stood so they were nose to nose. "You'll have to get those details yourself. Excuse me."

Avery wanted to think Chance was smarter than to ask an easy woman like Dru to model for him. As she stormed down the empty hall toward the front doors of the school, she fell into analyzing it, even though the sting of his refusal to paint her felt fresh as a slap now.

Having brothers had opened her eyes to how easily some men could be duped by the opposite sex, being caught like magnets in a field they couldn't resist. Though all of her brothers had married women with intelligence, Avery had witnessed countless times when they had each lost their minds to a pair of long legs or big boobs.

Emerging from the building out into the crisp afternoon air didn't take her mind off Chance. Neither did a greeting from one of her students as she made her way to her car.

A man with Chance's appeal had probably had every kind of proposition laid in those talented hands of his. Why did it scratch at her so? They were friends. She had no right to think of him and feel jealousy.

Having been witness to the casual manner in which most men viewed relationships, she had vowed in her teenage years never to search for happiness in the arms of a man. Ironically, it had been that carefree attitude that had attracted most men to her. She knew this because they told her. Avery saw herself as the one who held the reins in her relationships.

She liked being in control of that; it fit her disciplined way of life, and it kept her heart protected from men the likes of Chance Savage. Yet here she was, unable to stop thinking about him.

As she drove toward home, she convinced herself that whatever was going on at Chance's house was none of her business and that she didn't care. To rid her mind of him, she slipped in a CD.

The romantic Johnny Mathis song was a song they'd danced to in class, and the ballad did nothing but make her curiosity itch. She saw Chance in her mind again, the poignant look that lived on his face he tried so hard to cover but was too close to the surface to hide. He needed a woman who would be cautious of that, a woman who would care for that. Dru would only see him for what she could get from him and give no thought to the consequences.

Curiosity and concern overcame common sense and soon Avery found herself driving to Chance's apartment. *I'll say "hello" and go,* she told herself. *Since we're just friends, it would do me well to get over this silly misunderstanding and get on with it.*

His old green VW was nowhere in sight. Pondering whether or not she should wait considering how much her heart would benefit from seeing him and clearing the air between them, she was bothered again by Dru's implication, and the still-shocking fact that he'd refused to paint her. She put her car in park and idled on the empty street in front of his apartment.

Whether she wanted it to or not, Avery's stomach crimped as visions of Dru slithering around Chance's apartment flashed through her brain revving jealousy to a level she had never experienced. *This is what happens when you tangle with danger.*

Her life was about the safety of self control. For years she had forced herself to endure hours of training to perfect her skills as a dancer. She'd sacrificed a lot along the way, but one thing she'd never sacrificed was her dignity. This act was taking her perilously close.

Just as she was ready to pull her car into a U-turn and leave, his car came buzzing up the street. Quickly, she ducked, killing the engine. Her heart was racing. *This is ridiculous; I'm hiding like I have something to be ashamed of and I'm here because I want to apologize for behaving like a baby.*

Slowly she eased her head up and watched him get out of his car. He'd worn a charcoal sports coat over black clothing that day. It sent a too-pleasant trembling through her just looking at him and she let out a sigh. *It's time to settle this*, she thought. She would apologize and hope he'd not noticed the way she'd been ignoring him like a jealous lover.

She reached to open the door but her eye caught the bright red sports car zooming up the street. Dru.

Dru was tapping on her horn to catch his attention and Avery frowned. How desperate. Did the woman know she looked like a love-sick girl, chasing after him this way?

Chance stopped at the sound of the horn and was now coming slowly back down the walk to Dru's red car.

Dru was out in a flash. She'd changed her clothes, Avery noted. Gone was the tartan skirt and green sweater. Her long legs were bare to her upper thighs now in a short, flirty skirt with flowers plastered all over it, and she might as well have been naked for the tight blouse she was wearing. Her breasts plunged out like ripe grapefruit. The woman was merciless. Avery felt both angry and envy at the sight.

Chance had a smile on his face as he talked to her, those dimples deep and engaging. Avery wished she could hear what they were saying, but she had an idea. Body language could be very telling and Dru's was pressing toward his, those ripe breasts tantalizing as she stood evocatively before him.

Chance looked Dru up and down but he hadn't moved to take her inside.

Avery inched up a little more in her seat, hoping it wasn't

true—that Dru had just been fantasizing—just like she had—when she'd said he'd invited her to sit for him.

Dru reached out and laid a silky hand on Chance's arm and he looked at it. For a moment, they didn't speak. Then, to Avery's shock, he jerked his head slightly toward his place and turned.

Dru followed.

Avery's heart plunged. Her knuckles whitened on the steering wheel. She couldn't believe it. For a long time she sat, suffocated with disappointment. More than anything, she wished she hadn't seen what she had just seen. *This is what happens when you do something foolish,* she thought with humiliation.

Furious with herself, she started the car and drove away. Johnny Mathis was singing on the oldies radio station. It brought Chance's face into her mind, the feel of his body brushing hers as they danced, the dark sparkle of intensity in his brown eyes.

She reached over and flicked off the radio.

Inviting Dru inside was a mistake, he knew it. But it was so easy and he'd never been stupid. She was offering. He was alone, feeling like crap since he'd all but shoved Avery away, and he could use a diversion.

He'd been six weeks without the diversion of a drink now. A record. But his body craved something. Since Dru was poised as pretty and ripe as a peach he reached and plucked.

He heard the front door shut and his body started to hum. "Make yourself comfortable." He didn't look back at her as he peeled off his coat and headed to his bedroom. He was sweating already. "I'm just going to change."

"Great. I will."

Tossing his coat on the bed, he unbuttoned his shirt as he sifted through piles of clothes on his bed for jeans. Avery had been the last woman in his apartment. The thought of her had him pausing. He closed his eyes.

"Need some help?"

He turned around. Dru stood in the doorway with one arm up in the jamb, one shapely leg extended into his bedroom.

His heart began to thud. "Can't seem to find my jeans." The search continued, but out the corner of his eye he saw her slowly come toward him. The next thing he knew she was holding up something blue.

"Here they are." She held them near her breasts so that he had to graze them with his knuckles as he took them from her.

"Thanks." Her eyes made a very slow descent down his body. He felt it, fiery and fast, as he watched her eyes travel. She was smiling as her gaze moved. And as it dipped lower and lower, every ounce of blood in his system roared to his center, pooling there. He clutched his jeans. Her face was lit with brazen hunger. It was just how he was feeling inside.

But always there was this emptiness, a cavern somewhere he was helpless to fill that had been gouged out years ago by another female hand. He felt the vastness of it whenever a woman wanted him. His body would respond, momentary pleasure would be shared, but nothing ever filled the ugly hole gaping inside.

"Is this where you work?" she finally asked, but he knew it was just to pass the time. She was holding back, her body was as tight as his, as desperate as his for release.

He nodded.

"Why don't I turn around while you change?" She grinned and turned, her backside arching just enough to stir his blood into a faster whirl.

Just changing into his jeans was difficult. He did it fast, noting how she coyly turned her head once to look. "Keep your shirt unbuttoned like that."

He threw his pants onto the bed and studied her back. Her head was still turned slightly toward him. She had a Vargas Girl body—full, voluptuous. Her legs were long but not lean, more like stretched hourglasses, and his hands would fit nicely around her waist.

His steps were swift when he crossed to her. He stopped directly behind her back, and took in her scent. He hated it. Avery's light, floral scent was what he yearned for and to have musky gluck fill his senses stole his desire and slowed his blood as if he'd been slapped.

He took a step back as if he had, his desire in a quandary.

She didn't say anything, just turned to him. After a time, she said, "Where do you want me?"

Chance's heart began to drum again. He wanted to laugh because he was actually on the verge of turning her away. For the first time in his life, he wanted only one woman, and Dru wasn't her. He knew at that moment he would not indulge, and he looked to dig himself out.

"Why don't you, uh," he scratched his head. "Here." He reached behind her and brushed off everything that had collected on the one chair in the room, clearing it. Then he plopped it in front of her. "Sit here."

"Sit?"

"Uh-huh."

"Don't you want me on the bed?"

He pointed to the empty chair. "Go ahead. Sit."

She was taken aback, so it took her a moment to lower herself into the chair but she finally did.

Quickly, he set up his easel, gathered his tools. He should kick her supple body out, he knew it, but he was hungry inside. So hungry, for a moment he felt that hunger well behind his eyes, catch in his chest. The reaction was shocking, mortifying to feel tears, hot and wet, but they were there. He blinked hard, keeping his face turned but he heard her rise from the chair, felt her near.

"Hey." She had that soft tone women used when they wanted him to think they cared. But she barely knew him, and she only wanted what she saw, not what was inside.

In an abrupt shake-off, he was breathing better with distance between them. This was a game to her. A dangerous game that he'd played before. His hands were shaking. She was right behind him and he felt her hands stream up the tight muscles of his back. His drinking had been one ugly pattern he was still trying to break. Comfort sex was another he wanted to end, even knowing his body would be edgy.

Maybe he could have submitted—taking, trying to fill the void inside of him—but her perfume choked him, keeping him highly aware that she was not the one he wanted.

Her hands had slithered from behind and were now lingering on his abdominal muscles, tense and exposed because she'd told him to leave his shirt open. Her breasts pushed into his back. He could try not to breathe so he'd not take her in. He could drop his head back and let go of himself.

"You're so incredible," her voice lulled in his ear.

Where sudden will came from, he was never sure, but he was able to turn to her, even with her warm hands still caressing his skin, even with invitation in her eyes, lips just inches from his. He was able to take a step back.

His first impulse was to hurt her. It always whipped at him, no matter how he tried to see a woman as innocent. But he'd been innocent when a woman just like her had been the first to hurt him.

Though Dru was far from innocent, he'd not allow himself to give in to his need to lash out at her.

"Just sit in the chair," he told her.

She reluctantly did as he said.

She sat in the chair with her legs apart, her back arched. His stomach rolled with sudden disgust and he averted his eyes to his tools, busily setting them into place.

"Chance?"

His tongue wet his lips and he dared his eyes not to look. He wanted her gone, but knew well enough that she wouldn't leave unless he made it easy. He focused on her face and positioned himself in front of the canvas.

"How's this?" she purred.

Still refusing to let his eyes wander, he stuck his brush in between his teeth and felt the ache in his jaw intensify as he again adjusted the blank canvas. "It's fine."

"Or do you want me some other way?" Now she turned sideways on the chair, her right arm holding onto the back of it as she extended a leg.

He wanted to laugh, at her, at himself. "You practice this with a pole, Dru?"

Her eyes flashed and she sat up, adjusting her blouse. Fury colored her cheeks. "I thought you wanted to paint me."

He started brushing his canvas. "I never said that."

"Yes you did," she stammered.

"When did I say that? Remind me."

"Well." She leaned forward so the line between her breasts deepened. "You said you painted women."

He nodded, reached for another brush. "That's something I did say, yes."

"And I just assumed you, well, that you—"

"—That what?"

Her face bloomed red. "That you wanted me to pose for you."

"You assumed wrong," he said bluntly, then shrugged because he knew it would sting her. "But, whatever, right?"

Anger flowered on her face. "You could be nice about this."

"You show up here, come onto me, and then presume I want to paint you."

She shot up from the chair, steaming. "You're twisting things. I heard you ask me to sit for you."

"I never asked anyone at the school to sit for me."

She circled the chair, bubbling with it. It was a good thing his brush was stuck between his teeth, it kept him from shouting at her. He had hoped to make her angry—to get her mind off the game and out of his apartment.

"So you haven't asked any of the women at the school?" She stopped and he saw something mean glitter in her eye.

Because he still held his brush in his teeth, he shook his head, then took it out, swiping it once across the canvas. "Why?"

A smile of satisfaction covered her face then. She tilted her head at him. "Maybe another time would be better."

Finally. He took one last brush across the painting and then reached for the cloth that would cover it.

"I want to see it," she said as she quickly came to his side.

The cover fell into place and he hoisted it up, carrying it out of her reach before setting it down on the right side of the closet. "I never show my work until it's completely done," he lied.

For a moment she stood without what to say in reply and he busied himself with cleaning up.

"Oh. Well, when should I come back?"

"Let's keep that open." With a tender caress he ran his fingers over the brush bristles before setting them aside. Then he faced her, shoving his hands in his back pockets.

Her eyes were filling with black mischief again; they lingered on his bare chest. "You ever modeled?" she asked, taking a step toward him, her eyes feasting there. "Your body is perfect."

He could smell that horrendous perfume of hers again. She reached out her hand to stroke him and he snapped a hand around her wrist.

She seemed to like that. "You could be mean, Chance Savage," she said. Her gaze wasn't on his chest anymore, but looking into his. "Mean and cruel. That's worth getting deeper into."

A chord in his gut twisted. Yeah, he could be mean, and he'd been raised with cruel. He'd spent his adult life trying to figure out how to get away from both of those things.

"Maybe another time," he said. But that would never happen. He'd seen enough of Dru. After he finally gotten her out the door, he went back to the canvass, ripped off the covering and stared at the emptiness of it.

EIGHT

The beer grated his throat as it went down—fizzing bubbles, bitter and savory. Chance's head rolled back as an "Ah" escaped, purging him of everything that had been building inside since the last time he'd pressed the amber elixir to his lips.

Kurt was like a rabid bat lurking around. He knew he hadn't seen the end of the settlement of their parents' possessions.

The impossibility of everything beautiful and untouched that Avery presented was enough to drive him crazy. He'd no doubt scared her and whatever friendship they had off with his blunt refusal to paint her.

He stared at the liquid in his hands and considered this moment timely. He wouldn't allow himself to feel any guilt, not after successfully thwarting Dru's attempts to seduce him. He'd ignored every craving he'd had, including this one, for ten long weeks now. A shudder of gratification wracked his system as he savored another swallow.

Something twanged from the juke box in the corner and two guys in jeans and plaid shirts played pool under a dingy red light across the room.

"Another?" the bartender asked.

Chance wet his lips and stared at the glass. He'd only had one. He could push himself away right now if he wanted to. But the cold glass felt good in his hands. At least it was something to hold onto, chilling as it was. He shook his head.

Now that his gut was warm and that warmth was

spreading, he thought again about the emptiness inside, wishing he could find something that would fill that void for good.

Art had been that at first. Though he'd been the author of his own comfort by creating, it had been Mr.Tudo in sixth grade that had seen something more and encouraged him to develop his talent. *God bless the old man.*

Chelsea had been in his class a few years later, the year his life had changed. He closed his eyes. When things around him swirled too fast, too tight, he would find himself there because that had been the beginning of some things good, most things awful.

Brows pinched tight, Chance threw back the rest of the dark amber liquid and ran a hand over his face. The country music was loud enough that it drowned his groan. He signaled the bartender and his fingers tapped anxiously on the bar as he waited.

He could get up now and walk out; he could leave his money and just go.

Watching intently as the barrel-chested man behind the counter pulled the tap and the gold liquid filled another glass, his mouth watered and his veins opened with need. It was only then that he regretted not taking Dru up on what would have been an obvious night of temporary enjoyment for them both. Now that his senses were dulling, so was the sharp edge of determination he'd carried this afternoon.

He barely tasted the glass after it was placed before him. In his mind he saw her—Chelsea's mother—-and he was there again, a kid, afraid. He saw her as she'd come to him that day—the day everything in his life changed. Tilting his head back he drank the whole glass down.

The rehearsal with Scott was over and Avery stood alone

in the studio. They were getting close to Nationals, one of the largest competition in the country, when they would compete for a title in Standard. Putting in extra hours each night, fine-tuning their routines. Avery needed the extra practice tonight. She'd found it difficult to relieve her mind of the image of Chance and Dru.

Before she pushed the sweeper back and forth over the floor, she selected some tunes. She set her life to music and put on something light—old Frank Sinatra—to ease her mood. She appreciated all types of music, having been exposed to everything from hard rock, with her brothers, to Vivaldi, her parents' favorite. Often when she chose to unwind, she listened to Frank, finding his voice soothing, like warm milk.

When the door flew open, she froze, startled by the sight of black night and blowing snow. Quickly she jogged across the floor and reached outside to pull the heavy metal door shut. Icy flakes blew in her face and she squinted against the ravaging wind. A dark figure stumbled just a few feet away. At first frightened by the sight, she almost slammed the door shut to call nine-one-one. But she knew the carefree gait.

"Chance?"

Snow whitened him from heat to toe. He didn't even have a coat on over the same dark clothing she had seen him in earlier when he'd been outside his apartment with Dru.

"Chance? What are you doing here?" Avery trudged through the gathering snow and squinted up into his face, angry that he had the nerve to show up after his interlude with Dru.

He wobbled like a boxing toy. Instinctively, she reached out for him. "I was in the neighborhood."

"What happened to Dru?" She let heavy sarcasm line her tone.

"Wh—Dru?"

"Forget it." She tightened her grip around him. "Are you

all right?"

"I'm better than all right." He took her quick gesture as a signal and wrapped his arms around her in a tight bear hug. "Mmm, you smell good."

Avery's heart skittered in her chest. She wasn't sure if she should be alarmed. The strength in his body was like that of an anaconda. The sour smell of ingested alcohol warmed her face as he nuzzled her neck and the scent shot a hot buzz down her spine.

"Let's get inside, it's terrible out here."

Chance let out a laugh and stumbled, almost bringing them both down in the snow. "Whoa."

"It's icy. Careful." Her arms wound around him and she held on tight. He was cold, his muscled body wet snugged next to hers. Once they were in the warm room, she wiggled free and pulled the door shut against the foul wind.

It thudded shut and Frank Sinatra echoed off the spacious walls.

She looked at him, soaking-to-the-skin wet. His dark shirt clung to every curve in his arms, every ripple on his chest. His slacks sucked his skin, outlining long, muscled thighs and calves. Against the pale glow of glistening skin, his hair looked black, drenched as it was, and it lay in waves and curls against the strong lines of his face. Where he'd been pressed against her was wet and cold and she shivered, wrapping her arms around herself as her insides swarmed with uncertainty. His eyes were sharper than she expected for a man who'd obviously been drinking. Focused on her in a way she'd seen that first night he'd broken the dance between her and Scott.

Her blood streamed fast in her veins as she watched his breathing, hard and heavy. He stood tense and ready.

"Are you all right?" Her voice echoed too meekly for her liking.

He blinked heavily then started to move, slow as a snake, toward her. Avery's eyes widened, and her arms, wrapped around her body, clutched more tightly. Her heart banged against her ribs. She wouldn't act afraid, even if she was, but it wasn't Chance she feared. He was someone else tonight; the abrupt, demanding and angry man she'd met that first night at Bruisers.

He stopped just inches away from her. She smelled the wet of his clothes mixed with the breath of beer. His eyes darted over her face, finally coming to a stop on her mouth, where they narrowed, sending another tingle of pleasure through her.

"I want you."

"Oh. Well, I'm flattered." She went to take a breath before she continued, but he pulled her against him in a move so fast breath caught in her throat.

His lips covered hers in a kiss that was hot and greedy. Stunned, she first fought against him, but the sparkling sensations jamming her body caused her to go nearly limp in his arms. When she did, his grip intensified as if he was trying to absorb her into the soaking wetness of him.

The lingering taste of beer flavored the kiss. His lips challenged as they moved over hers. She'd not had time to prepare herself for this, and part of her heart was torn in disappointment. This was not how she'd fantasized her first kiss with Chance would be.

His hands drove over her body somewhere between gentle and jagged. She couldn't relax, not sure what those hands were capable of. Then he thrust his tongue deep and stumbled, moving them forward, lips still fastened, and she knew he was spiraling out of control.

She hadn't been raised a wimp, not with three brothers, and she shoved hard at him. She expected him to let her go. When he did not, she flung her head back breaking the firm seal of their mouths. "Chance, stop."

His eyes were murky and dark when they slid to hers momentarily. He still had her flush against him and as she arched back, he only squeezed harder. "Don't play at this."

"I'm not playing." She shoved harder. He held on tighter, his face hard-edged with anger that now sent a ribbon of fear through her.

He dove again for her lips but she jerked her head to the side. "Let me go," she demanded her heart pounding.

"I just want a little kiss," he growled against her neck. Then he shoved her away and paced, panting hard. "What?" He shouted, seeing her wide-eyes. "You can teach me to dance but you're too good for me to kiss?"

He was spiteful as a wet cat. She knew better than to scream at him. There was trouble brooding in his eyes. "Chance, did something happen tonight?" She expected if he'd spent the evening with Dru that he'd be in a much different mood.

He wasn't as out of it as he'd been that night in Bruisers and Avery felt a little tug of relief. "I just came here to see you, but I can see you don't want what I want so I'll just leave." Irritably, he crossed the floor, faltering once and cursing under his breath.

"You can't leave like this. You can barely walk. And you're angry."

"Damn right I'm angry." In a second he was back in her face. "Why are you too good for me?"

"I do not think that I'm too good for you. I would have thought you knew me well enough—"

"I know what you think of me." Chance brought his face within inches of hers.

"And what do I think?" she asked. "Tell me."

"What difference does it make?" He stormed away from her, rocky and tense.

"Please talk to me."

"What's there to talk about? You're a Michelangelo. I'm a—"

"—Michelangelo?"

"Forget it."

"Tell me why you…did this to yourself."

"I don't need a reason to drink, Avery. I do it because I like it. It makes me feel good. I can't dance my way clear of problems like you."

"That's an easy out, Chance."

"Excuse me?"

"Sure. How hard is it to drive yourself to the nearest bar, sit and pickle your brains so you don't have to face what's in it?" He stared at her incredulously, unable to speak. "Or storm in here and take something that doesn't belong to you. That was – that kiss was disappointing to me."

His eyes narrowed sharply and he brought himself close enough that she swallowed another jag of fear. "Is that right?"

"I won't lie," her voice trembled. "I've thought about what it would be like to kiss you, and the scenario in my mind was nothing like that."

"Let me guess—candles, moonlight—some romantic park somewhere. You wouldn't kiss anybody unless the surroundings were absolutely perfect. You wouldn't have anybody that was less than perfect."

"That isn't true. I like romance like anyone else but—"

"—But you've never been taken." He reached out and grabbed her by both shoulders, crushing her against him. "Without anything more than need driving the moment." His voracious gaze ate her face. "No candles. No music, Avery, just the sound of insatiable need."

Her eyes widened with shocked. To her dismay, she began to quiver. His fingers dug into her arms until her face twisted from pain. His eyes were filled with emotions—fierce anger, need, hate—but as she watched them score his face, they changed, helplessly changed to tainted sorrow that stilled her trembling and tore at her heart. With another hard dig of his fingers, he pushed her away.

"I should go."

She knew that he should, but she wanted to help him more than she feared for her own safety. Whatever the risk, she cared enough about him to take it. He started for the door and she grabbed his wet sleeve. He glared at her under eyes taut with misery and pain. "Don't do that."

"You're not fit to drive."

"I got here, didn't I?"

"Please, Chance, for your own good."

He let out a sneering laugh. "You sound like my mother." He jerked his arm free.

"Because I care about you."

"Well, she never cared."

"That can't be true."

"Not everybody grows up surrounded by love, Avery. Open those sheltered eyes of yours."

"You were her child, she had to have some feelings for you."

"Yeah, utter disdain and contempt."

Avery considered him for a moment. He was desperate. Lost. She walked to the door, her chin lifted with resolve. He'd opened up to her, another layer of the package was peeling away, and what she saw underneath was proving to be more fragile than the last. She was not about to let him go now. She turned and faced him and pressed her back against the door.

"I'm letting you out this door on one condition." His fractured glare sharpened. "The floor in here is pretty hard to sleep on, I know," she said. "I've had to do it."

Shaking his head, he slowly crossed to her. His lids thickened heavily. "Not you." He reached out and his finger gently traced her cheek. "You'd only sleep on the softest mattress, in the nicest house—a castle, maybe. Like a princess."

Heaven help her, but that face of his tripped through her bones and made them soft. "Let me drive you home," she said.

For a moment, gratitude hovered in his face, childlike and guileless. Somewhere, deep inside, was a man desperate to be understood, maybe even loved. And Avery was determined to find him.

He closed his eyes and leaned his head back. Avery stole glances as she drove, wondering if he was asleep. The smudges of grey under his eyes pinched her heart, made her wonder what had happened to drive him back to the bottle? He was still wearing those wet clothes. Though the heater was on, he was shaking. She needed to get him dry and warm.

When she pulled up to his apartment, he finally opened his eyes. For a moment, he was disoriented and sat up, looking around. Rubbing the heels of his hands to his eyes, he let out a groan. "I must have fallen asleep."

She was glad she'd insisted on driving.

He stumbled with her alongside of him, from the car to the apartment. His hands shook as he dug into his pocket for keys and they rattled into the lock. Inside, he fumbled for the light switch. "Justin must be at Inessa's," he said. When the lights finally flicked on, he stood momentarily at a loss. Avery weighed the wisdom of staying any longer. She took off her coat and laid it over the back of one of two charcoal couches in the living room.

"Does he often spend the night?" she asked because it was so quiet between them.

"Never. Value's his sleep too much. The most disciplined guy I know."

"Yes. Justin's a good man." Chance was still wet, so she

went to him. "Cold?"

Chance pointed down the hall with one hand, his other lazily rubbed his damp hair. "Wet. I'm going to go change."

"Yes." Avery tried to ignore his easy sex appeal. "That's a good idea."

She watched him disappear down the hall. His damp clothes clung to his lean form, and she took a deep breath.

She decided to venture into the small, bare kitchen. Most men could eat at any hour she knew that from having three brothers. There wasn't much in the fridge, a half gallon of milk, some eggs, orange juice and some leftover Chinese in white cartons. One glance in the pantry and she knew her options for creating something were limited.

He had peanut butter so she toasted two slices of bread then spread the peanut butter thin, like she preferred it.

The bachelor's life amused her. Though her brothers had all moved out in their early twenties, she'd had plenty of opportunities to see how they lived post-home: sparse, sometimes not even with the necessities, and no decor to speak of.

These two men lived that way.

This place with its blank white walls and dark-toned furnishings wouldn't say much about either one of them. But Chance's bedroom was just another layer of wrapping. It didn't bug her that he was messy. He was too absorbed in watching what was going on around him, how it could potentially color his art, to care about whether his bed was made or his clothes were hung up.

She preferred someone she could assist in that area anyway—it put the finishing touches of possession on a man. He was neat about himself, dressed as if he took care in that. But it was too early to be thinking like that way, she decided. She liked him the way he was—casual, easy-going, yet deeply intense—like tonight.

She touched her lips, remembering the way he'd kissed

her. Even now it shot liquid heat from her lips to her belly, where it quivered and waited. She tried to dismiss the warmth she felt swarming there. The kiss had been exciting, she couldn't deny it, but tainted.

He'd been verbally aggressive under the influence. She could deal with that. What she wasn't sure she could deal with was his physical power. In dance, he was gentle, still getting his footing, not much of a lead. But tonight there'd been an unleashing. Now, standing in his apartment, she wondered if he tried anything again, if she'd be able to stop him.

He came around the corner in loose-fitting flannel pajama pants in grey and ivory plaid. They barely sat on the angled bones of his hips, baring a faint feathering of dark hair just beneath his belly button that disappeared beyond the elastic waist.

He was grinning when Avery's eyes finished their admiring trek from his navel, along the curves and contours of his bare chest and shoulders to his face.

"Hey," he said.

She cleared her throat and quickly picked up the plate of open-faced peanut butter toast. "I wasn't sure if you were hungry, but I made you one of my favorites."

"That was nice." He crossed to her and stopped so only the distance of the plate was between them. Then he looked into her eyes. His dimples creased deep and Avery's heart fluttered.

"You won't be warm without your—" Her gaze fell to the smooth skin of his chest and wanted to stay there. "Without any...maybe you should put on a shirt." She looked back up at him.

Chance was enjoying that Avery seemed distracted. "I'm plenty warm." He took the plate with one hand, the other skimmed her arm. "You?"

"Of course. I'm not the one who was caught in a snow

storm without a jacket."

"Okay, Mom. Want to sit?"

He led them both to the couches where he plopped onto one like a teenager home from a late night.

"Hungry?" he asked, extending the plate to her as she sat down. He'd just taken a bite and was chewing. Avery wondered how she could find even this act exciting. His full lips spread even wider moving in a leisurely, delicious circle. The bones in his jaw contracted, a movement she found sexy in a man.

"No." Her stomach was a whirl of different things, but the hunger for food was not one of them. "You're safely home. And feeling better, it seems."

"Yeah, that little nap must have done it."

"Then I should go." She stood.

"Already?" He looked genuinely disappointed. When she stood, he immediately put down the plate and was up in a flash. His hands took hers. "Not yet, Avery. Please."

She could no sooner turn away a homeless child begging at her door than say no to him. His fingers slowly grazed her hands, and the air around them thickened.

"I need to apologize for earlier." Pain crossed his face, deepening the crease between his brows. "I promised Justin I wouldn't drink during my substitute gig. I—" He released her hands and scraped his fingers down face. "It's not easy for me. I know you think it's an easy out and you're right. But even knowing that doesn't stop me."

"But you did stop for, what, ten weeks? Chance, that's commendable."

He looked at her, hesitant to take the compliment, then ran one finger alongside her face with gratitude in his smile. "You're seeing things I guess I don't see."

"Then look harder." Closing the space between them, she looked up at him with her heart starting to open. "If you want it, you can do it. What do you want?" Again emotions flickered over his face like clouds dashing across a windy sky: sorrow, disbelief, hope, need.

There were so many things he wanted; Chance could hear them running through his mind like a tape on fast forward.

Freedom from the chains of cankering memories.

Control over body and mind-wasting habits.

To settle amicably with a brother who wouldn't stop until he'd taken everything away from him. All of these things were so huge, so encompassing, he saw no way out from under any of them except by means of easy escape.

And here she was telling him to face it all without any buffer.

"I can't look deep," he said on a raw whisper, knowing how hope had once crushed him. "It—"

"It what?"

She moved closer, and his heart clipped in his chest. She was offering, but not what he wanted. "What do you want from me?" he asked.

To help you, was her first thought. Avery's gaze lingered on the scars she saw deep behind his eyes. But that endeavor would be silent. There were other things she wanted, and she wondered if sharing them with him would make her sound like a dreamer. "I want you to open up to me, to let me be your friend."

His fingers traced her cheek again. "It's hard for me."

"Yes, I can see that. And that will make our friendship all the more valuable." But just as she said that, something murky and angry hovered in his eyes.

"You should go." His voice was a whisper caught between desperation and frustration.

"Is that what you want?" she asked.

I want to make love to you, he thought, but knew even that was just another temporary fix. *I want you to be mine. I could live with the pain. I could suffer any affliction if you were there.* So strong were the emotions welling inside of him, he felt them rush up the back of his throat, into his eyes. He'd never expose her to the ugliness of his past, the sure bleakness of his future.

They could never be and so he nodded.

She hesitated and he almost grabbed her and buried his sorrow in the curve of her neck, sought solace in her lips. But he only watched her go to the couch and gather her coat.

"I'll see you tomorrow at school." It hurt when she walked to the front door. He'd be alone, and empty pain would surround him.

She opened the front door and stopped with a gasp of surprise.

NINE

The face staring back at her was rough and white as used sandpaper, with ash-blonde hair and brows, and skin that looked slapped by a harsh wind. Blue eyes the color of pale marbles and just as unyielding stared back at her. The man's large form boxed the doorway as he looked over her shoulder and his stare hardened on Chance.

"Little brother."

Avery turned and looked at Chance who had tensed. He was behind her in two fast strides, so close, for a moment she thought he was being protective and she couldn't imagine why.

"You never return my calls," Kurt said.

"There's nothing to talk about."

"You're wrong."

"I should go." Avery took a step out the door but Kurt didn't move aside for her.

He smiled. "Excuse my brother's manners. I'm Kurt Savage." He extended a hand and Avery shook it.

"Avery—"Before she could get out her last name, Chance was tight at her side, with his arm around her.

"Thanks for tonight, Avery." He gave her a quick squeeze then escorted her safely past Kurt and onto the porch.

"Be careful in that snow," Kurt laughed before he swung his head around to Chance. "It's deadly."

Chance's nerves started to thrum. Kurt passed him, shouldering him in the chest and entered the apartment. Chance slammed the door. "What do you want?"

"Same-old, same-old. I'm not going to let up." Kurt's eyes

narrowed. "Who was that bomb, anyway?"

"A friend." Chance took his plate into the kitchen and tossed it into the sink, then thought better of leaving it there and rinsed it. The menacing presence of his brother came up behind him.

"She's hot."

Coming from Kurt, the words caused Chance's gut to clench. He opened the dishwasher. "Let's not dance around this. I'm not signing over any part of what Mom and Dad left me to you—ever."

Leaning back against the counter, Kurt crossed his legs at the ankles. "What do you want? Come on, name your price."

"I'm getting what I want. And you're getting what you deserve." Reading Kurt had become second nature to Chance—for survival. He wasn't buying his brother's easy stance and knew a fight was coming. He figured the living room would be a better spot—less corners to gouge flesh.

Chance started for the living room and the move caused Kurt to shove, landing a palm on his bare shoulder and Chance whirled around with his left arm deflecting any more attempts like a sword in swing. "Don't touch me," he hissed.

Kurt's face flushed red, another sign he was readying. "I'll never let you have the house."

Chance headed to the other side of the living room. It had always been his way, to stave off a fight with as much talk as possible. It had taken him years to be able to say what he really wanted to say to his brother, and even then, it always ended up with fists finishing. But for some reason he couldn't explain, it seemed ridiculous to him now, the fighting—their hostile history. It shamed him. People, families, didn't treat each other like this.

"Think of someone other than yourself, Kurt," Chance started, watching his brother's tiniest moves, still hoping to work it out with words. "It's the way they wanted it."

"So what." When Kurt took a step his direction, Chance's body tightened. "You don't deserve a dime, let alone the property. Why would you want it? Nobody in the neighborhood will take you back, you're the plague."

Chance fought the roving anger he felt starting. Words he'd been badgered with for years ripped the tender scabs off old wounds deep inside. "That's old news."

"They'll care if a rapist moves back into the neighborhood."

That was all it took for Chance to lunge, for his hands to wrap around Kurt's throat and squeeze.

They fell back, toppling to the floor like toy soldiers. Chance's mind raced with anger, hurt, deprivation. His fists pounded into Kurt's face without mercy. Kurt bucked and twisted, but Chance recalled Justin's moves and wrapped his legs around Kurt's thick trunk to keep him pinned.

Blood spewed from Kurt's nose and split lip. Chance could feel his brother's strength waning but he kept hammering, blow after blow until Kurt's hands stopped fighting back and flew up to cover his face.

Neither of them heard the door open, and Chance was still pounding his fists into Kurt when he felt two arms wrap around his chest, pulling him off from behind.

Still in fight mode, he struggled only to have his throat wrapped in a choke hold that left his body twisting, his breath sputtering, until he slapped the floor and signaled submission.

Kurt, Chance and Justin lay in the thick aftermath, breath racing, air filling with the scent of blood and sweat. Kurt was still on his back groaning as scarlet streamed between his fingers.

Chance scrambled up, braced to continue. A calm but firm hand on his shoulder gave him cause to hold back. "Dude, you need to stop."

Chance's gray eyes burned bright. His body was so rigid

that Justin took his hand away, afraid he might snap.

"Get out of here," Chance told Kurt.

Kurt eased up to his elbow with a growl, looking at his bloodied palm before his icy blue eyes shifted to Chance. "You're so going to pay for this."

"I've already paid for it," Chance shouted. "I spent my life paying." That his brother knew how he'd suffered, been a part of it in fact, had Chance storming over for more. Reaching down, he saw the flash of fear in his brother's eyes and couldn't help but enjoy it for a moment.

He grabbed Kurt's shirt and pulled, bringing Kurt's face to his. "Don't ever say that again. It was a lie and you know it."

"Who cares?" Kurt shoved away. "Nobody believed you then and nobody would believe you now."

Because it still hurt so deeply, Chance did what he was trying so hard not to do, and shoved at Kurt. "Get out!" He kept shoving, as the two of them started in again.

Justin leapt into the snarling fight, hopping on Chance's back to pull him away. It threw Chance off balance and off-guard, opening his abdomen up for a direct hit from Kurt.

Chance fell back with Justin, the two of them landing on the floor in a cracking thud. Justin was up faster, and stood with one palm toward Chance, one toward Kurt. "Enough!"

"Get out of the way," Kurt ordered, advancing.

In an angry flash, Justin had the front of Kurt's shirt in his palms and was pushing him toward the front door. "I'm telling you now, it's over, or I call the police."

Still boiling, Kurt wiped the back of his hand across his oozing lip. He pointed a white-haired finger at Chance. "I'm not through with you."

Chance rose to his feet, trying to suck in air after Kurt had expelled it with the heavy blow. "Get out."

"You just try to reclaim what you lost," Kurt hissed from the door. "They'll tear you apart again. And I'll be there to watch."

Chance would have lunged for him, so ragged were his emotions. But Justin blocked him with two firm hands. They both waited for the door to shut and when it did, Chance jerked free.

His past was a nightmare that never left him. It had changed his life, ruined his family and stolen everything from a boy still in need of love and guidance. He'd sequestered the memories, time after time.

But Kurt thrived on yanking them back out into the open.

Chance drove his hands through his hair and let out a heavy sigh. He really needed a drink. He needed to anesthetize his brain and sleep forever. Let Kurt have the house, let him have it all. He didn't care anymore. Besides, Kurt was probably right, the exclusive behind-the-gates neighborhood he had grown up in would sooner let a pack of wolves into the area than the likes of him.

Chance was at the refrigerator in four slick strides. But the six-pack he'd kept there for visual moral support was gone. He glared at Justin who had quietly followed him into the kitchen. "Where is it?"

"Somewhere in the landfill, dude." Justin settled against the counter.

Chance paced the tiny kitchen as if he was trapped, even though he knew Justin would let him walk any time. He couldn't deny that he needed to talk this out, but he'd trusted no one since he'd last told his mother what had happened those years ago and she'd refused to believe him.

He knew he could trust Justin. Indeed, Justin had saved him in too many ways to discount how much he needed his friendship. But the feeling was the same as it always was whenever he thought about his past: the ugly, dark, clawing of something uncertain, something that, as a teenager, he hadn't been fully capable of understanding, something that had eaten his life and his dreams away. The darkness was there again, fresh as if he'd stepped back into that place and found himself at Chelsea Drake's front door.

"He wants the house along with everything else," he started. "I won't let him have it. It's not that I care about having the house or anything that was theirs. They kicked me out so long ago none of it means anything anyway. It's a pride thing, I guess. I can't let him have it all. I can't."

Justin gave a nod. "And it's what they wanted that's important."

"He could care less about last wishes. This is about him and me. It always has been and always will be, until he has it all." He shook his head. "I don't know."

"What?"

"Maybe it'd be worth it to get him off my back." But unlike Kurt, and in spite of all the injustice, Chance would not leave his mother resting in her grave thinking that their last wishes had been met when they hadn't.

Because the whole evening had worn him to a thread, Chance left the kitchen, hoping Justin would leave it alone. He went back to his bedroom but heard the faint rustling of movement and knew he was out of luck. Justin was following him. Something deep inside was of him glad.

"What happened, Chance?" Justin asked.

Chance did something he rarely did: he picked up his clothes and put them away. Justin, he noted, had made himself comfortable in his doorway.

"Nothing. We just had a fight."

"I'm not talking about that. What happened in the neighborhood?"

He couldn't believe Justin hadn't heard—everyone had, and it had driven his socially paranoid parents into fury. Regardless of their money and efforts to keep the scandal quiet, people had found out.

"When I was fifteen, I met this girl in my art class." He plucked a shirt from the pile on his bed. "Her name was Chelsea Drake." He could still see her, Chelsea. Her blue eyes had captivated him from the first day he'd looked into them and needed to commit them to memory, known he'd have to put them on a canvas.

"She was one year younger than me, but, you know how classes in high school are, mixed and all. She and I kind of liked each other." Slipping the shirt on a hanger, he took it to his closet.

"I sketched her for fun. They were great sketches. Anyway, I gave them to her, you know, because I liked her, wanted to impress her." He started back in on the piles of clothes covering his bed.

His hands slowed as he sorted through the pile. "Her mom saw the sketch and she liked it—loved it, actually." In his hand was a black tee shirt. He squeezed it, stared off for a moment. "Ginger Drake." He looked over at Justin for any sign of recognition but when Justin just lifted a shoulder, he looked at the black tee in his hands and closed his eyes.

"Chelsea invited me over one afternoon to meet her mom. The place she lived in was like a museum. I mean, I walked in and couldn't move. There was marble everywhere. Everything was gold and white."

"Ginger had the most extensive art collection I'd seen. Not a lot of triple A stuff, but enough B and C class to be impressive."

"Anyway, she sat me down in this all-glass solarium they had off the back. Chelsea was there." Chance took the black tee shirt and hung it in the closet. "Ginger offered me two thousand dollars to paint her and Chelsea."

Justin let out an appreciative whistle.

"I couldn't imagine why she'd offer me so much. I mean,

I'd barely wet my brushes, you know?" He returned to the pile of clothes on his bed. "But she really believed I could do it. Told me all great artists have mentors and she wanted to be mine."

Plucking a striped shirt from his bed, he shook it out. "For days I thought about it, wondering what I should do. I didn't tell my parents, because I knew they'd freak. They had this quiet rivalry going with the Drakes.

"Ginger's collection was private, but that didn't mean that the whole upper crust community didn't know about it. And Mom's way to maintain her social status was to support the cause. She and dad donated hundreds of thousands to the museum for enlargement and acquisitions."

"Your mom was friends with Mrs. Drake then?" Justin asked.

Chance shook his head, and tossed the last remaining clothing left on the bed into the drawer of his dresser. "Too much of an age difference. There was also an income difference. Mr. Drake was a plastic surgeon." Chance shut the drawer with a thud, looking down at it. "He was never around."

With the bed mostly cleared, Chance lowered himself onto the foot of it, his gaze on the floor. "I took her offer. I wanted to surprise Mom. I thought she'd love that one of her sons had made something of himself at such a young age. Nobody in our circle of friends had kids that did anything but live off daddy's money. " He buried his face in his hands and kept it there for a long moment.

Pausing to collect thoughts, he pressed his fingers together, brows cinching, jaw hard. "At first, things were totally up and up. Ginger had me start with Chelsea. She suggested I take photos and she bought me this top of the line, totally decked-out Pentax. Whatever I wanted, she'd buy. Then she arranged Chelsea in settings and I took the pictures."

"Finally, we got the shot—in the living room next to their grand piano. Chelsea wore this long, dark velvet dress. You know, traditional down to her patent leather shoes."

"I started painting right away. Ginger had a place made for me in the house, a studio. It was just an extra bedroom she'd had converted into an artist's dream back near the master—" Chance paused, rubbing his hands down his face as he let out a sharp laugh. "Anyway, I had this place to work. Most of the time I was alone. Chelsea's mom didn't want me to be distracted. She knew that Chelsea and I liked each other—but it didn't bother her. Let's just say she was a progressive woman.

"I spent every waking hour there for three weeks working on the thing but I was determined to finish it so I could have half of the money. That's what she'd told me, that she'd give me half when I'd finished Chelsea's and half when I finished hers."

Chance looked up at Justin for a moment that stretched empty between them. Patiently, Justin didn't move.

"When I finished, Ginger was thrilled. Ecstatic. Told me how great I was—she'd never seen anyone like me, that I was a natural. Filled my head with ego candy."

"I still hadn't told my parents what I was doing or where I'd been going every afternoon and evening. Mom was involved in her ladies groups; she didn't notice my absences and Dad didn't seem to care one way or the other if Kurt and I were around."

Every muscle in his body clenched now as the flesh of the memory neared. Chance wet his lips, then bit them. His fingers pressed into each other until the tips whitened. He kept his eyes on the floor where he knew there would be no judgment. As much as he trusted Justin, it was too humiliating to elaborate. But it was too late not to go there in his mind, and as he loitered near the sharp cliff of the memory, he was as anxious as the boy who'd fallen into the abyss that day. "Let's just say, things got freaky between Ginger and I."

"I'm sorry." Justin moved from the door, closer.

Chance stared down at the carpet, his fingers still pushing against each other. But he gave a nod.

"If I can do anything, let me know." Justin's tone brightened. "Too tired to take me on?"

Chance lifted his head. The wag of Justin's eyebrows brought a weary smile to his face. He let out a sigh and stood.

Justin jerked his head toward the door. "In the living room. We'll need some space."

He was sore the next day—to the bone, sore. And looked, he thought, like an old man, slow and embarrassingly feeble as he walked down the hall of the school toward the lunchroom. Chance was careful not to bump unnecessarily into the mass of bodies filing around him but it was inevitable in a relatively narrow space packed with enthusiastic teenagers.

Justin had twisted him into every lock and choke-hold imaginable, in every contorted position a body could possibly go. He'd done it over and over again until Chance had understood the concepts of finishing a competitor. You had to get them on the ground, and then you could take them.

He hadn't perfected the moves in the two-hour sparring workout, but he would eventually. Justin promised they'd work at it as long as they had to until he felt confident.

It wasn't over with Kurt. Chance could talk until he was blue in the face, but the only language Kurt spoke was physical. When Kurt made a threat, he kept it. It wasn't fear that made Chance want to learn the finishing techniques, but the desire to put an end to the hostility once and for all.

"Hey."

His heart flipped just hearing her voice and he turned. Avery's smile caused his heart to flip again.

"Hey." He slowed, dodged a student so they would be shoulder to shoulder. So willing was his soul to go to hers, he entertained thoughts of lunching with her until he reminded himself that he shouldn't, not if he was going to keep her away from the ugliness that tarnished his life.

"Want to eat together?" she asked.

I want to do so much more than that, he thought, and looked into her waiting eyes. "Sure." He'd said it without hesitation, and followed her through the door to the teacher's lounge. The air behind her was scented with delicate carnations and spice, luring his conscience into forgetfulness.

"You bring your lunch today?" She searched him for any sign of food.

He held up his brown lunch sack. It pleased him that she led the way to the furthermost corner where a table for two was stashed.

"You made your lunch?" She laughed lightly, sat. "That's a first for you, isn't it?"

He was experiencing a lot of firsts since she'd come into his life. "I had peanut butter and bread and no money. It was a natural."

Avery spread out her own sack lunch: fruit and a lemon Yoplait Custard yogurt. "Will that hold you?" she asked.

There was real concern in her eyes and it caused fingers of warmth to spread around his heart. He should ignore them. He hated that he wanted to enjoy the way she cared. He lifted a shoulder. "I don't have much of an appetite these days."

Avery dug in her bag for a plastic fork then nudged her fruit salad toward him. "We can share." She handed him the fork.

Touched, he reluctantly took it and paused before piercing a chunk of melon. "This is good." Food had never been a priority. He didn't care what he ate, considering himself lucky to shove down a banana. Her pretty little salad only reminded him of what he'd miss if he stuck to his resolve to move on without her.

"So." When she began, he knew by the tentative tone in her voice that she was going to ask about something she wasn't sure she should ask about. "That was your brother I met last night."

"That was him."

"Does he visit you often?"

"Only when he wants something."

"Oh."

"My parents left me the property, him the money. But that's not enough for him. He wants the house too."

"Did they leave these legally to you?"

"Yes."

"And he doesn't like that."

"Hates it."

"There's nothing he can do unless the two of you agree to change it."

"Or I die."

Avery swallowed deep. "Has he threatened you?" Because her face went white, he lied.

"Not in words. How do you know so much?"

"My father's a lawyer. Who's older?"

"Kurt."

"He looks nothing like you. You look like your mother."

Chance stopped chewing and stared at her. Her eyes widened before fluttering to her food. "That was an interesting comment," he said. Her face was now bright pink and he found it amusing. "Been checking up on me, have we?"

She dabbed daintily at her mouth with her napkin. "All right," she looked at him behind a flush. "I'll admit I did some investigating."

He sat back with a pleased grin. "Is that right?"

"Don't look so flattered." She propped her elbows on the table and leaned toward him, noting Dru's keen stare from across the room. "You've been rather evasive about your life. I was curious."

"So you snooped?"

Her cheeks were still a beautiful shade of magenta and he decided his vow to end their friendship would just have to wait. She was too lovely, so out of reach, one more day wouldn't hurt either of them. "I'm forced to wonder how you came to the conclusion that I look like my mom. Did you scrounge up a photo somewhere?"

Avery bristled. "I – okay, maybe it was scrounging. My brother, Alex, is editor of the *Daily Herald*. I had him email me some stuff."

"Stuff?" Chance's stomach tightened.

"Your parents' obituaries. I'm sorry, I hope you don't think that's—I suppose it sounds—"

"No, no. It's okay." He was more flattered than he should be that she wanted to know anything at all about him. "I'm sorry if I've been evasive. It's just that we come from such different backgrounds I didn't think there would be a point."

Her brows puckered and she set down her yogurt. "From what little you've told me and what I got from the obituary, our backgrounds are very similar, Chance."

"Maybe socially, economically, but when it comes to our families we're as different as oil and watercolor, Avery."

"And that means?"

"That means, well..." He couldn't very well tell her it meant they could never be together, like he'd dreamed. She'd think he'd inhaled too much of his paint. He was sure that particular dream had never entered her mind. "It means that you and I are different in ways that are not compatible."

"That's the most ridiculous thing I've ever heard." She

picked her yogurt up. "We don't know enough about each other to know whether or not we're compatible, so why would you make such an assumption?"

The passion behind her conviction surprised and pleased him a little.

"Besides, different doesn't scare me," she continued. "And I can't believe it scares you but if it does, that's okay. You do rather remind me of a hermit crab."

He nearly spit out the last bite of her lovely fruit salad. "Excuse me?"

"Yes. I think you need some coaxing out of that protective shell you live in."

"I don't live in a shell."

"You do and you don't know that you do. You're the hardest kind of man to coax."

"For a woman who just said we don't know each other very well, you seem to have me figured out. Or at least you think you have me figured out."

"It's my way, to analyze. I had to—with brothers. They were the most complicated group, continually making my life impossible. It was a necessity for me to understand everything about each one of them so I could manipulate them and function."

"You're fascinating." She blushed again and he enjoyed the innocent reaction. "Fascinating and beautiful."

"I imagine complimenting women comes naturally for you in that you would have to speak their language to lure them into posing."

"I never lure."

"Pardon me, that wasn't the right word."

"That word would mean I have ulterior motives. And I don't."

"Never?"

"Let's not make this about my reasons to paint. That's

only gotten us into trouble."

"You have to understand that it's a fascinating part of you, Chance. In a way, it is a lure—like dangling a sparkling diamond under a woman's nose. She'd want to touch it, examine it, know every facet of it."

"I'm no diamond."

"I see deeper than you, remember?"

"That's beyond deep. That's seeing in dreamland."

"My ratio is ninety-nine out of one-hundred percent accurate."

"For what?"

"Seeing men. Ninety-nine times out of one-hundred, what I see in a man is there. It may be deep, it may be something even he doesn't see, but it's there."

"You got a Ouija board hidden somewhere on that body of yours?"

"Comes with the territory—from practice."

"On your brothers or other men?"

"Both."

"Huh." He hadn't figured her as the type to have a bevy of men, not that she couldn't. It was obvious she could have anything she wanted. But her aloof manner almost spoke of exclusivity: well-chosen, carefully selected companionship.

Avery let out a breath, noticed that Dru was still watching them intently. "I need to get to the gym. Scott and I have to squeeze in a practice before we leave tonight."

"Where are you going?" He stood, and ignored the little pang he felt from the news that she was leaving. He walked with her out of the lounge.

"We have a competition in San Francisco over the weekend."

"Yeah? Wow."

They greeted students as they walked together through the hall. Chance had that familiar feeling again, the one he got whenever he looked at the calendar and checked to see just how much longer he had before this job would be over, and so would so many good things he'd come to look forward to.

"We're hallway gossip," Avery told him as she scanned the faces of students.

"I'm glad you said nothing scared you." He gave her elbow a squeeze before the hall broke in two. He wasn't ready to let her go yet, and they stood in the stream of bodies looking at each other. What could he say? That he would miss her? The timing couldn't be more perfect, her leaving for San Francisco. It would force him to let go once and for all.

"Good luck this weekend." With one last gentle squeeze, he released her.

"Thanks, we'll need it. See you on Monday." She started off the opposite direction with a smile he would try not to forget.

TEN

He hadn't felt sore at all during lunch and mused that it must have been the company. Now, pain was beginning to creep in again, reminding him of who he was, and that no matter how much his soul yearned for rest in the ordered and peaceful life of a woman like Avery Glenn, their relationship would most definitely mean bad things for her. She didn't deserve that. She deserved a perfect porcelain man in a black tuxedo.

Everything around him felt heavier as the thought of losing her for good hovered. He wondered if he'd be able to get through the last class without being a grouch.

The art room was just beginning to fill when he groaned his aching body through the door. The worst part of sparring was that he knew it would be a long time before he wrangled a win from Justin, which meant he'd be feeling like crap until then.

He nodded a smile at the handful of students who sat ready. The eager ones—there were a few in every class.

A small white envelope was on top of the tidy desk. He picked it up and opened it with a glance at the students' faces in the room, faces too engrossed in chit-chat to notice.

How about tonight?

-Dru

The question caused a ripple of uncertainty to stream

through him. He crushed the note into a ball before tossing it into the trash. However unappealing Dru was, at least she shared the same egalitarian floor he did. He didn't want her, but she might wear him down offering.

He wished things were different, that he and Avery could have a chance. Wishing had been his m.o. for as long as he could remember. He'd dared to dream about a lifetime—what he'd gotten was a moment.

He lost his tangled thoughts in teaching. It was satisfying to share what he loved with those willing to learn. He was enjoying the temporary gig, even if his audiences were captive.

His last class of the day was his wildest. It was as if all of the kids who thought Foundations in Art would be an easy A signed up so that they could end the day with a laugh or a yawn. The boys were disinterested in anything art unless it was graphic or nudes. The girls either cloistered together and gossiped or brazenly flirted with him.

"When are you gonna bring in your stuff again?" one of the girls asked.

"If it would get you guys off your butts, I just might."

"Is it true you do nudes?" The petite blonde sitting up front crossed two bare legs that shimmered with some sort of fine glitter. For weeks she'd been in short skirts and tight tops sitting like a candied apple.

"I've done them." He was in the middle of drawing a diagram on the board that had nothing to do with either subject so he didn't turn around, thereby encouraging a discussion.

The boys hooted and whistled but Chance didn't even react. "This is how you show depth," he said, demonstrating the most basic principles in shading and angling.

"So," one boy began, "do you, like, use live models?"

"Sometimes." With his chalk, Chance shaded the areas that would make the squares he'd drawn look like blocks.

"Hot." He heard one boy say. Others followed with nasty

talk.

Chance bowled on. "You can change the mood of the piece depending on where the light is coming from."

"Sketch us a naked woman."

Chance covered a laugh with a cough. He knew from experience sex was on the teenage mind 24/7. A few months ago he wouldn't have thought a thing about joking with these kids about stuff. But things had changed. It bothered him now to think that most of them were driven by their hormones and little else.

Life had infinitely so much more to offer.

He turned, placed his hands on the desk top and looked into their faces. Some were still innocent. Their eyes glittered with curiosity that had not been exposed to things that clouded the clarity of purity. There were a few with eyes that hungered; eyes that had seen too much, too soon, and were ravenous in spite of the danger of wanting more.

Miss Blondie in front all dolled up with glitter and scent was still innocent. He was glad for her, and wished with all his might that he could warn her. Tell her to stay away from boys with hungry eyes, because they'd do nothing but eat her alive and leave her in scraps she alone would have to piece back together.

"It's an art form," Chance began. Suddenly he wished he wasn't feeling the need to defend his livelihood. "It's been done tastefully for centuries."

"But it's meant to turn on." One of the wolves in the back barked.

Chance looked right at him. "How many of you would find Michelangelo's *David*, for example, titillating?"

"I'm no homo," the one boy who had brought it up said, and sat back with disgust. The other boys concurred. They'd have argued about it but Chance held up his hands to quiet them.

"If you look at it, really study it—"

"Mmm, I could study it all day long. It's definitely hot." A girl who sat back near the wolves grinned when they acknowledged her.

"If you really study it," Chance began again. "Notice the skill in the finest details, like the curls in his hair, the creases in his fingers, even the lines in his lips; you can't be anything but awed. And I'd suggest to you that there would be no sexual reaction. This was all done with marble and tools, sweat and exhaustion for both Michelangelo and his model. It's a perfect piece."

"Perfect piece of meat," a girl replied.

When the bell shrilled, the class hurried out like they usually did, except Miss Blondie, who, Chance noticed, was taking her time gathering her books into her backpack. Accidentally she dropped a charcoal pencil to the floor. Instinct had him retrieving it for her. He had second thoughts when he recognized the indisputable glint of mischief in her eye.

"Thank you, Mr. Savage."

He continued up to the front of the room. "You're welcome." Then he picked up the eraser and swiped it across the blackboard.

"Do you ever paint your students?" Her voice was like strawberries and marshmallow, sweet and soft. He didn't stop erasing, going over spots already clean.

"Never."

"How come?"

Setting the eraser in the ledge, he wiped his hands on a rag until they were clean and turned. "It's against my personal philosophy."

She'd amped up her candied apple smile, he noticed. Her legs were posed, one straight, the other curved, toe tapping daintily behind, and she was leaning over his desk just enough for her youthful cleavage to make a show. *Oh, honey,* he thought, but kept his eyes from wandering, *you're playing with fire and you don't have the faintest idea how to use an extinguisher.*

"I'll volunteer," she said. "You wouldn't even have to pay me."

Suddenly, his face was slapped with heat. He smiled and zipped up his briefcase. "Careful, Aubrey."

He almost reached out and glanced a knuckle on her chin but didn't even want to touch her, afraid she might glom onto something that didn't exist.

"I'm being careful." She scurried behind him as he strode up one of the aisles to the door. "We could keep it just between you and me."

"That would suggest that there was something illicit going on between us." He reached for the door and she did too, not backing away when her hand covered his. She looked up at him, her blue eyes round and blinking.

The door knob slipped from both of their hands as the door swung open and exposed Dru. Her green eyes instantly shot to their bodies, suspiciously close.

"Dru." Chance stood back, gripping his briefcase with both hands on the handle.

She tilted her head with a smile that was curious and might be hazardous if that curiosity wasn't satisfied.

"So," Aubrey said boldly. "You'll think about it? Won't you Mr. Savage?"

"You have my answer, Aubrey. See you tomorrow."

With obvious disappointment, Aubrey headed through the door. Dru's smile was big. She walked with Chance down the hall busy with students escaping the confines of school.

"What was that all about?"

"She wanted to pose for me."

"My, you do have your dilemmas, don't you?"

"It's not a problem, I told her no."

"And is that the answer I'm going to get?"

"If that was what your note was referring to, yes."

"But you've already started my portrait."

"My closet's full of unfinished pieces."

Dru's eyes narrowed for a moment. "So what reason did you give that poor, love-struck girl back there?"

"The same one I'd give anyone—I don't paint women I work with. I most definitely don't paint pubescent girls."

"Hmm. You broke your own rule for me. How flattering. That means we'll have to finish it."

He thought of the blank canvas and the fact that he wouldn't be inviting her to do anything, much less pose for him, ever again. "When my substitute gig is over."

"Well, do you eat dinner with women you work with?"

"If the offer's right."

How does anything you feel like sound?"

He swallowed a laugh. "Anything?"

They stopped just outside the main entrance of the school. Her eyes wandered his face, held on his mouth. "Anything."

Dinner would get his mind off Avery, at least temporarily, he rationalized. "Can't say no to that."

Her tongue wet her lips in one, slow stroke. "Good. When do you want me to come get you?"

"How about I come get you?"

"Absolutely not. This is my treat, my gas."

"But my choice of dining destinations?"

"Your choice—completely."

"Pick me up at six."

"It's a date."

"It's dinner," he said, "because you asked."

"So? It's still a date."

"A date's when I ask."

"Chance Savage, are you sexist?"

"No. Just a man who prefers things to stay the way they appear. You asked, I accepted. It's not a date, it's dinner."

"Whatever you say."

Avery always packed for a competition the night before so she wasn't rushed now as she left the high school and headed for home. She and Scott had been to enough competitions around the country that they had traveling down to a science. After the pleasant lunch she'd shared with Chance, her heart was light and, she admitted, woozy.

She warned herself not to let her feelings go to her head—or her heart. She needed to take her time, be cautious and smart.

She never regretted not being a woman of the world. Retaining control of her feelings was one of her strongest accomplishments. She could leave wild relationships and experiences to more worldly women like Dru.

The woman was heading right for her, with a smile bigger than the Cheshire cat's.

"Hey, Avery." Dru stopped, so Avery did also. "Doing anything this weekend?"

"Scott and I have a competition."

"You're going out of town?"

"To San Francisco."

"Sexy city."

"Yes, well." Avery couldn't help but notice Dru's grin. "You look very pleased."

"I have a date."

"That's nice."

Dru nodded. "I haven't had a man in so long; I'm ripe as a peach."

Avery shifted, uncomfortable with the honest admittance.

"Oh."

"Don't you ever get starved for a man?"

"Well, I—"

"You spend so much time with Scott maybe you don't miss it. All I know is I'm ravenous. I could eat one alive."

"And it sounds like you've found one."

"Oh, I have. Yes, I have."

Avery turned to continue on. "Well, good luck."

"You too. Oh, by the way, since we're friends and all, I'll let you in on a little secret but you have to keep your lips sealed." She leaned as if to whisper but didn't.

"I'm sinking my teeth into Chance Savage this weekend. Yeah, him."

"Really?" Avery stammered. "How nice for…you both."

Dru slipped her arm in Avery's and began to walk with her toward the parking lot. "I've had these totally hot fantasies of him painting me and—"

"I'm sure that's very private." *And a complete waste of paint,* Avery thought as she pulled her arm free.

Dru let out a throaty laugh. "Come on, you can't tell me you haven't had a few fantasies of your own about that gorgeous man."

Avery's face was heating. "If you'll excuse me, I'm going to be late."

"With a man like him there would be no limit to the imagination." Dru let out a satisfied sigh. "I'm going to go home and spend the next two hours soaking in a nice, hot, scented bath." She clutched her overcoat around her, before veering toward her car. "Have fun in San Fran."

Avery ached inside but it wasn't from the cold. The news seemed impossible: Chance and Dru. But she couldn't ignore the flicker of doubt inside of her with the shocking outline of Dru's plans. Dru's summary of the weekend was not congruous with what had happened between her and Chance at lunch.

He'd been friendly – flirty even. That little squeeze to her elbow had been a squeeze of encouragement, hadn't it? Avery knew better than to pick apart every word, every physical act. Those puzzles almost always remained just to tease and torment. She'd never let them torment her before and she wasn't about to start now. The only way to know for sure was to go to the source.

Waiting until she returned from San Francisco was not an option. She was the kind of woman who never procrastinated. Time wasn't on her side: she and Scott were going to catch a plane in three hours and with security delays at the airport, they had to arrive two hours early. That would barely leave her enough time to stop by Chance's while Dru soaked in her hot, bubbly bath. Just what she would do when she got there, she didn't know.

This is crazy, she told herself but laughed aloud even as she turned her car in the direction of Chance's apartment. Spontaneity had never been her sentiment of choice, but she'd been doing lots of things out of character where Chance was concerned. That in and of itself was oddly assuring to a woman who preferred things to be just so.

She hesitated for a breath when she pulled up to the curb in front of his place. During that breath she considered being there, knocking on his door with questions. It made her look dreadfully female and suspicious. Who was she to tell him what he could and couldn't do with his weekend?

She was his friend. She cared about whether or not he got used by the most aggressive maneater she'd ever met. She was watching out for him.

He's not your brother, Avery. He's not your anything. He doesn't need you, and he is perfectly capable of handling Dru, if that's what he chooses to do. Turn around while your self respect is still in tact.

She did. But it was too late.

His old green VW was rattling toward her. He'd seen her. In fact, he was looking right at her, so any hopes of being just another woman in a beige Toyota Camry were dashed.

She was surprised to see how quickly he got out of his car and strode over. She rolled down the window, her mind scrambling for what to say.

"Hey." When he leaned in with that casual smile, her body both buzzed and sighed. His heavenly scent trickled in the air and into her head. "Thought you were going out of town?"

"I am." She swallowed, laughed, and looked out her windshield. She'd been raised with honesty as the best policy, but at this juncture, she knew it would make her look insane.

"You want to come in? I have—well, I don't have much in the way of anything to offer you, but—"

"I really shouldn't. I'm short on time as it is." He was gracious enough not to ask why she was there. "I just wanted to say good-bye."

He nodded and his dimples creased deep. His gray eyes were lit with something that made her heart thud. "I'm glad. Can I give you a kiss good-bye, Avery?"

She looked at his full mouth; his lips looked soft and enticing. For a second she debated.

Chance opened the door. "I have yet to make up for that kiss the other night."

"Oh. That."

"Yes, that." He extended one of his skilled hands to her and she couldn't resist taking it.

Suddenly she was standing outside her car, the scent of his cologne dancing on the air between them. As tempting as he was, her thoughts betrayed the concerns of her heart and Dru's face came to her mind.

"Let's save that kiss of contrition for another time," she

said.

He moved closer. "Why?"

"I – my time is short and I—"

She couldn't say another word; his body smothered her, enveloping her next to him with his arms. That mouth, so soft and luscious, was hot and supple—searching, invading, luring. Her bones wanted to melt but she managed to curl her arms around his neck and hold on.

She loved the way he felt against her, solid and strong, taking the curves of her body to his in perfect fusion. His lips fit flawlessly with hers, responding to her yearnings with the right mix of gentleness and need.

There was nothing of the tainted kiss they had shared before in this kiss. His lips moved carefully, with seductive calculation, drawing her into a fist so tight she could do nothing but press into the hardness of him in search of release.

His hands, so magnificent, so skilled, skimmed her back with the keenness of the artist to whom they belonged, as if memorizing each bone and sinew, leaving a fiery track of want in their wake.

"Chance." She stole a breath and said his name because she liked saying it, wanted him to know that.

No one had ever felt like this: familiar and comforting, yet fresh and new—like an undiscovered work of art that drew him helplessly to admire. His fingers danced lightly over the softness of her clothes, feeling the hint of curve, the warmth of feminine softness lighting a fiery need inside to explore deeper.

Slipping his hands under her coat, he searched through the fine-ribbing of her turtle neck sweater. He wanted to tear the barrier away so heat could meet heat, flesh could memorize flesh. But they were outside and he reminded himself of who she was.

Withdrawing his hands, he allowed them only her face and cupped the smoothness of her cheeks, deepening the kiss with more urgency.

"Come inside," he whispered, dragging his lips from hers, along her jaw. His fingers gently pulled away the confining neck of her sweater, exposing pale white throat underneath. He pressed his lips there.

A moan squeezed from her that nearly sent his arms scooping to carry her inside.

He eased back instead, lightly touching her cheek. He let out a sigh. Just looking at her soothed him. He'd never begged a woman, but knew at that moment, he'd beg. He'd give anything to have her in his life. His heart, that well-protected part of him that he'd sworn years ago he would never again share, he was willing to give to her, no questions asked, no conditions required.

"You're so beautiful," he murmured.

He wondered at the confusion crossing her face then. Surely she knew this, had been told before. When confusion shifted to something akin to distance, he felt a trickle of worry. Whatever desire she'd had was gone, replaced by uncertainty that now drew her fine features taut.

Avery wanted to ask him about his weekend but the kiss had sealed the impossibility of it. "That kiss made up for it."

"Did it?"

"It was very nice."

He laughed. "Only from you would I hear very nice."

"Is that not good enough?"

"No. No, that's great." He traced the details of her face with his fingers. He would think of her every moment she was gone. Knowing it was better this way made the moment more painful and he stepped back, finally releasing her. "I thought it was incredible."

"Let's not get caught up on adjectives."

"Yeah."

"So," she ventured, "what have you got planned this

weekend?"

He lifted a shoulder. "Stacks of homework, pencils to sharpen – you know."

She nodded, looked away, trying to ignore the way her stomach was churning. The quiet vacancy of the street whispered between them. "I should be going," she said after a time.

He nodded and held the door open for her, taking in every detail of her that he could. "Bye, Avery." He stayed to watch her car disappear, holding it in his vision until he closed his eyes.

Avery stared out the small, rectangular window of the airplane into darkness. Usually, she enjoyed flying, stealing the quiet time to nap or read. She could smell coffee, heard the pop and crackle of soda pouring over ice. She was ready for a bit of refreshment, she decided. She hadn't thought about anything but Chance, and that made her irritable.

She'd been spontaneous going to his apartment. But then she'd lost her head, and her purpose, when he kissed her. It wasn't like her to lose her head. The visit left her wanting, and without knowing.

Thankfully, Scott knew to leave her alone with her thoughts. He'd carried her luggage when she'd absentmindedly left it at the curb, grabbed her purse after she'd left it at the airport store while purchasing a magazine for the flight. She'd not opened the magazine once.

She was disappointed in herself. But then how could she be? She'd experienced the most thrilling kiss because she'd been moved beyond reason to go to Chance. It whet her appetite for more. It suffocated her common sense, and connected her to him.

Leaning back, she closed her eyes, hoping to doze and relieve her crowded mind of thoughts of Chance. Instead, she was barraged with flashes of Dru. She couldn't let these things interfere with her life, calm and collected as it was. They would distract her and ruin her concentration for competition. She could hardly wait for her feet to hit the streets of San Francisco so she would forget all of this.

"You okay?"

She opened her eyes and found Scott watching her guardedly.

"Fine. Why?"

He glanced at her fingers. "You're digging into those arm rests like you want to kill somebody."

Instantly she relaxed her hands and tried to laugh. I do, she thought, seeing Dru's face again. "Just tense."

"It's Chance Savage, isn't it?" He shook his head. "You and him... Avery, I've never pried in your personal life before, because I appreciate that you don't pry into mine. But I can't sit here and let you tangle with the devil. I won't do it. I'll kill the guy first."

"Thank you, Scottie." She patted his hand, flattered he was so protective but he ripped it out from underneath hers, his blue eyes flashing with anger.

"That guy is bad news. Have you heard about him? Do you even know what he's really like?"

She enflamed with the need to defend. "I'm getting to know him, Scott. He's not what you think. Not anything like he was that night at Bruisers."

"He's not what you think either," he sneered. "Look. I wasn't going to say anything because it's not what you and I do. But I did some digging."

"And?"

Scott leaned close, his voice dropped. "Did you know that he was tangled up in some sex scandal a few years ago?"

Avery's stomach clenched but she kept her face calm. A kernel of alarm stole under her skin. "Tell me about it."

"Some girl—they say he raped her. Her family wanted to have him sent to juvie but they could never get the truth out of the girl."

She lifted her chin. "How did you find out about this?"

"I was talking to one of my friends – he knows the girl's family."

"You talk to your friends about my personal life?"

"It's not like that, Avery."

"It sounds very much like that, Scott. With all there is in the world to discuss, why would you discuss me?"

"How about because I dance with you? Have danced with you for six years now. That kind of qualifies me to know about you, doesn't it?"

"To know maybe, but not to make me bathroom fodder." She turned away, angry, frustrated and hurt.

"It wasn't fodder, Avery. You're part of my life, for crying-out-loud. Everyone I know knows that I dance, that I have a partner and that partner is you. If it wasn't that way in both of our lives, I'd figure us to be pretty superficial."

"It's none of your business who I see or who I have feelings for."

He sat back. "You can't...Avery, *feelings?*" He let out a loud sigh. "I've never seen anything but red flags when I've seen Chance Savage. This news confirms that the guy is—"

"The only thing it confirms is that your friend likes to spread horrible things. How could you believe that? He would never do that, never."

"My friend knew this girl's family personally, Ave. He remembers when it happened."

"And when did it happen?"

"Like, twelve years ago. The point is it happened. The guy can't be trusted."

"I won't believe it until I understand it from him."

"You shouldn't go near him again."

"I won't let something like a story stop me from finding out what's truth and what is not."

"Do your parents know?"

"They haven't met him yet."

"Because you, in your dissecting way, know there is something very wrong here."

Her mouth fell open. "That is absolutely not true. I have never once had a bad feeling about Chance. Not in that way, anyway. I'll admit, when I first met him, I could see that he was troubled."

"I'll say. He's walking around with an assault on his hands, Avery. That'll trouble a guy plenty. It's probably just the tip of the iceberg. He's probably a sex offender."

"Would you stop?" She couldn't hear anymore, couldn't let the dark idea of something so awful shroud her mind and all that was good in it about Chance.

"In any regard," Scott began. "You should not see him alone."

"I'm perfectly capable of taking care of myself. And don't you dare tell my parents or call any of my brothers. If you do, our partnership is over."

He stared at her. "What has he done to you?"

"He hasn't done anything. You know I would never pass judgment without adequate facts."

"Even at the risk of your virtue?"

She flushed, and looked out the window. Partnerships came with just as many drawbacks as perks, and the fact that Scott knew personal details of her life because he'd been around for so long was unavoidable.

"Does he know you're still a virgin?"

"This conversation is over now."

"He's probably setting you up. Avery, don't you see? He's

waiting. He knows, and in his sick mind he's waiting to—"

"Stop it!" She stood and squeezed out of the confining window seat, away from him. She walked unsteadily to the back of the plane. Her hand fluttered against her heart and she tried to breathe deep. Tears filled her eyes.

"Are you all right?" The stewardess asked.

Avery nodded, blinking to keep the tears from falling. Instinctively she dug into her pocket, pulled out her cell phone before realizing she couldn't make the call thirty-two thousand feet up in the air. That was fine, she could wait. It would give her heart a chance to slow, her mind some time to clear. Then she'd have the presence of mind to find out the truth in a calm, respectable manner.

ELEVEN

Chance chose the most unromantic, utilitarian place he could think of. Hot, fast, and predictable, McDonalds wouldn't do anything more than fill his empty stomach. He made sure they sat in the playland, where there happened to be a birthday party in progress—lots of screaming children, wandering balloons and frantic parents.

The look on Dru's face amused him.

"This was not what I had in mind for dinner." Dru ducked to miss being hit by a child's sock flying through the air.

Chance unfolded the yellow wrappers and looked at his two cheeseburgers. "Well, it was just what I was hungry for." He took one in his fingers and brought it to his mouth.

"Could we sit in the main lobby?"

"You don't like kids, Dru?"

"I teach, don't I?"

Dru didn't seem like the motherly type. Avery had that hands down over her, and that was part of what Chance liked about her. Though he'd not spent a lot of time around young children, he had spent a little time pondering the idea of family, of finally having the power to create something he'd been denied.

"You don't strike me as the fatherly kind." Dru poked at her side salad with nominal interest.

Chance couldn't say why the comment bothered him, but it did. Maybe it was because he was trying to change things in his life. He'd seen the shallowness of his self-centered existence. Indeed, he'd spent so much time floating on the surface he had been perilously close to drowning, and would have had it not been for Justin and for this substituting gig and for Avery and dance.

It didn't surprise him that a fellow surface skimmer like Dru would still see those things in him. That was all she would see. But whether or not she saw him as the fatherly type wasn't worth debating – with her, anyway.

"This is great." He meant to keep their evening just as superficial as the woman, and chewed, nodded, and eyed the burger poised in front of his mouth.

"Glad you're enjoying it."

"You're not?"

Her eyes narrowed. She set down her plastic fork. For a moment she just looked at him.

"What?" He knew the look in her eye, had seen it before in women with specific agendas he'd turned away.

"I don't know what this is all about but I don't appreciate it."

"It's about dinner—eating."

"Yes. But I had something else in mind for the menu."

Chance swallowed a thick bite.

"You know, I would have thought you were more, I don't know – more of a man than this. I'm disappointed."

He shrugged.

"You had no intention of satisfying me tonight."

Chance looked around though he kept his expression even, his voice calm. "Keep your voice down."

"You knew that's what I wanted. So why this twisted game? Or is this your idea of foreplay?"

"This is my idea of dinner, Dru. You asked me, remember? You gave me the choice."

"With the very obvious overture that I wanted you, not some brainless burger in a child's playland."

Chance finished chewing the last bite of cheeseburger and reached for a fry. The children were laughing, running, playing. Carefree and innocent, their delighted faces reminded him of Avery, and he had the quick flash of her pregnant, of him by her side. The yearning suddenly flushed through him so fast, he had to stop chewing. He looked away, emptiness aching inside of him.

He took another fry but Dru's hand snapped out and wrapped around his, bringing his eyes to hers. There was fury building there, but she was masking it with a seductive smile. "I'm sorry," she said with about as much sincerity as the cold in her hand. "Look, maybe I've been too aggressive. I just thought it would get you hot."

Maybe a few months ago, he thought, looking at her with tepid disgust. Gently he pulled his hand free, noting that she watched.

"Do you mind telling me what gets you hot?" She positioned herself closer, folding her hands on the table.

He grabbed another fry. Everything about Avery Glen heated him. She could be girlfriend, lover and something more. She was forbidden, like a mother is forbidden, but could touch that place every man had deep inside reserved for angels.

It disgusted him to think about Avery in the same breath he used to converse with Dru – seemed sacrilegious somehow. "You say it like you want it, don't you?" he said, finishing his fries and wiping his hands of salt.

"I don't believe in wasting time."

"I can see that."

Her mood changed instantly. "You like to keep me guessing, don't you? I like that."

She was so off track it was comical, but he didn't have the interest to correct her. "Uh, right."

"Let's go back to your place." She stood, her eyes glittering with dark trouble.

Her full bowl of salad sat untouched. "You haven't eaten."

She reached out her hand and he looked at it. Her behavior could not drown out the happy laughter, the scuffling of little feet around them. Nothing would change the fact that Avery was hundreds of miles away and he was there, with Dru.

Avery stared at the lights of San Francisco from the cab as they drove across the Golden Gate Bridge. The city sparkled in breath-stealing majesty, spreading out like a glittering fairy-tale metropolis.

The competition would be stiff, so she had to focus. It would require every ounce of energy, every bit of will, and all the positive thinking she could muster to go out on that floor and keep her and Scott's current ranking or earn them a notch up. She was ready, they were ready, but she had to have her peace of mind or it would be ufair to Scott, not to mention their partnership.

Reaching into her pocket, she pulled out her phone. Scott shot her an electric glare she could see even in the darkness of the cab, but she turned away.

"Yeah?" Alex's gruff greeting didn't faze her.

"Could you do me a big favor?"

"I thought you were in-flight?"

"We just landed."

"And you haven't called Mom? She'll—"

"I know, and I will. But this comes first. Can you find me something in the archives?"

"Depends. What are you looking for?"

"Anything on Chance Savage."

"Isn't that the name you gave me a while back? The obit?"

"Yes. But this is their son."

"I'll see what I find."

"Then call me, okay?"

"Must be pretty important to cut into your schedule."

"Don't ask."

"If I want to know, I'll find out."

She figured he would, now that he'd caught the scent of something. She'd debated the dangers of having Alex do a search – if there was something about Chance; he'd have a conniption. Most women would give anything to be as adored and protected. Avery knew she should consider herself blessed to have so many men in her life that cared. Only occasionally, like now, did she feel rebellion rise up in response to such adoration.

She and Scott always shared a room when they traveled—neither wanted to fork out more money to have their own space. Tonight, Avery wished she had, still angry at him.

But they'd been angry before. They'd work through the awkwardness; they couldn't not work it out and dance successfully. Both understood the importance of ditching pride for the sake of common goals.

They rehearsed in an empty corner of one of the hotel ballrooms. Other couples were doing the same. Avery enjoyed the first mental reprieve from Chance she'd had since she left Utah.

The minute her feet hit the floor, her mind clicked over to dance. She didn't need music, lights, the buzz of competition; the simple steps were always enough to take her to that revered place in her soul only dance occupied.

After the hour it took to run through their routines to both of their satisfaction, they decided to see some sights.

Tracks for the red, green and gold-colored cable cars ran directly in front of the hotel and they hopped on. They rode to Chinatown, the smells of fried food, fermenting garbage and steamy vendors filling the air.

Scott's hand closed over hers as she held onto one of the poles inside the standing-room-only car. He let out a sigh, looked off into the night before he met her gaze. "Just promise me you'll be careful."

She kissed his cheek. "You have a promise."

When the car stopped, he took her hand and led her into the bustling that was the center of Chinatown. The streets were narrow, packed with people scouring stores with the fever of finding a deal. Merchandise of every type spilled from bright store fronts and into the crowded streets. Voices shouted, horns blared from cars impatiently trying to make their way. An occasional bling-bling of a cyclist with a large delivery box attached to his bike wove through the herding bodies.

Scott always picked up souvenirs for his girlfriend when they traveled. Particular to key chains and scarves, Avery enjoyed finding little trinkets for her nieces and nephews; toys and odd toys like the Chinese finger lock she was now stuck in.

And her phone was ringing.

Scott laughed and pressed her fingers together so that she could free herself. She plucked out her phone, still laughing. "Hello?"

"It's me," Alex said.

Avery covered her ear, trying to hear. She looked at Scott, and jerked her head toward the darkness of a nearby alley. "I need to get some place quiet."

Scott led her through the crowd until they found a dark corner and ducked into its depths.

"There wasn't anything major," Alex began. "Some press notice for art awards and stuff like that. He's a talented guy, this Chance Savage. The only mention of Savage anywhere other than that was Mrs. Savage who made hefty, undisclosed donations to the Springville Art museum for expansion. Gotta run. That all?"

The relief Avery felt was huge and she grinned into the phone. "Yeah. Thanks. I appreciate it."

"Good luck with the comp."

"Thanks." She clicked off the phone, noticed that Scott had listened to every word and now he looked perturbed. "You had Alex do a check that didn't show anything, right?"

"Right."

He shook his head. They were standing on a corner, cars and people streamed around them but he wasn't distracted. "That doesn't mean anything, Ave. He was a minor. His records would have been sealed." He took her elbow and escorted her back into the rush of bodies.

"The story could also be a lie." How horrible, she thought, feeling the weight of it.

"People don't generally make up stuff like that about fifteen year-olds. What would be the point?"

Avery thought about Chance being so evasive about his family, about the look of betrayal she'd seen in his eyes when he'd told her most emphatically that his mother hadn't cared about him. She'd not believed it.

"Not all families are happy and close like ours are, Scott. A lie, some deception, nothing could destroy a family faster than that."

"Yeah, I'd disown my kid too, if he did something like that."

But Chance hadn't. She suddenly felt empty inside, even surrounded by the commotion. Soon Scott was tugging her into another open shop, and she was glad. She had one more person she wanted to find something for, and she felt a lift in her heart just pondering what he would like.

"You sure you don't want to go get a drink?"

"No thanks." The evening had been an exercise in refutation and Chance had made promises to both Justin and himself he intended to keep.

"How about a movie?"

"Dru—"

"I suggested that already, didn't I? I meant how about a rental? We could watch it at your place."

"I'm a little beat. Besides, I've got piles of projects to look over and grade before Monday."

"I'm all caught up. How about I help?" She pulled up to his apartment, killed the engine and faced him. "Why don't I come in? We'll go through the projects together."

"Dru." He meant to stop her but wouldn't touch her to do it. She was out of the car and halfway up the walk before he had to tap her on the arm. "Dru—"

When she turned, she pressed into him and wound her arms around his neck. "You make me crazy, Chance. I have no pride, no will when I'm with you. I'm just this woman with a craving so deep I'd do whatever you tell me." She leaned up to kiss his mouth but his hands wrapped around her wrists and tugged.

She forced her lips on his.

More abruptly than he intended, he pushed her away, and they stood staring at each other in the darkness. A car drove by, its lights casting an eerie beam onto her face, wracked with frustration and anger, the site sent a cold shudder through Chance's system.

"What do you want?" she demanded.

"I don't want anything." He ran a hand through his hair. "I'm sorry if you got the wrong impression, but this was not about anything happening between us other than dinner."

"Men break my door down, Chance. This does not happen to me and I won't stand for it. I won't."

He stood unable to respond.

"You think you're too good for me?" she snapped, coming in close. "You're this artist who can pick and choose whom he paints, who he sleeps with? I can have any man I want. You're not going to come along and change that."

"I don't want to. Just don't expect one of those men to be me." He started up the walk, more than ready for the evening to end.

"I know all about your dirty past." Her eyes glittered with triumph when he stopped halfway up the stairs. "That's right. Twelve years ago Provo was a much smaller town. News spread fast. Don't think I won't tell Principal Ackerman about your little incident if I'm forced to."

Chance wet his lips. "You want to tell me what you're talking about?"

"You know what I'm talking about," she said. "But if it turns you on to hear me say it than I will."

"This evening is over." Chance headed up the stairs, his hand shaking as he dug in his pocket for keys.

"It's called rape, or have you conveniently forgotten that girl?"

His body filled with slick, black dread. He turned from the door and looked down at her. "We're done."

Slowly she shook her head. She came up the stairs with calculation in her step and trouble on her lips. "It's old news, I know that." Again she stopped close to him. "News that will stay old and not threaten your job if you'll consider what I'm offering."

Her hands started at his abdomen and slithered up the front of his chest. She smiled when she felt his breath hitch under her fingertips. "See, you do want me. Take me inside, Chance."

His breath had hitched because he was filled with loathing – for her, for himself, for a past he could never outrun. Because he sensed Dru was a live cannon, he gentled his voice.

"You're an interesting, if not complex woman, Dru." He'd have to choose his words and actions carefully if he didn't want to be caught in her aim. "I really didn't see any of this coming. I'm not prepared, and when I am, I'll make sure to give you some notice."

"I don't need any notice," she breathed out quickly, gears shifting from anger to hunger. "Please. I hope I didn't ruin the moment but you really do make me crazy. I lose my head when I'm around you, I want you that much."

"I'm bushed." His hand set on his door knob. "But I'll see you tomorrow, right?"

"Sure there's no way I could change your mind?"

Not in this lifetime, he thought. "I'm beat."

"How about I give you a rub down? I could make you some hot chocolate, run you a steamy bath."

"You're full of surprises, Dru."

"And I'll show you sometime." She backed down the stairs. "I had a great time tonight."

"Yeah." He opened the door.

"Oh, Chance." His heart almost stopped when she took a step up. "I was angry earlier. That wasn't really me."

But it was, he thought, and tried to smile. "No problem." He started to shut the door when she spoke again.

"Your secret's safe, Chance."

"It's not a secret," he told her. "Secrets are about things that happened." Then he shut the door and leaned against it, closing his eyes on a sigh.

Chance pulled off his shirt and strode back to his bedroom. Dru had made him sweat; brought back that sickening hopelessness he was trying so desperately to keep from his life. His body, his soul, felt suffocated.

The apartment was empty and he hated that he was alone. It was too quiet. It would be too easy for him to fall into self-pity.

Peeling off his clothes, he threw them on the bed and sat, burying his face in his hands. He wouldn't give in, even with a body craving the escape of liquid anesthesia.

He flicked on some music and rock blared from speakers. He thought of Avery, missed her, wanted her, so he pressed the scan button on the stereo system, searching.

When Frank Sinatra's calming voice sung about stepping out of a dream, he stopped and closed his eyes. In his mind he saw her dancing, floating around the studio, too far away to touch. Breathing stopped, and he tried to quell the emotion swelling in his chest. Always, she was too far away to touch.

Letting out a breath, he went to his tabaret. His easel was empty so he thumbed through his closet and pulled out Avery's canvas.

Chance ripped off the cover and stared. His blood skittered seeing her, even though nothing was there but slashes and shadows of what would be. But she was in his mind, waiting, ready – close. Lightly he stroked the empty spot, as if by so doing, she would materialize.

He began with her body.

His vision of her was still the same, lying relaxed, poised, longing only for him. He barely fleshed her in – the details could wait. What drove him, challenged him, caused his blood to hum now was her face.

Using his finest brushes, alternating three in one hand, one waiting for use between clenched teeth. Feathering first the oval shape of her head, he brought out her cheekbones, then painted her blue eyes, mixing color over and over until he got the midnight-sky color exact. Her lips were easy, with their natural pout and ripe strawberry color. Shading, darkening, his heart pounded as she came to life under his fingers. Sweat trickled down his neck, gathered the length of his spine.

Her brows were slightly arched, like the wings of a dove taking flight. Lightening the blue in her pupils gave her eyes just enough of that innocence and vulnerability that kept him thinking about no one and nothing else but her. Wanting no one and nothing else but her.

Johnny Mathis sang in the background now, words he'd heard in the studio, a melody that would forever remind him of her. He stood back, breathing heavily, drenched with sweat as he stared at her image.

She would never look at him that way, and he wouldn't ask her for more. But this was his creation, his vision. Only his eyes would see it. And so her gaze would be colored with all the acceptance, love and desire he hoped for. Her skin glowed with passion she would never feel for anyone but him.

Satisfied, at least for the time being, he finished with her hair falling seductively around her shoulders. He wet his lips, imagining soft skin, womanly heat.

"Wow."

Chance's heart skidded. The brush in his hand fell to the floor and he whirled around. Justin had a smile on his face as he came into the room, looking at the painting. "You're amazing, dude."

Retrieving, the brush, the sweat sheathing Chance's skin cooled him. He stuck the brush between his teeth again and adjusted the canvas for better viewing. "You like it?"

"It's—no seriously, I'm speechless. She's gonna love it."

"She'll never see it."

"Dude, you can't keep it from her, it's, it's—"

"It's mine. And you can't say anything or I'll ream you. Seriously."

"But it's insanely perfect. You have to give it to her."

"*No,* I don't."

"Any woman would find it cool, dude. It looks like a Met

piece. Seriously."

"And she's seriously not going to see it. I didn't mean for anyone to see it, but since you have, you keep that mouth of yours shut or I'll stuff it with one of my disgusting paint rags."

"Because she's naked? You've done nudes before. What's the biggie?"

"The biggie is that Avery's different."

"Avery's conservative but she's not a prude."

But she is untouchable. Chance wanted to make sure nothing tainted that. "Whatever. She's not going to see the painting. It's my fantasy of her and that's all it will ever be."

"Do you always paint in your boxers, dude?"

Chance looked down and shrugged. "I was hot."

"I bet. And you're not even finished with the piece." Justin wagged his brows, gesturing to Avery's fragmented body. He slapped his palm on Chance's bare shoulder. "You could use some solid exertion. Let's hit the floor."

Chance snickered and set down his brushes before following Justin out in the hallway. "Inessa kick you out?"

Justin's walk was cocky. " 'Course not."

"I'm kind of beat, and I have homework to grade."

"Dude, you're tight as a drum. You've said painting relaxes you but I think your subject matter got in the way tonight."

Once they hit the openness of the living room Justin turned with his arms poised, and ready to dive at Chance.

"I have projects to grade—" The excuse was lost in a grunt when Justin's shoulder rammed him in the abdomen, and stole his breath. They both fell backward with a thud and a laugh.

TWELVE

Avery was anxious to see Chance and was disappointed when she didn't even catch a glimpse of him at school. Curiosity had her checking the computer for the teachers' attendance log. She felt an instant settling knowing he was there – somewhere.

Now that the school day was over, she made her way to his classroom just for the purpose of laying her eyes on him.

Of course she'd not been able to completely forget that he was supposed to have spent Friday night with Dru. Finally able to compartmentalize that information so she and Scott could compete without distraction, they'd done well. Not as well as they would have liked, but at least their performance had nothing to do with where her head had been. She and Scott had stayed alive until the final heat, a feat for two teachers who squeezed in as much time as they could to perfect their craft. They'd placed sixth, and she was happy with the accomplishment. The direction she and Scott were consistently going was up.

With this competition over, she could settle the situation with Chance and proudly tell Scott he'd been wrong.

And she would find out what had happened Friday night.

The art room was dark, locked and empty. Avery frowned, peering through the glass panel in the door. Not that he owed her anything – not even a welcome back greeting. But that kiss. Surely a kiss like that meant something?

She thought she knew men fairly well, and as she walked through the door of her basement apartment fifteen minutes later, she began to feel challenged. No man had been a puzzle for her. Most had been easy in fact, opening their hearts and minds so fast she'd moved on, yawning from lack of stimulation.

She washed her hands in the kitchen sink. Before she knew it, her fingers were at her mouth and she was imagining the consuming kiss Chance had left on her lips. The memory sent fever-pitched jags through her body that needed only the reminder to fire up again.

Slowly, her hands skimmed her arms. She took a deep breath, as if by so doing she could feel some of that heat. She simply had to know what that kiss had meant.

In another hour she would see him in class, and readied to change into her dance clothes without thought. Tonight they would be dancing tango. The close, fiery dance could only mean one color. She smiled, picked just the right ensemble and enjoyed the sizzle of anticipation.

"You're back?"

Avery turned; her mother stood with a grin on her face and a laundry basket full of her clothes.

"Mom."

Charlotte Glenn's blue eyes twinkled in a bed of fine lines. Her lips curved, revealing pearly teeth. She set down the laundry and embraced her daughter. "When did you get in?"

"Late last night. It was too late to wake you."

"How did the competition go?"

Avery pulled the snug-fitting tee over her head. "Great. We placed sixth."

"Wonderful, wonderful."

"We're getting there. Mom." Avery nodded toward the full basket of clean, folded laundry. "You didn't have to do my laundry. I'd have gotten around to it eventually."

"You're a working woman, my little girl, and I'm retired with nothing to do but weed when the weather permits and read when it doesn't. Oh, did I say that I baby sit my grandchildren when I'm available?"

Avery laughed. "You have plenty to do without having to pick up after me."

"I stopped picking up after you years ago. Laundry's just a perk, but if you'd rather I not—"

"Oh, no." Avery kissed her cheek. "Squeeze me in between books. Does this look all right?"

Charlotte stepped back admiring her daughter's slim, perfect figure with a sigh. "It's enviable, Avery. I never looked that good, even before I started having babies. But then I never danced."

"The color okay?"

"More than okay. Are we wearing it to tempt?"

Avery recognized the glittering curiosity in her mother's face. "Maybe."

"This sounds better than getting back to my book." She sat down on the foot of Avery's bed with rounded eyes and hands clasped resolutely over her crossed knees.

"It's nothing – yet. But I'm kind of interested in this man I met a while back."

"Where did you meet him?"

"He's Justin's roommate."

"Then he's a nice boy."

Avery didn't look her mother in the eye. If she did, her mother would see she was still figuring that part out. But her pause gave her away.

"He's not a nice boy?" Charlotte asked lightly and without a thread of concern.

"No, he is, of course. I—well, he's, not like the other men I've been attracted to."

"Oh. You mean he's not practical, predictable and average? Good. I was beginning to worry about you."

"Mom."

"I was afraid you'd spent too many hours locked away in that school or worse, in the dance studio with Scott. Not that I have anything against dear Scott. The boy's bland enough to please any mother." She rose, standing behind Avery so that they looked at each other in the mirror. "But, I thought with three brothers you'd pick somebody with a little more spice."

"I can't believe I'm hearing this from you. You've never said anything before."

"You weren't twenty-five before."

"I'm still young."

"Yes, I suppose."

"Suppose? You really think I'm getting old?"

"I didn't say that. It's just that when a mother has four boys all marry and settle down by the time they're twenty-five, she starts glancing at the calendar when her youngest, a girl, reaches that same age and is not even seeing anyone seriously."

"I've been busy."

"Exactly. And you hole up with Scott in that studio for years on end and, voila, before you know it, zip! Your time is up. You're twenty-five and boringly alone."

"Thanks."

"I only mean to give you rude reminders, darling."

"Uh-huh."

"Tell me about Mr. Spice."

"Well, he'd be a deep, flavorful bay leaf if I had to describe him."

"Bay leaves are delicious, aromatic and absolutely necessary. Mmm. Now, what does he look like?"

"He's gorgeous. Dark hair, kind of messy and wild, like he's not sure what to do with it—"

"—Perfect."

"And the cutest smile with these dimples—"

"—Dimples? How precious. Good teeth?"

"Great teeth."

"Eyes?"

"Stormy gray."

Charlotte's brow arched over a smile. "I love a good storm."

"He reminds me of a little boy in ways I can't put my finger on exactly."

"As long as you don't want to mother him." Charlotte waved a hand dismissively. "That kind of man can be a pain in your back all of your life."

"No. Not like that," Avery said thoughtfully. Chance was far too feisty and independent for that. "More like—lost."

"Oh. That's different altogether."

"Bad or good?"

"Depends on the man—on how lost he really is. You can't save anyone, darling, no matter how much your heart aches for them. But a woman can help a man find his way. And visa versa of course."

Only a part of Avery's heart ached, and it ached for what she figured he lost when his family stopped caring for him. But she couldn't believe that, it was like listening to music played backwards. It only made her more determined to dig deeper into Chance so she could have a better look.

"Be careful." Charlotte wrapped an arm around her shoulder. "You're a nurturer by nature. Just don't let your heart beat for him unless it's for love. And I mean good, strong love, the kind between a man and a woman that lights a fire inside. So by all means, wear this, you look stunning. And bring this young man home, will you? I want to meet Mr. Bay Leaf."

It relieved some of Avery's angst now that her mother knew. It would only be a matter of hours before the rest of the family found out, her mother being the kind that shared good news via frequent phone calls.

Avery hardly noticed that she and her mother were at the door—that her mother had tucked her purse under her arm, kissed her cheek, had her hand on her rump and was nudging her out.

Avery was late on purpose. It was her first time – ever, being late to teach a class, but she wanted to make an entrance.

She opened the door with a smile, nerves jittering, and greeted the group at large the same way she did each class. "Good evening ladies and gentlemen."

She searched for Chance. He stood at the back of the studio, a dark figure casually leaning against the wall, his hands tucked away in his pockets. Justin and Inessa were with him and they all looked her way as she sent him a small nod.

When her eyes met his, he pulled away from the wall, and stood erect.

"Tonight," she began, a skittering of pleasure rifling through her, "we review tango." The room fell to a hush and she leafed through her CDs, feeling Chance's eyes tear through her back like lasers, causing her insides to quiver. "I know it's been a while since we went over these steps, and for some of you, this will be completely new. But I thought it would be a nice change for us."

She put on *Roxanne* from *Moulin Rouge*. The beat strummed her blood, her mood, and she faced the class.

"Tango is rigid but sensual." Slowly she walked in front of the class as the music teased. "The position is closed, fused pelvis to pelvis. You're never open in this dance, rather pressed body to body.

"Tango is not a dance for the faint." She smiled when everyone whispered. "But it's not about power, men. Those tacky tangos you've seen on TV, in most movies, look like you could be in traction by the time you're done dancing. If done right, tango is just as fluid and smooth as waltz or fox trot or quickstep. We'll start with the basic position. Men, take your ladies in your arms please. Chance?" She stretched out her hand to him.

His eyes were sharp as a hawk. He made his way through the couples like an animal on the prowl and something deep inside of her trembled. He stood tauntingly near, she felt his breath, smelled the faint sweet of mint mixed with his tantalizing cologne.

"Welcome back," he said so that only she could hear.

She held her hand out as if to shake his. "It's good to be here."

He looked at her hand, then at her before flashing a grin. "We've already met."

"Stand in position class." She looked out over the group. "Mr. Savage was not here during our beginning tango classes so I will be working with him on the basics." Her eyes slid back to his. "Give me your hand, Chance."

He set his hand in hers, as if they were going to shake in greeting. It was then she twisted herself around so that when she finished their bodies were close. "It's called hand shake positioning," she told him. Then she slipped her left arm slightly underneath his, her palm nestled at his arm pit as she extended her right arm out, holding his hand.

"You may begin," she announced to the class. Couples jagged around the room in promenade. Avery looked up into Chance's eyes and slid herself close, her arm twining with his tense one. "Relax, Chance. Get used to the feel of me."

"Impossible."

Fire sparked through her. The hardness of his chest, pelvis and thighs was hot along the full length of her. "In tango," she said, her eyes locked on his, "thighs stay close, like this. Knees stay bent, like this."

He gripped her hands hard. "Easy, easy," she said softly. "Remember to keep your hands gentle. We haven't started moving yet, when we do, I'll need to feel strength there."

His hands tightened anyway, sending an explosive shuddering down low to her belly. She'd danced for too long to be reacting like this; heart fluttering, palms sweating. She would bet her cheeks were red, and they were so close, she couldn't hide them from those razor-sharp eyes of his.

"Now, we move." She urged him forward. "The count is slow, slow, quick, quick. Two walks and a link, like so. Yes, you've got it." Slowly she nudged him along, his stance stiff yet as she strove to keep her own body fluid.

There was no smile of accomplishment on his face, even after her compliment. His face was drawn tight with something exciting she found hard to bear looking at. Pearls of sweat budded at her hairline, around her neck, and she forced her look out toward the class.

"Very good." But her voice trembled and when it did, she felt his body press deeper into hers.

"Why, Ms. Glenn," his voice was low in her ear. "You're trembling."

"I'm a little cold," she lied.

"In that outfit, I wouldn't doubt it. There's not much between you and the air." His voice was rough. "I like it."

She did tremble then, from the delicious heat his words sent through her. "You're doing very well for someone who has never done tango."

"Thank you."

"This step is the basic promenade step."

Chance glanced at the other couples. Justin and Inessa were heading their direction, with smiles on their faces. "When will you teach me that thing they're doing with their heads?"

Taking two slow, long steps together, Justin and Inessa jerked their heads when they took shorter, quick steps, angling their bodies in another direction.

"Someday you'll be as good as me, dude," Justin called to him with a grin.

"I'm on your tail." Chance pulled Avery closer without even thinking about it, a possessive move she liked. He looked at her, his eyes skimming her face with an intimacy that spoke of familiarity. "How was the competition?"

"We did well."

"What is well in this business?"

"Great is placing first. Well is staying in the rounds as long as you can and placing. At least that's according to Avery Glenn."

"That's all I care about," he said.

She trembled again. "What a nice thing to say."

"That's what you said about my kiss, that it was nice. Tell me about kissing according to Avery Glenn. Just what is *nice*, exactly?"

Warmth flushed to her cheeks. "Nice is—"

"Ms. Glenn?"

A couple had neared, and both looked frustrated. "We can't seem to get the quick, quick right. When we do it, we come apart," the man said, blinking hard behind his bottle bottom glasses.

"I keep telling him we're supposed to stay together and he keeps moving his hips away." His wife's face twisted into annoyance.

Avery looked up at Chance. "Excuse me for a moment." She eased back but he tugged her in close for a moment more. The move caused her heart to thump.

"You're going to finish that thought about the kiss," he whispered before letting her go.

She was glad to have a moment to catch her breath and

collect thoughts so wildly scattered. Out the corner of her eye, he hung like a dark temptation at the edge of the dance floor. She went from couple to couple, checking form and step. Everything around him was electric, drawing her into a magnetic field she was less able to resist.

When she allowed the class a five-minute break, she was as jittery as she had been when she'd first walked into class, and with him now coming her direction, her palms began to sweat again.

"I haven't forgotten you," she said. "It's just that it's been a few months since we covered this in class, and most of my students needed some reminders. If you don't practice, well, it gets lost in the shuffle of life just like everything else."

Something sad colored his gray eyes then and she felt it right in her heart. Instinctively, she reached out and took his hand and moved closer to him, lowering her voice. "Are you all right?"

Even with a slight crease in his dimples, the sorrow remained in his eyes. "Yeah."

"Would you like to go over the steps again?"

He looked around at everyone drinking ice water from white-cone cups, some talking, a few still practicing; Justin was stealing a kiss from Inessa. Chance pulled her hand close to his chest, wrapping his other arm around her to lead her in a private walk around the floor.

Her neck shivered when he leaned his lips close for a quiet whisper. "You look beautiful tonight, did I tell you that?"

The compliments, the feelings, were all too intoxicating and before Avery let herself really enjoy them, she wanted the answers to her questions. "Can we talk after class?" she asked. He stopped, cautious for a moment. "It's just that there are some things I want to talk to you about and this isn't the right time," she added.

"Okay." His arms slipped from hers and he gave her

some space. Wariness brought his brows together. The class was growing restless; there was no time to reassure him.

She crossed to the front of the room and demonstrated the next step.

He shouldn't have come to class. He'd decided to sever things, knew it was best for her, even though he could go on torturing himself indefinitely just to be near her. Now he was torturing himself with having to look at her, feel her, smell her knowing he couldn't have any part of her.

She was red heat in motion tonight, wearing something so close to skin he'd been tempted to skim her body with the palms of his hands to see if he could discover the differences. What little he had felt had warned him to keep his hands where she told him to, anything more would place him dangerously close to being unable to stop a corporeal exploration.

Circles, that's what he was going in, and it needed to stop.

Justin sauntered over. Inessa hung from his shoulder with stars in her eyes. The obvious display of love slugged Chance with envy. "You look tense," Justin told him.

Chance avoided looking at Avery who stood talking to a couple as *Roxanne* began to play again. More than tense, Chance mused, glancing at Avery's sleek red form. It was time to start looking for another job, what, he wasn't sure.

"You're doing great, by the way," Justin said.

"Avery's a great teacher."

"That, too." Justin laughed at Chance's obvious attempt to cover up his preoccupation with Avery. "But I meant the job, dude. The kids love you."

And he'd grown to like the kids – a lot. Chance looked at Justin feeling a sudden surge of gratitude. "Thanks to you."

"It hasn't been all that bad – the dance class, has it?" Justin nodded Avery's direction with a grin. "You and Avery."

"There is no me and Avery."

Inessa made a little noise and Chance looked at her with raised brows. She shrugged, hiding demurely behind Justin's shoulder. "It's just so apparent that you two like each other," she said.

Chance looked across the room at Avery, their eyes held for a few taut moments. "Yeah, well, she's way out of my league." Because his throat was dry, he crossed to the water cooler. Justin whispered something into Inessa's ear and followed Chance alone.

"I recognize that look, dude and don't do it."

Chance tugged a paper cone-cup free. "Don't do what?" He filled it with water.

"Don't ditch something that's good for you."

Chance drank the water down. "What?"

"You got that same look when I told you about the sub gig and look how great that's been."

He couldn't deny Justin was right. It just caught him off guard that he was becoming that transparent. For years he'd protected his feelings and his emotions from everyone - even himself. Only with Justin's friendship had he'd come to know Avery and begun to feel safe again.

Justin's palm landed on his shoulder in a hearty pat. "She's hot for you. It's so obvious I need sunscreen."

Chance laughed, taking too much pleasure in Justin's appraisal.

Avery started class again. Justin had gone back to Inessa, the two of them nuzzling, kissing. The room boomed with the beat of *Roxanne* and soon couples were starting across the floor in the dance of tango.

Avery was looking at him, her hand outstretched. The gesture caused his blood to whirl through his system. Crushing the cup in his fist, he crossed to her.

Chance hung by the back wall while she answered the last questions, satisfying straggling issues of steps and form. As he watched her speak patiently with over zealous students, he saw the love she had for them, the passion for what she was trying to teach.

Few people in his life had cared that much for anything he'd done. He was envious until he reminded himself she was his teacher, too. It moved him in ways that drove deep into his system, finally settling around his heart.

Maybe there was nothing wrong with pursuing a relationship.

He ran his tongue over his lips as the last couple finally left. Finally, they would be alone. The door thudded closed and she turned, looking right at him as if she'd been just as anxious as him to be alone.

She'd turned off the music some time ago and silence tiptoed in the air, but he heard his heart beating fast and hard. He started toward her, taking in every curve of her through the thin red fabric.

She reached both hands behind her back and he heard the click of the door being locked. "I don't want to be interrupted," she said.

He was so near now that he could see her chest rise and fall a little faster with his approach. Why was she wearing something that alluded to perfection, followed every muscle and bone with exquisite attention to detail? Had she any idea what it was doing to him? He wanted to take the flimsy fabric in his hands and gently peel it away, leaving nothing between the two of them but what his own flesh held captive.

But she was here to talk, not to be prey to his desire. He stopped close enough to catch the sweet scent of perfume she wore. "You wanted to talk?"

She took in a deep breath. "Yes. I hope you don't think I'm too forward for saying what I'm going to say. I believe in talking things out. I've had to, with partnerships, with coaches and students. One thing I've learned is that it's better to know than to be left guessing. It's black and white and I know that it's black and white or I'm confused and unsettled, two things I hate to be."

Chance fought reaching out and running a calming finger along her cheek. "I can tell that. You like things on the table."

She nodded. "It's just the way my family is. Does that scare you?"

Petrify was more like it, but he shrugged. "It's not what I grew up with, but then I've already told you we're different that way."

"I know you've said that, but my intention here is not to scare you with my honesty. I don't want that."

"Hey." He did reach out then, and touching her calmed him as well. "It takes a lot to scare me away." Indeed, he was finding it increasingly difficult to end the relationship, even with his recurring reasons.

"I've enjoyed getting to know you, Chance. You're very different than anyone I've ever known, in ways I like very much." She smiled, hearing her mother say the word 'spicy' in her mind.

This was by far the most difficult thing she'd ever done. But then she'd never known someone that had rumors like his floating out there. Would he hate her for doubting? He was stormy, feral, yet so much of him was simply achingly unreachable. No matter how intriguing she found him, Scott was right. She had to know.

"Do you mind if we dance?" Nothing else would calm her as she delved into the unknown.

"If that's what you want." He waited while she selected

music. Closing her eyes for a moment, she searched for what she wanted and she pulled out something classical. Sweet violins pierced the air, weaving the melody straight to her heart.

"Waltz?" he asked. She nodded.

They moved with ease around the room, skirting the edge of the studio.

"You feel uptight." His voice was as soft as the violins. "Is this not helping?"

"It will. Chance?" She eased back, looked up at him. "Tell me about what happened twelve years ago."

He stiffened instantly, gripping her in a flash that eased only when he looked away. She waited, still encouraging him to dance with gentle urgings from her hands and body that went uninterrupted.

"Twelve years ago I was in high school. I imagine you were too."

"Yes."

He shrugged casually, but it didn't disguise the tenseness still in him. *I was in the fight of my life,* he thought but wouldn't tell her. In fact, anger simmered that she might be alluding to that god-awful period. "It was high school, typical stuff."

She kept her gaze steady on his face. "It's painful for you to talk about your family and your life, I can see that—"

Suddenly he pushed her away and moved restlessly. "You can't see anything." Then he paused, softening some. "You think you know but you can't. You couldn't possibly know." Part of him wanted a woman to finally understand, to believe. It was the hardest, thinking about sharing his past with a woman, for it had been a woman he'd first trusted and been deceived by. But when he looked at Avery, the space between them vanished. Her eyes, accepting and full of care, pulled the words from a place he had kept them safely locked.

"I was fifteen when I met this girl. We liked each other. I

sketched her, for fun – pencil stuff, charcoals. She took them home and showed them to her mom and the next thing I knew, I was meeting her mother." He lowered his head for a moment before continuing.

She was slowly coming toward him and he willed his feet not to flee. His eyes stayed with hers, reaching for the open caring he saw there. "Her mother wanted me to do portraits of them. They had tons of money. They lived in this huge place on the bench. Same neighborhood as us, it's just they had the biggest and best of everything. My mom was all about old, established family money. They were new money so in her book, they weren't even on the same page. But that's not how Ginger saw it. Ginger, that was Chelsea's mother."

Avery nodded. She was next to him now, setting her arms out for him to take her. He considered for a moment before conceding. He could try. He could try to hold her while he explained. He moved at her gentle urging.

"Mom had these visions of me being something great someday. She was all for supporting me, until she found out I liked Chelsea, and that Ginger had discovered me. I guess when it came down to it, she didn't want my talent nurtured by anyone but her. She thought mothers were owed that.

"I was the typical rebellious teen. When she forbid me to see Chelsea, I saw her anyway. That was when Ginger offered to pay me two thousand dollars to paint her and Chelsea's portraits and I agreed."

Avery let out a small wisp of appreciation. "You must have really impressed her."

His sharp laugh came from a well of anger and hurt instead of adulation. He stopped dancing and moved away from her, rubbing his hands down his face with an aching groan. He looked at her. "How did you hear about this?"

"Someone that cares about me."

"Warned you? Told you I was a rapist, right?"

Avery stood perfectly still in the center of the room, her blood flowing cold.

He set his hands on his hips and shook his lowered head. "You sure you want to hear about this?"

"Yes."

He kept his distance. It was better this way. Now she would know, and then she would be done with him and they could both get on with their lives. "I took the commission because I wanted to prove to my parents I could do something. Long story short—"

"I'd like the long version, please. This is important to me." When he looked over, her eyes darkened with something he couldn't read.

Avery could see his struggle to continue. His expression was painfully troubled as he walked toward her. He stood before her like a child confessing, as if he had everything in the world to lose. "Ginger offered to mentor me. She paid for more classes and I took them. Anything I wanted, she got for me. Portraiture was easy, incredibly easy to do, and I loved it. I loved the process, the intimacy between creator and subject." He looked off for a moment, as if searching for something in a dark corner of his mind. "Ginger wanted it done a certain way, and I did what she told me to do."

The anguish on his face was tight. Avery's stomach began to hollow.

"Chelsea and I got closer because her mother insisted she pose live while I painted her. Even though I'd taken photographs, she didn't want me to use them. She said they'd change the integrity of the piece.

"Ginger was always with us. Not because she didn't trust us. I was naive. I mean, I liked Chelsea a lot, but it would never have occurred to me to do anything. We only kissed maybe a half dozen times, you know? Ginger hung by because she liked to watch me work.

"After I finished Chelsea's portrait, Ginger was supposed to give me half of the money. But she kept putting it off. I couldn't figure it out. I'd sweat blood painting that portrait. I'd spent every free, waking hour in that studio. I even fell asleep there."

Rubbing his forearm, he lowered his head again. "At first I thought she was withholding the money because she wasn't happy with my work, but I knew she loved it. I thought it was because of the money, that's how naive I was, how stupid I was." He covered his face with his hands then dropped them, leaving behind red and white finger marks. "I came to the house one day and Chelsea wasn't there. Ginger said she was at a friend's house.

"It didn't faze me to be there alone with Ginger, she was Chelsea's mother, you know? But the mood was off. She was acting different. Mr. Drake wasn't around—he was never around. He's a doctor who commuted to L.A. four weeks out of five. I asked her about the money because I was starting to wonder if I'd ever see it." He let out a groan and turned away. "This—it's hard for me to talk about this."

Avery drew closer. "I'm sorry that it is. It's something I feel strongly about understanding, Chance."

He closed his eyes, knowing the revelation would shock and repulse her, and end the sweetness between them. "She told me she'd pay me when I was done painting her. I was upset. I reminded her of our deal and she just...smiled.

"I didn't understand then. I thought maybe she was joking, or she was high or something. She wasn't herself. When she came close to me, I could smell what I later found out was alcohol. My parents didn't drink, my friends didn't drink – I'd never been around anybody drunk before.

"She kissed me." He let the sentence sit on the thick air between them for awhile before continuing. "I was so shocked, I was unable to move. I would never have expected it and I didn't see it coming. She told me if I wanted the payment, it was time for me to pay her back. I didn't understand what she meant at first but she started touching me and I – it scared me." Shame kept his head bowed, his voice almost a whisper. "She told me I owed her. That I was foolish if I'd thought all this time it was for free. 'Nothing's for free', she said, and she expected payment."

Time stretched in quiet sorrow as he fought memories and emotions. Utterly still, trying to keep her expression even, Avery waited.

"She said if I didn't sleep with her, she'd ruin my name." His eyes were glistening, his shoulders hunched with guilt, and regret.

Avery didn't know if she was still breathing. Her breath had caught, was locked in her chest along with her heart. So many questions rang through her head, vivid scenes of faces she had never seen, places she had never been as the idea of the distorted scene played in her mind.

He looked beaten, as if he were reliving the entire episode in telling it. "I know it sounds like I should have run from the place and afterwards, I did, I was so freaked. But she got in her car and came after me. I knew she'd been drinking and she was driving like a crazy. She nearly killed me with the car. She was crying, upset, swearing. She demanded I drive her home because it was my fault that she was on the street. So I drove her home, even though I didn't have a license and I was scared."

"There's no reason to go into the rest of the story, Avery. The details aren't important anymore. It was an ugly mess." His eyes finally dared a look into hers where he found nothing but compassion waiting. "She accused me of things when I wouldn't do what she wanted. Just know that I didn't rape her daughter. I'd never even been with a girl."

She believed him—completely. She only wished he looked

relieved now after telling her. Slowly she eased toward him and rested her hand on his arm. "I'm sorry seems dreadfully insufficient to say."

The words were more than he'd heard from either of his parents. No one involved had said anything of that nature to him, in fact. "Say you believe me, that's all I need to hear."

"I believe you."

There, in the quiet of the studio, she felt the urge to wrap around him and so she did, feeling him tense at first, only to savor the way he yielded, finally burying his face in her neck.

As if he'd dragged himself across an unforgiving desert with no hope for anything that would bring comfort, Chance fell into the warmth she offered with the ease of falling into bed from exhaustion. It wasn't the stirring of desire he felt trusting himself to her arms, but the unconditional love he'd not allowed himself to feel again for another human being after being abandoned those years ago.

It seemed impossible that someone finally understood and a swelling of tears filled his eyes. The flicker of hope was now lit, urging him to give more of himself to her. But doubt stood in too many shadows and he couldn't bring himself to hurt her with what still lay in those dark places.

Her body soon stirred his desire into a voracious need to become one with her, as if in doing so he would take that understanding and love he'd been denied and finally fill the void he'd carried for so long.

Hands eager for more, yet painfully aware that they could be left empty—skimmed her as if feeling her for the first time. Her neck was at his lips and so he kissed her there, light fluttering kisses, until he found her jaw. It gave him a punch of pleasure when she moaned and her head fell back, exposing more of that long, lush throat.

Eagerly, his hands roamed, tracing her shoulders, the length of her arms, finally twining fingers with hers when his lips found her mouth. Emotion welled in his chest, sang through his veins, mixing with the storm of desire inside, creating a tempest he was sure to get lost in.

Tears flushed behind his eyes again. He was ready to break, right there. He couldn't, and pushed back from her, walking as far away as he could. He needed to face her and take what was coming; it was part of why he'd told her.

He wanted to thank her for believing. Yet, the words would sound so ludicrous, he stopped himself from saying them but the magnitude of her simple belief—she would never understand what it meant to him. For that reason, her simple trust, as well as too many other things he loved about her, he did what he had to do.

"Even though you believe me," he began with his back to her. "It doesn't change anything. There are still people out there that believe and will always believe Ginger."

"And?"

He turned. "There'll always be whispers. You haven't had to live with the tentacles of scandal, Avery. They reach deep. Their hold is so tight it steals your life."

"You're still here."

"And I've fought for every thing I've had. After it happened, I was sent to the Boys School. Locked away for my own safety as well as the safety of every teenage girl in this county, at least that's what Ginger said. What my parents agreed to."

"But I thought the girl never confirmed the allegations."

He stared at her and she realized she had not told him all that she had heard from Scott.

"None of this was ever made public," Chance said after a moment, obvious speculation in his eyes. "Drake money kept it quiet. Except of course what she wanted out there. She didn't bring in the police because she knew as well as I did that I'd never touched her daughter." Chance wanted to laugh at the irony, that it should have been Ginger Drake locked away, but the shame of it kept him from telling Avery the whole truth. "So she set the rumor loose. She wanted to ruin me. She got what she wanted."

"What happened to Chelsea?"

"She tried to tell everyone that we never had sex. She even snuck to her doctor so that he could verify that she was still a virgin. Her mother swooped down and sent her back east to boarding school. That was the last I saw of her. I was in the home, with restrictions. I couldn't even use a phone."

Avery could imagine the helplessness of being locked away while outside, a rumor devastated and spread without being able to do anything to stop it. She started toward him. "You've made something of yourself in spite of what happened. You can be proud of that."

"I've had to dodge a lot of bullets along the way. It's not that a lot of people knew, Avery, it's the ones who knew. They were the money, the positions, the ones who mattered in this valley. Believe it or not, they're so bored they still stir it up if they feel like it."

"Where are the Drakes now?"

"Around. I saw Ginger a few years back. I was at an opening and she showed up."

"That was bold."

"Yeah, well, that was Ginger."

"Did you speak to her?"

"I tried not to but she caught up with me in the bathroom." Avery's eyes flashed and Chance sneered. "Look, this whole thing was a nightmare, one that I've done my best to forget, and the best way I've found is to distance myself from anything and everyone who knows anything about it. That way nobody gets hurt."

"I hope you're not including me in that tidy sweep because I won't let you do it."

"It's for your own good."

"You said you didn't touch her. I believe you. What am I in danger of?"

"Didn't your mother ever tell you if you lay down with dogs, you come up with fleas? These fleas are still biting me and they always will."

"Is that why you push everybody away?"

"What choice do I have?"

"Take a flea bath, I don't know. But that sounds like a pretty convenient cop-out to me."

The way his eyes sharpened and he jerked toward her almost had her taking a step back. Her heart pounded hard, but she didn't move. If he wanted a fight, she was prepared to fight – for him. "It may be harsh but that's the way I see it," she told him.

His first instinct was to lash out, to scream in her face unloading the extent of the injustices his life had known since Ginger Drake had let loose her serpent's tongue. But he didn't want to expose her that was why he was forcing himself out of her life.

Knowing she had no idea the extent of what he'd suffered, he couldn't blame her and he didn't want to. He just knew how weak it would look when he turned and left her now. How cold and indifferent he'd appear tomorrow and any day thereafter when he ignored her.

He started for the door.

"Chance?"

He stole the sound of her voice, tucking it away in the deepest corner of his heart as he crossed the floor. It was time for another door to shut and lock and when this one echoed closed, it tore to the center of him.

THIRTEEN

The solitary life he'd led—surrounding himself with blank canvases he could color and paint, images that kept him silent company—meant that he'd insulated himself from anything good as well as anything like the pointed words of truth Avery had said to him.

Chance found himself avoiding his reflection in the burnished mirror hanging along the back wall of the bar. His body was practically shaking as he sat, the back of his hand blocking his mouth, staring at the full bottle sitting in front of him. His mouth salivated, and the craving was seeping into his system like a fever. He closed his eyes.

It was right that he leave her alone. She had no idea what it would mean to have a man at her side she had to take a breath for every time she introduced him to someone, afraid of what that person might say, think.

Chance reached out and wrapped his hand around the cold, sweaty bottle. The chill screamed up his arm, settled in a shiver in his gut and without another thought, he put the bottle to his lips, his tongue running along the rim once, tasting a hint of the sharp flavor his body was waiting for.

"Well, well."

Chance froze. He pulled the bottle away from his lips just far enough so he could speak because he knew he'd have to.

"It's always easy to find you, little brother."

"Go find another rat corner."

"Why? I can see you squirm in this one." Kurt slid some money across to the waiting bartender and ordered before he sat. "Yeah, the heat's gonna turn up again under your pathetic life. I just can't wait to watch you burn."

Chance still held the bottle, twisting in his fingers. He could see Avery in his mind; he could still hear her voice saying his name and was relieved she would never be exposed to the derangement of his family.

Kurt nodded to the bartender who brought him his drink. "I'm finally wearing you down. Which is good because I'm getting tired of this little dance."

Because he was feeling dangerously worn, Chance didn't look at him, knowing one look at those icy eyes could either break him or send him over the edge and into a fist fight.

Kurt drank, set down his bottle with a thunk. "It was always so satisfying to fight with you because you always took so long to beat down. It was the process, watching you slowly crumble."

Chance turned his face away, rubbing the back of his fist to lips eager to scream or drown. It was hard to believe they were brothers, that once they had shared a bedroom, traded scary stories late into the night. Eaten each other's birthday cakes.

"But, hey," Kurt continued, "I got the stamina. I can keep at it for as long as you want."

When Chance didn't reply, Kurt took another drink and let out a hissing belch. "I'm bringing papers over. Sign them."

"I'm not signing anything."

Kurt's fingers flexed. "Did you know that in the unfortunate event that anything happens to you, I get everything?" He leaned close. "Everything – like it should have been in the first place."

Chance kept his stare on the bottle warming in his hands. He knew it would come down to this. Still, the shock of warning that spread through him now was tremulous. "I guess it goes both ways, doesn't it?" He slid his first look at his brother and their eyes locked.

Kurt's slivered, the corner of his mouth twitched. The stare was long, impenetrable by the rousing country tune pounding from a juke box or the half-dozen other patrons sitting at the bar or wandering in silent loneliness around them.

Finally Kurt stood, moving close enough to remind Chance of the power he'd always had physically over him. He threw back the last of his drink, slamming the bottle to the bar top. Chance started in spite of anticipating such an act.

One side of Kurt's lip curled. "Then we'll just have to see who comes out alive." He turned and strolled out the bar and into the night.

Chance turned and faced the bar, and caught his reflection. He still held the bottle in his hands. It was room temperature now, and because his stomach was clutched in a fist, he wouldn't drink it. Watching himself through the mirror, he brought it to his lips and inhaled deep before he left it, untouched.

Avery drove straight to his apartment after he'd walked out. Her worry pushed her to do something she didn't consider spontaneous as much as necessary. It was out of character. When she cared for someone, she followed her instincts and her instincts told her Chance might put himself in danger.

She was still trying to figure out why he'd left. They'd not even finished their conversation, at least not the way she was accustomed to finishing a conversation, with every end neatly tied. He'd left an uncertain mood in the air and she hated uncertainty. She couldn't be angry about it; she was coming to understand that he'd had very little in the way of diplomatic training of any kind.

It still seemed unbelievable to her that a parent could

abandon a child because of a lie. Even though he'd not entrusted her with anything more about his family's reaction to what had happened, she deduced as much from what he had eluded to so far.

Her parents would have fought with their teeth and nails for her or any of her brothers.

Only one light was on in the apartment. Justin opened the door in grey sweats, a stack of papers under his arm, a smile on his face. "Hey, Avery. What brings you out this time of night?"

"Chance here by any chance?" They both smiled at her choice of words and he stood back so she could enter.

"Haven't seen him—not since class anyway." When he saw her face tighten, he asked, "Everything okay?"

"We were talking after class. He was upset. I was worried. But then I'm probably looking in the wrong place." She turned for the door and Justin tossed down his papers.

"Let me get my shoes, we can go together." He disappeared to the back of the apartment.

Teeth and nails. Avery looked at her hands; she had plenty long nails for a good fight.

Justin was back and tugging on his tennis shoes when the front door opened and Chance walked in. He stopped when he laid eyes on Avery.

"Chance." She would never have expected his face to change when she said his name but it did. The hard look he'd worn through the door softened for just an instant before it turned to stone again.

He strode past her. "I thought I told you I wouldn't be in your life anymore."

"And I told you that kind of push-broom sweep doesn't work for me."

"I don't want you here."

"I don't believe that. Not after the way you held me. "

"Uh." Justin slipped off the shoe he'd just put on. "That was—"

"—That was you, opening up to me, Chance."

"A mistake." He shook his head.

"It wasn't a mistake. Did you think your admission would change things? That I'd be appalled, shocked, repulsed?"

Finished putting on his shoe again, Justin cleared his throat. "I'm gonna head out for a few minutes." Then he disappeared out the front door.

Chance crossed to Avery and looked down into her face. It had only been an hour, maybe two since he'd seen her but it felt like months, and he took in every detail with excruciating care. "You should go."

"No until we talk about this."

"There isn't any point."

"There is, Chance. I care about you. I'm your friend. Friends don't leave in the middle of something just because it's messy or ugly or bad."

But family does, and he would never be able to forget or forgive that. "Why do you care?"

Because I see inside of you, she thought. *I can see that you're aching, you're alone.* There were so many reasons Avery felt compelled to him, she was ashamed for feeling so much so fast. *You're beautiful, and what you create is beautiful. It comes from inside, and that means what's in you is not something you should keep locked away.*

"You want me to embarrass you?" she finally said amidst her whirling thoughts. "I may not have scared you earlier, but I will now."

He held up his palms. "No. Don't."

"My feelings for you grow each day, Chance."

"Avery, stop."

"I think you're exciting, mysterious, wonderful, complex. I'm not stopping there."

"Please."

She shook her head. A faint smile crested her lips. "What you do with your hands, it's unlike anything I've ever seen. It's because that beauty comes from inside of you."

"You're wrong."

"No." Carefully, she laid her hand on his tense forearm. "I told you, I'm ninety-nine percent accurate where men are concerned."

"I'm the one percent."

"You are in that you're the most extraordinary man I've ever known and that's why I—" She stopped what came in her mind from flowing from her lips. For a moment the air heated and thickened.

"Why what?" His voice was desperate. "Tell me."

With caution she ran her hand along his cheek, felt it harden to rock under her fingertips. She shivered with pleasure when he closed his eyes. Bravely she let her fingers wander to his lips. His eyes fluttered open and she saw the fight to believe clashing with what had always been a reality for him.

"It's why I'm going to fight for you."

His eyes glistened before he could look away. He shook his head. "I'm not worth the fight," he murmured.

She couldn't imagine who would have told him such a thing. Daring to soothe, she inched closer so her body fused the rigid length of him. "I've already decided that you are. And just so you know, when I fight, I win. One hundred times out of one hundred."

Their eyes locked and he moved in so he could breathe and take her inside of him. "I want you."

"That's good," she said just as softly as his whisper had been. She leaned up, kissed his cheek lightly. "I'm going to be here."

He wanted to bring her against him in a squeeze he knew

would crush her, he wanted her that much, needed to have her be a part of him to his core.

"I have a private with Scott but I'll cancel it, if you need me."

The offer humbled him. "No. You should take it."

She turned and headed for the door, leaving him with only the softest kiss lingering on his cheek.

"I'll see you tomorrow," she said, opening the door. Her smile was pure and honest. "I'm glad you came home," she told him. After the door closed behind her, he stood staring. It was the first time he had ever heard those words from anyone, and his heart wept in his chest.

Chance had placed the easel close enough to his bed so that as he lay on the mattress, with only the light of the moon streaming through his window, he could look at her face as sleep overtook him.

He'd awakened the next morning hanging halfway off the bed, facing the portrait, arms and hands spread as if reaching for it. In the hush of dawn, he stared long and hard at her face, knowing that he could guiltlessly spend the entire day lying there, looking at her.

But Justin hustled him off to school. Chance didn't mind. The everyday routine was something he hadn't experienced since his round of odd jobs waiting tables and tending bar, and he enjoyed the security and satisfaction of teaching.

Avery was ever-present in his mind as he went through the day. Every movement he caught through the small pane in his classroom door drew his eye in hopes he would find her there.

When he finally saw her, she was walking toward the lunchroom talking with Dru of all people. Avery lit up like a searchlight when she noticed him in the crowd of students, an innocent reaction that didn't go unnoticed by him. The three of them stopped outside the door of the teachers' lounge.

"Well, hello, stranger." Dru ran her hand from his shoulder to his wrist, where she squeezed.

"Hey." He allowed Dru a brief glance before focusing on Avery. His stomach fluttered when her eyes met his. "Can I take you to lunch?"

Avery blinked, her mouth opened and held for a moment before she smiled and turned what Chance thought was a lovely shade of pink. "I'd love that. Thank you."

"My." Dru folded her arms with her lifted brow aimed at Avery. "Lucky you."

Gently Chance reached out for the brown bag Avery held in her fingers. He loved the light dancing behind her lavender eyes. "You won't need this." Then he tilted his head toward the front doors. "Let's go."

Dru's eyes narrowed. "Wait – are the two of you?"

"We are." Without looking at Dru, Chance placed his hand at the small of Avery's back. "Have a nice lunch, Dru."

The air was filled with laughter, talking, and flirtatious play as students hurried to their cars and drove to the nearest hang-outs for a quick break from school. Chance couldn't take his eyes off Avery, and led her to his car more nervous than the teenaged boys surrounding them that did this every day.

Spring was in the air and the day was warm. Feeling the sun mix with what looking at her did inside of him, Chance knew he'd be sweating with his jacket on. He pulled it off and loosened his tie. He'd decided to believe what she'd said – though he could hardly bring the words to his thoughts – that she would fight for him. Because of that, he was taking a tentative step and trusting her.

"What a pleasant surprise." Avery's eyes lit the soft planes of her face, and that glow drew Chance's protected heart to the surface.

"I wanted to be alone with you."

She didn't say anything, but the kindness in her face, in the gentle way she reached out and lightly touched his arm, caused his breath to lock in his lungs. He opened the door of his car and held it for her.

Avery slid in. "This is the first time I've ever ridden in a Volkswagen."

"Not much of anything, but, hey." Chance stole another look at her before shutting the door. It was still like a dream that she was with him, that they were going somewhere together.

He got in, started the engine and it buzzed. He took Battle Creek Drive, the narrow road was lined with small brick and siding houses, wistful trees and orchards that stretched like blankets over the rising mountainside. Cars packed with students passed and honked, and Avery waved at faces she recognized.

"Oh," she said on a sigh.

His eyes met hers. "What?"

"Nothing. I'm glad we're doing this. That's all."

His dimples creased deep under sparkling brown eyes. He wore all chocolate today; slacks and shirt now open at the throat where he'd loosened his black tie. Another deep breath sighed from her system. Their lunch date would stir questions, but she didn't care. In fact, the idea pleased her. She looked around the inside of his car. There were a few wrappers from meals eaten on the run; a Mexican blanket in white, forest green and black stripes had been thrown in the back seat along with a tattered pillow.

"Do you sleep in your car often?" she teased.

The blanket was something he'd learned the hard way to keep on hand in case he was too smashed to drive, he'd find a secluded place and sleep it off. "Not any more," he said, and the truth felt good.

The main road narrowed as they headed further up, winding through bushes and wild shrubs finally coming to a clearing.

"Kinsdale Park?"

"Kinda." He pulled the car around and parked. Soft waves of excitement rolled through Avery's blood. A roofed picnic area was neatly hidden behind some trees and another car sat empty in a nook of the mountain, no doubt belonging to some teens out for more than just a lunch break.

He opened her door for her, rounded to the front and popped the hood. Her eyes widened when he pulled out a large, round wicker basket. Something was hidden under the hand towels she recognized from his kitchen.

The wind barely moved along the foothills, tickling the bushes and trees. It lifted his waves and curls, showcasing the smoothness of his jaw, the fullness of his mouth. Another wave, this one warmer, stronger, pulsed through her. Then his eyes were locked on hers.

"Did I tell you how beautiful you look today?" he asked, extending his hand.

She could say the same about him. "Thank you. What a great basket."

He lifted it. "One of my props." He handed her the blanket which she held folded over her arm before he led her through the bushes and spindly trees. He followed a small trail that led to a clearing whose view overlooked the entire valley.

"Where are you taking me?" She was completely thrilled to be following his lead. She had to stop and take a breath. "Oh."

"Great, isn't it?"

She could see the lake, a mirror asleep, with nothing in its reflection but endless slate sky. The mountains on the other side of the lake weren't as dramatic and craggy as the ones on which they stood, but more soft and rolling. The air was clear and every town in the valley could be seen, along with farmland in giant patches of green and brown and gold.

"What a spot."

"Found it a few years ago when I spent about three seconds thinking I'd paint landscape." He flapped out the Mexican blanket and placed the basket in the center, holding out his palm in gesture for her to sit.

She did, and he sat next to her, their knees brushing as they situated themselves cross-legged on the blanket. The moment, the place, the man brought a smile to her lips. "I haven't been on a real picnic in years."

"But you've been on, what, fake picnics?"

She laughed and watched his exquisite hands peel back the kitchen towels with the gentleness of a surgeon, revealing an artistic assortment of small, triangular sandwiches, some fresh fruit and two bottles of fruit juice.

"I'm not much of a cook," he said. "I actually went shopping late last night. Isn't it great that grocery stores stay open all night now?"

She picked up a triangle, anxious to eat anything his hands had created, sure it would be superb. "Deviled ham?"

"I thought I was the only one who'd ever eaten it." He opened her bottle top, propped the bottle next to her thigh.

"My mom used to put it in my lunches."

"I'll bet you were a girlie girl, pretty dresses, ribbons and dolls."

"I was all those things and more." She took a bite, pleased to taste something of his making that brought her memories of her youth. "You're forgetting I had three older brothers."

"Who no doubt protected you from everything?"

"I was lucky. Being the only girl, they all pretty much took care of me."

"You'd have been easy to take care of," he said, his gaze steady.

She eyed him as she lifted her bottle and drank. The wind tousled his caramel-colored hair. His eyes squinted in the sun. With every move of his mouth his dimples winked, and she imagined her lips there. She wanted to ask him about his family, know more about his past. It had been a fascinating story what he'd told her, and it had only made her anxious for more. But the hesitancy was still there, vulnerable and afraid.

"You have an older brother. He must have taught you a few things."

Chance laughed. "Yeah."

"I take it you weren't close."

"In age only," he laughed bitterly.

"Some siblings are here merely to test our patience and endurance."

He expected an answer like that from her. His relationship with Kurt had been that and so much more, but she could never fathom the ugliness, so he did what he always did when he thought of his family and sifted the painful memories away.

"Tell me about him, about you two."

"I'd rather not ruin a perfect lunch."

They shared a moment looking at each other.

"I'm sorry. I didn't mean to upset you."

"Forget about it."

"I want you to meet my family." She would show him what family love could be like, she decided. His jaw froze for a moment before he swallowed.

"Okay."

It pleased her that he agreed. Her mind flashed scenes of him shaking hands with her brothers, sitting around the dinner table with her mother and father.

"Sunday," she said. "Everyone comes over for dinner on

Sunday."

He picked up his bottle, looked at it as if he wished it were something else before setting his eyes on her. "Wow. You sure?"

"Yes." Sensing his apprehension she added, "Casual. It's very casual." This fight for him would be best approached with great care, she decided then. To make sure he knew she wanted this, she leaned over. His gray eyes widened then narrowed some, staying with hers, shifting to her mouth. It was not her way to be physically aggressive with a man, but with Chance she felt a need – his need, she supposed. It ran deep into her, colliding with her own blossoming. She skimmed his hard jaw with a soft kiss, taking in the smell of citrus shampoo as the breeze tickled his hair.

The dusting of growth on his face scratched her lips; she could smell the tangy scent he'd shaved with. Her mind dazed a moment with the thrill of his roughening skin on her mouth. She was shocked out of that daze when his palms wrapped around her upper arms.

Dark desire was in his face, in his gaze slipping from her eyes to her mouth. His arms wrapped her tight, as if his next breath depended on what he could squeeze from her. Lips that had moments ago looked soft and inviting, ravished hers with fury more greedy than a man starved for a meal. She submitted completely, her body caving to his with utter willingness. When his hands moved eagerly from her back to her waist then suddenly to her face, she shuddered. She'd never felt anything like the bolt that jagged through her, liquefying her limbs.

Slowly he eased her back, as if the consuming nature of his possession meant he would take her right there. Their lips hungrily passed over and into each others, exploring lightly, then more deeply, until she was lying on her back, eager to feel the weight of him.

Instinctively he granted her that wish, half of him resting on her. Gently, he angled her head and his lips sought, searched. Every part of her was lit with fire. The heat and hardness of his body so torturously close created a rushing storm that had no outlet except to be burned away by the afternoon sun.

"Chance." She managed to whisper his name between kisses. She loved saying it. Loved what her body did when she spoke it.

His kisses slowed, more torture now, she thought, as he gently took her lower lip in a teasing seduction, before moving up, taking her upper lip. He lifted his head, keeping her lips a brush away. "What?"

"I like saying your name."

"So you don't want me to stop?"

Never, she thought, wrapping her arms around his neck. In his eyes she saw flickers of joy. "I'd love you to keep kissing me but, we do have students waiting for us."

"Yeah." One of his arms slipped out from underneath her and he checked his watch. "Yeah." He sat up, pulling her up with him. "I didn't mean for that to happen, I'm sorry."

"Don't be sorry."

"Avery, I didn't bring you up here to kiss you."

"I kissed you first." She leaned over, brushed her hand against his tense cheek. The gesture brought his face around to hers. "And I'm not sorry. Thank you for this."

"I've never been to this place with anyone," he told her. "It seemed like a good place to bring you."

The admission touched her, knowing that he'd shared something exclusive. She began to put leftover lunch in the basket. Together, they folded the blanket and snagged trash. After the basket was filled, he stood, reached for her hand and brought her against him. "One more thing." He took her in the waltz position.

It was he that took the lead, gently moving them around the clearing to nothing but the sounds of the rustling breeze as it wove through the trees and bushes that cradled the place.

"I've never danced without music," he said.

"You can hear any tune in your head."

"That's not what I'm listening to."

His gaze was so intense, breath fluttered from her chest. They danced until a rock caught under Avery's shoe, causing them both to lose footing and laugh. "You're getting good, Chance."

He reached for the basket and stopped when he saw that she was standing, staring at him. "What?" he asked.

"I'm proud of you."

She was a teacher, used to sharing hope with students. But compliments hit him with simple profundity that dove deep into his soul and he found himself averting his eyes, unable to look at her.

"This was very romantic." She took one last glance at the spot. "Perhaps this will be our place," she said. At first he thought he'd imagined it, that the breeze had whispered the phrase audaciously into his ear. But she was looking right at him. "A place only we know."

The very idea of sharing something with her and only her was more intimate than the kiss they had exchanged, and it stirred everything inside of him. He wanted her in his life, not just in this place and not just for this wisp of a moment.

FOURTEEN

Chance stood in front of the painting, brushes in hand—afraid to touch her. He'd created her, like dozens of other paintings, but she was so real to him languishing with that expression that held both promises and secrets. He was afraid to do anything but look.

Sweat began to cover him; it always did when his mind roared along with his blood while he worked. He ripped off his shirt and stepped closer.

If he was lucky, someday she would look at him that way.

But luck had nothing to do with it, that he knew. If he wanted her in his life, and he did, he alone would have to make that happen. Again he was besieged with snaring whispers that all of this was wrong and couldn't possibly work. Avery was right; fear was why he pushed every opportunity away.

He smiled at her face then, thinking again of what she'd told him—that she would fight for him. Like a child holds onto the hope of a wish, he found himself circling back to those words. It still seemed unreal. If it was a dream, he'd take it while he could and wake up only if he had to.

Hope.

It was not a name he would give just any piece. But she had come into his life and he'd never felt like he could give up so many things that had enslaved him at the same time. Avery's strengths, the way she looked at things, black and white, the very foundation she was made of, was the lifeline he found himself reaching for. The new direction he wanted his life to take.

Knowing that nothing more would become of them other than friendship if she so chose, he thought about what he would do, where he would go, when the job ended and his life as he'd known it was all he had.

He looked into the dusky blue of her eyes. He'd never go back. The last few weeks had been too liberating. He would have never believed it, but there he was, talking himself into something better because he suddenly felt like he deserved it.

He shook his head, grinning at the portrait. "What have you done to me?"

Paint still glistened on the canvas so he didn't reach out and touch it even though he wanted to.

He heard the doorbell and grabbed his shirt, tugging it over his head. It was Saturday and Justin was already off on a run. He had invited him to go along but Chance wanted to finish the portrait.

He saw Kurt's face distorted through the peek-hole and paused before opening the door. He could ignore the tightness in his stomach that came whenever he and his brother were within a mile of each other.

Kurt had papers in his hand and held them out.

"I told you, I'm not signing anything."

Kurt let out a sigh and stood in that anxious way that warned. "You're going to regret this if you don't sign little brother."

"You want to fight, come in; we'll get it over with."

"I'm not talking about fighting." His eyes steeled.

"Sounds like extortion."

"Just try screaming it. You won't have a day to breathe."

"I'm not signing. I want the house, and I'll be taking ownership in two weeks, on schedule."

When Kurt backed off, Chance's eyes narrowed with suspicion. Kurt never backed down from a fight and the tight band around his stomach pulled hard.

"Your way then," Kurt said over his shoulder as he took the stairs down. He stopped halfway. "Just don't think you can beg your way out when things get rough. I've given you your chances." Then he continued, whistling as he strolled, papers in hand, to his car.

Chance slammed the door with a growl. Picking up the cordless phone, he dialed Frank Nesbitt, his parents' lawyer.

"Frank, Chance Savage."

"Yes, Chance. What can I do for you? Are you holding up all right?"

"Yeah. Kurt's pulling my bones out about issues of property, rights, and stuff in the will. Is there something – has he been talking to you about anything I should know about?"

"You know how your brother is. He's been in here every week since the funeral. I've tried to talk to him but he's deaf in both ears when it comes to your parents' holdings."

"He's greedy."

"This is between you and Kurt. But I believe your parent's will was an accurate reflection of their desires for their estate."

Chance thought about how often he and Kurt had fought and how neither one of their parents had ever done anything to stop it. They had to have known their assets would be a fiery topic between them. But it was too depraved to think they would encourage it beyond the grave.

Chance wasn't sure whose side Frank was on so he didn't bother mentioning Kurt's threats. He'd been left to fight his own battles and he would continue to.

"I want something written up that leaves my assets in a trust for AOM."

"Artists on the Move? I can draw up preliminary papers but your parents' will specifically states that if anything happens to you, your portion goes directly to—"

"I know, but I don't want him to have any of it."

Frank let out a sigh. "You sure this is what you want?"

"Definitely. And I want Kurt to receive a copy of the papers."

"Sounds like war."

It's always been war, Chance thought. "Thanks, Frank."

"You're still taking ownership on the fifteenth, correct?"

"That's the date."

"All right then. I'll get the papers drawn up and be in touch. Let me know if I can be of any further service."

Like you are to Kurt, Chance thought grimly before hanging up. Lawyers were just too pleasingly neutral for his liking.

Justin came in, dripping with sweat and catching breath. "Was that Kurt that passed me down the street?"

Chance nodded.

"I take it he wasn't here for a friendly visit."

Flexing his fingers, Chance rubbed out a cramp in his right forearm. "Nope."

Noting the gesture, Justin asked, "Things get ugly?"

"Not yet."

Crossing to the kitchen, Justin stripped out of his sweatshirt and opened the refrigerator. "He still after you?"

"You know how he is." Joining him in the kitchen, Chance realized he'd not eaten breakfast because he'd been working on Avery's painting. With Justin's inquisitive stare, he dug into the empty fridge. "We need food, man."

"What did he say?"

Chance pulled out the bread, eggs, and milk and didn't say anything, prompting Justin to move closer. " 'Cause if you need any help kicking his butt—"

"Right now, I could use your help making some French toast." He was still getting used to people caring enough to check up on him, to offer their help. "How about it?"

Justin jerked his head toward the cupboard where the

frying pan was kept. "No wonder you're a wimp, you can't feed yourself."

"Hey, I made French toast for Avery."

Justin thrust the loaf of bread at him. "I like mine crispy around the edges." Then he headed down the hall.

Chance's grin stretched. "Where you going?"

Justin's teeth flashed over his shoulder as he pulled off his wet tee-shirt. "To shower. I expect to taste some of what you call food in about ten."

The numbers on the dusty red bricks matched the numbers on the yellow post-it Avery had given him. Half a dozen cars were spread out between the driveway and the curb. This had to be the place.

It was a welcoming house, a place where a little girl like Avery could grow up and plant dreams and watch them grow. Chance liked the all-American red brick, black shutters and colonial white trim that accented the windows and covered porch. It was formal, just as he imagined Avery's parents might be. Yet an oval twig wreath hung on the front door and that added a friendly greeting.

He got out of his car and straightened his tie. He'd worn one knowing it was always better to be overdressed than underdressed – something his mother had taught him.

Even with the distance he was from the house he heard laughter, talking and the screaming of youngsters. He broke out in a sweat. He'd spent so little time around young children—it wasn't as if he didn't like them, he just got nervous with the unpredictability of them.

When he knocked on the door, somebody peeked through the curtained side panel. The face was gone before he could smile and he waited, hands tight around the bouquet of wildflowers he'd brought.

He let out a sigh when the door opened and Avery's face greeted him. She stole his breath. He leaned close, filling himself with her perfume, and placed a kiss on her cheek. "Hey, beautiful," he whispered. Her eyes were still closed when he pulled back.

"That was very nice," she murmured.

She wore the same lavender slacks and sheer shirt he'd seen her in that first night at Bruisers. He took a deep breath. "You look great."

"So do you."

Chance stepped inside and the place went silent.

Through an arched doorway to his right he glimpsed a mahogany dining room set, the table set in ivory, candles lit. To his left was a formal living room. A curved stair went up the right side of a hardwood entry. Something comforting scented the air; meat of some kind cooking; bread, vanilla. He heard whispers, saw a head or two peek out upstairs, from the back of the house where he heard voices pick up again and his nerves rattled.

"Come in, I want you to meet everyone." She extended her hand and when he slipped his in hers it settled him a little.

There were so many faces; he stopped under the curved archway from the hall, and clutched the flowers. Men, women, and what seemed like dozens of children of all ages stared at him. Avery squeezed his hand.

He saw her in the faces looking back at him. Every one of them looked like they belonged in a painting, and for an instant his mind flashed a gathering of love, laughter and welcoming under wispy shade trees alongside a river bank.

The little children gathered around as if he was Santa. Avery spun off their names, none of which he would remember without prompting, but he paid close attention to the three sharp-eyed men standing ready to meet him.

"These are my brothers, Alex, Matt and Dan."

Chance shook their hands, noting the keen way they studied him. Their wives were spread out; Alex's wife, Jan, was in the kitchen helping Avery's mother. Matt's wife, Debbie, was breastfeeding an infant in the open adjoining great room. She sent a wave. Dan's wife, Diane, waddled over, round and ready to have a child of her own.

"We've heard a lot about you." The man making his way through the crowd had Avery's deep blue eyes. Gray and white peppered his thick hair. Her father looked like a lawyer, Chance mused inwardly; staunch and discerning, but his gaze was warm.

"I've heard a lot about you as well." Chance resisted the impulse to swipe the sweat from his hand before offering it.

"An artist." From the back of the kitchen Charlotte Glenn maneuvered pans, platters and everything else needed to create a meal with the expertise of a professional chef.

She quickly wiped her right hand on a perfectly clean white apron before crossing to him. "And a very good artist at that." Her cheeks colored when he handed her the flowers. "How lovely. An artist and gentleman. Thank you, Chance."

"You're welcome."

The air was so thick he could choke, and Chance knew it was coming from her three brothers. They stayed close as guard dogs, all ears and few comments while their children scattered back to play.

"You're from Springville?" Alex asked.

Chance knew the condemning tone well. Springville had a reputation for wild kids and Chance had been one of them so he couldn't disagree with the label.

"Guilty."

The brothers exchanged wary glances and Chance's defenses prickled.

Charlotte Glenn searched for a vase. "Tell us how you became interested in art, Chance."

"Boredom."

"Then you realized you had a gift?"

"I realized it kept me busy."

"And out of trouble, no doubt," Charlotte laughed. Chance glanced at Avery who caught the grin of irony on his face.

Avery kept her hand in his. "I'm going to show Chance around."

Her brothers mumbled amongst each other before breaking up and joining their wives.

Avery led Chance out of the frying pan and into a wide hall where a wall of windows opened onto an expansive back yard shaded with towering trees. Chance pulled at his tie to loosen it as they walked through two double French doors and onto a patio. "Whew."

"They can be overwhelming, I know."

"I'm not breakable, Avery."

"No, but you aren't used to the Glenn onslaught."

He looked back over his shoulder through the window, saw that her brothers had their heads together over some dip and vegetables Charlotte had laid out, and they were watching. "Your brothers—the vibe is stronger than turpentine."

"Ignore them." She turned him to face her. "You look hot."

Slowly, his dimples creased, his dark eyes glittered. "That's the first time I've heard you say anything other than *nice*."

"Nice isn't...descriptive enough for you today." The urge to touch him hit her fast and hard and lifted her to her toes. "I have something for you."

"Yeah?"

Before she could change her mind, she put her arms

around him and pressed her head against his chest. He stood utterly still wrapped in her embrace and she closed her eyes, smiling, because she could feel that he'd stopped breathing.

"I'm glad you're here." She whispered then eased back. His eyes were dark with emotion.

It was a simple gift, her holding him like that. He couldn't tell her that being there was like a dream. Family, the warm, comforting quintessence of it, had not been a part of his life for so long, he felt like a foreigner in a strange land. He wanted to soak it all up as fast as he could. He slipped his arms around her.

Conscientiously aware that they were being watched, he drew back but kept her hand in his. "Show me where you became you."

Through the spacious back yard, under towering trees where her father had built his only daughter a charming playhouse, a miniature replica of their family home, she recalled memories. Now, the little house was occupied by some giggling, curly-haired nieces that dashed by, arms filled with dolls.

She pointed out the tree house in the upper branches of one of the largest trees. A haphazard ladder nailed to the trunk led the way up. Chance had wanted one just like that so badly he'd begged endlessly for it. His mother had refused because the existence of one would lower the aesthetic value of the Savage property.

"Want to go up?" Avery asked. He looked at her with eyes sparkling. "It's still useable," she said, reading his expression. "My nephews go up all the time. I'm surprised they're not out here, in fact."

Looking up, Chance felt the rush just like he had when he was a kid. "You sure it's strong enough?"

She nudged him. "Go on. The view's great."

"How about you?"

"Sure. I'll follow you."

He started his climb, feeling foolish he couldn't wipe the smile from his face. When he made it to the door, he peered in, thrill bubbling through his veins. The place was about five feet across and eight feet long. Good sized, Chance mused and pulled himself inside. He couldn't stand in it, it was only tall enough for a boy of thirteen maybe. So he sat himself down against one of the wood walls and looked around.

The moment was as plain and pure as a boy receiving the gift of a lifetime, the look on his face. The way he sat, taking in the details as if in a dream. Avery couldn't help that her chest drew tight watching him.

"My brothers were so proud of this place. They spent every hour constructing it one summer. Dad helped on Saturdays, but it was their project."

It would be just what he'd do if he had sons, Chance thought.

There were two windows in addition to the door, a door that hung open but had a latch for closing. Ragged red-checked curtains hung in the windows and somebody had made a table out of wood scraps.

"They ever sleep up here?" he asked.

"All the time." Avery ditched concerns over ruining her outfit and climbed in. She settled next to him, feeling his enthusiasm like an electric current. "Once a year, they have a guy thing out here. They sleep, eat, stay up all hours telling stories, harassing each other."

"Seriously?"

She nodded, sighed. "Guys and their rituals."

"That's so cool." He'd dreamt of nights like that, wished he'd had a brother who would have cared enough to want the same.

Taking her hand, he looked at her fingers. He could visualize her playing in her playhouse, making up voices, pretending, with her brothers watchfully nearby. One at a time, he kissed her fingers, enjoying the way the blue in her eyes flickered to lavender. Turning her palm, he ran soft kisses there next, lingering at the delicate flesh on the inside of her wrist.

For a moment they looked at each other, his lips poised at her wrist. Reaching behind her neck, he cupped his palm and gently brought her closer. When her breath caught, his blood skipped hot through his system.

"You're—" he whispered. *You're everything I could ever hope for and I would spend my life on my knees to have you*, he thought but fear kept his lips still as he looked at her.

When her hands took his face, his cheeks burned. She pulled his mouth to hers and kissed him, wrapping her arms around his neck. He'd take her right there on the rough floor of the tree house if there was no one to account to. The throbbing need was ubiquitous in him, pushing his body now to cover hers as he pressed her against the wall. He tore his arms from her soft curves and pressed his palms to the safety of the wall, caging her.

"Don't stop," she said.

Dropping his brow to hers, he let out a raw laugh. "This isn't the place."

"This is a wonderful place, Chance." Her eyes were anxious; her breath coming in and out fast, the rhythm churned his craving. He shook his head. With her, it had to be different. He'd have her his way or he would leave her untouched.

He moved, settling his back against the wall with his knees up, leaving Avery just out of reach.

Their breath slowed, but their gazes remained tightly locked. Girls' laughter and childish play trickled up through the windows and the open door.

There was resolve on his face and Avery didn't mind that, she just wanted to make sure it wasn't about them. "So we don't make out in the tree house." She slid closer. "I still want to kiss you." Leaning up, she placed a slow kiss on the tense corner of his jaw. "Right there," she murmured against his skin. "I love that spot on your face."

She drew back just far enough to see the place on his cheek contract when he closed his eyes. "And right here." This time she kissed where his skin creased into a dimple when he smiled.

He wasn't sure she was even aware that she might find herself consumed if the fire got out of control. His head fell back, and he kept his focus on the insides of the tree house, fighting the urge to grab her like a cat grabs a mouse playing too close for its own good.

He had to divert his thoughts. "So they built it, huh?" his voice rasped, giving him away.

She laughed and with her mouth so close to his neck, his blood thrummed. She coursed his neck with kisses. "Yes, Chance. They built it."

Exquisite torture, that's what her kisses were. He reached out and scooped her against him, ready to abandon himself to her when they both heard a timid voice.

"Aunt Avery?"

Chance let out a low laugh of relief and Avery moved to the door and peeked out. "Yes, honey?"

"Grandma says it's time for dinner."

"We'll be right down."

She smiled at him then, innocence rounding her eyes. The way she extended her hand to him, naively beckoning, Chance wondered if she'd had any idea how far she'd pressed him. The liability blanketed his shoulders.

He followed her down and they crossed the grassy yard with the handful of little girls behind them, giggling.

"What are you guys laughing about?" Avery finally turned, walking backward next to Chance as she waited for their answer.

The girls exchanged glances before breaking into song, "Avery and Chance sitting in a tree, k-i-s-s-i-n-g…"

It was custom at the Glenn house to sit around the dinner table and talk after sharing a meal together. And so, dirty plates piled high, chandelier dimmed to a flicker, conversation that had begun during dinner, continued.

Children too young to enjoy the adult topics soon wandered off to play. Only once did Charlotte leave the table, merely to return with two warm pound cakes, dripping with fresh hot fudge. She sliced and served as she listened to her husband discuss one of his firm's latest cases.

"It's not right, but there's nothing I can do to convince the man to hand over the property to his aunt."

"One of my writers covered that story." Alex nodded gratefully at his mother when she laid a plate in front of him. "Said the guy was a real jerk."

"And his aunt is the nicest little lady," Barry said before forking a bite.

"Chance is in the same situation," Avery's comment inadvertently brought all eyes to him sitting next to her.

He had been a quiet observer most of dinner, answering what few questions had been asked of him, none of them personal. Now he felt the hair on the back of his neck prickle.

"Is that so?"

Chance saw eagerness in Barry, and suspicion in the eyes of her three brothers. "Similar," he said, hoping the short answer would be message enough that he didn't care to discuss it.

"Chance's parents passed away in a plane crash a few months ago," Avery went on matter-of-factly. "His brother wants the entire estate, even what was willed to Chance. He's trying to talk him into signing his part over."

As if the whole family was used to discussing whatever, whenever, nobody noticed Chance shifting uncomfortably, tugging at his tie under the magnifying glass.

"I'm sure your family doesn't care about my—"

Avery laid her hand over his. "Maybe Dad can help."

Anger simmered then, shame mixed with it. The more people knew, the more dangerous it became. All he needed was for her growling brothers to find out about his past and they'd kick him out so fast he'd never remember what hit him.

Charlotte set a plate in front of him. The fuggy chocolate steamed his face, and he felt the first sprouting of sweat.

Barry was all ears. "These kind of family situations are never comfortable. But if your parents' will is valid and states what they wanted for you, legally there's nothing your brother can do about it without your agreement. Unless you sign papers, transferring the property to him, it belongs to you."

Chance took a bite of the chocolaty dessert, hoping not to have to answer any more questions with his mouth full.

"Does he have legal counsel giving him incorrect information?" Barry asked.

The sweat on Chance's brow was pearling. "No. Kurt just doesn't give up."

After serving everyone, Charlotte settled at the opposite end of the table. A skilled hostess, she could see the panic on Chance's face and turned the subject in another direction. "I want to hear about your work. Avery says you paint women."

"That's all he paints," Avery said, spearing a bite of the pound cake. The room fell silent.

Matt's brow lifted. "No kidding?"

"How did you get so lucky?" Dan grinned with new admiration, until his wife elbowed his ribs.

Sweat threatened to drench his shirt and soak through to his coat. Chance reached for his tie and tugged, bringing a laugh all around. Usually talking about his work relaxed him, but not in the presence of this audience.

"He does beautiful work," Avery said.

"Are they all hotties, the women?" Dan asked, shaking his head on a chuckle. "What's a guy to do?"

Chance tried to laugh. "Uh...So when's the baby due?" He hoped to change the subject – permanently, and was relieved when everyone chuckled.

"Any day now." Diane glowed. Both she and Dan rubbed her enlarged stomach.

"Do you know what you're having?"

"A girl." Dan's pride was obvious.

"So you just have the one brother then?" Barry asked Chance.

Chance nodded. "But I think big families like this are great."

"Your family owned Savage Enterprises." Alex changed the mood from the lightness of fun to the thickness of questions lining up in the air.

"Yes."

"They're a world-wide distribution company, aren't they?" Barry asked.

"They are."

"So what's happening to the company?" Dan asked.

"We're in the process of selling it." Chance took his last bite of the scrumptious dessert wishing he'd eaten more slowly so his mouth was full. "It's what they wanted."

As a boy growing up in the Savage house, chores weren't equally meted. Because Kurt put up a stink whenever he was asked to do anything, he was rarely asked. That left Chance.

So when the Glenn women finally began to clear the

table, he stood, gathering glasses.

"A well-trained young man is always a welcome guest in our home." Charlotte threw a look at her husband and sons, still sitting—and cleared her throat.

Dan got up. "You're making me look bad, Chance. How'd you get that name, anyway?"

"It was a better name than mistake." At least that's what his dad had told him more than once. His offer to assist in the cleanup was two-fold: to help, and to get himself away from the inevitable line of questioning that would continue if he sat there.

Not to be left behind, Alex and Matt joined.

"It's been nice being huge." Diane patted her tummy. "Dan's off his butt more often."

Jan nodded in agreement. "I'm surprised Alex isn't cracking the whip. We always share K.P. duty."

"He wants to make a good impression," Diane whispered.

Avery and Jan laughed; Alex could care less about impressions. In fact, Avery was sure Alex was up to some needling. She excused herself and went straight into the kitchen.

Four men with their sleeves rolled up doing domestic work – something about that appealed to her idea of what was fair in the world. She paused in the door, to hear just how her brothers were treating Chance.

Alex was rinsing dishes, handing them to Chance who loaded them into the dishwasher. Matt scrubbed pans and Dan was sweeping.

"Avery says you're filling a sub job at the high school." Alex handed him a plate dripping with suds.

"I am."

"So you teach and paint?" Alex asked.

"I'm subbing."

"Anybody can sub," Matt piped. "My buddy, Steve, did it for three weeks when his brother had a hernia."

"My roommate teaches there," Chance said. "He got me the spot."

Alex glanced over. "They do any background checks?"

Avery cleared her throat, stepping into the conversation. "They knew Chance had a degree in art," she said.

Pleasure was in Chance's gaze as it met Avery's then. "Justin's recommendation carried a lot of weight," he continued, pointedly at Alex. "Even with Springville being my hometown."

"Just wondered." Alex's eyes narrowed briefly. "I have a teenager set to go to high school next year, you know?"

"Don't blame you there." Chance took the last plate from Alex.

"So, you gonna paint Avery?" Dan asked.

"Yeah, what's with only painting women?" Matt stopped scrubbing, Alex's hands stilled in the suds and Dan's broom came to a halt. They looked at him and waited.

Avery saw Chance's back tense underneath the smooth fabric of his shirt. "He doesn't paint women he works with," she said, crossing to him. "Personal policy, isn't it, Chance?" She came up behind him, her smile taunting. "But I'm going to try to change that."

"Whoa," Dan whistled. "Better be careful, Chance. That look means she's on the war path and I can tell you from experience that she fights to win."

"Definitely." Matt went back to scrubbing.

Alex leaned toward Chance. "Tip – hold out. She's spoiled. Needs to be kept where she belongs."

Avery gasped over a laugh. "And just where is that?"

"You've got to dangle the bait long enough that you get what you want first."

"You're annoying," Avery fumed, teasing. "I don't know how Jan lives with you, but then I warned her."

"Warned me about what?" Jan asked, coming in from the

dining room with Charlotte and Barry.

"About marrying this sexist."

Jan slid her arms around Alex's middle and laid her head against his back. "And it was a good thing I didn't listen to a sixteen year-old."

Avery grabbed Chance's hand. "I'm taking him away from you guys. You'll taint his beautiful, pure mind."

She dragged him to the quiet of the living room before she stopped. The laugh Chance let out was lost when he looked at the gallery of family photos taken through the years hanging on one of the pale, cream walls. His parents had never hung anything but what his mother considered art on the hallowed halls of the Savage house, keeping their home in a perpetually reverent atmosphere more like a museum than a home.

He moved close. "Look at all of these. Avery, this is great."

"We have a giant extended family."

There were faces he didn't recognize but plenty he did; her brothers, her mom and dad, and her, at various ages, in different settings.

"You traveled a lot," he murmured, looking at a section of the wall devoted to pictures taken around the world: the family at the base of the Eiffel Tower, near the clock tower in London, in front of Anne Franks' house in Amsterdam.

"Every summer we'd head somewhere."

He nodded. Envy tried to slither in but he wouldn't let it. She'd been surrounded by love, and she was who she was because of that. That was part of why he wanted to belong to her.

"You have a great family." He turned to her. His mind was telling him they were too good. They would never want someone with a past like his to have anything to do with the precious daughter they had cultivated and protected like a rare flower.

"Don't look like that." Reaching out, she touched his face as her own drew tight.

Even though he wanted something between them, old whispers thrived inside, taunting him, reminding him that anything at all between them simply would never be.

Carefully he wrapped his hand around her wrist and eased it away from his face. "I think I should go now."

"We watch family movies, pop popcorn." She covered his hand with hers then held it against her heart. "Stay."

"I have things I need to do," he lied, and his fingers slipped free. It would be too torturous to see her as a child. To watch her growing in those treasured family films, becoming the beautiful woman he would never have.

"If you say grading papers—"

"No—other things."

"Do you need help?"

He shook his head.

"All right." She walked with him to find his coat. He thanked her parents, said goodbye to her brothers and stood with her at the front door. The scent of popping corn trickled invitingly in the air from the kitchen where there was still plenty of laughter and talking. This had to end, he told himself with one last look at her face, so lovely and sweet. Dirty oil and clean rain would never mix.

Leaning, he held his lips against the softness of her cheek. "Thank you."

When he turned to go, he was startled to feel her hand wrap tightly around his arm, bringing him back to her. She took only one second to look at him before she took his face in her hands and kissed him long and deep.

His head spun, sending a whirl through him that he took like a hammer to the knees. Hope beckoned with wisps of love, twining around his heart. She cared. Cared too much for her own good now, and it would hurt even more when she stood back long enough to realize she could do better.

Her kiss was the last they would share and so he didn't stop her, rather took from her lips every detail of soft sweetness he could store away in his memory.

FIFTEEN

He was back to square one.

He didn't want to have to convince Avery he was wrong for her, they would only get into a debate about it and he'd lose. He'd give her whatever she wanted and anything else he could grab for her along the way – forget what her brothers said. They didn't want her in the way that he wanted her.

If she was any other woman, by now he'd have turned her off with his selfish lifestyle. There'd been no woman who could compete with his relationship with the bottle or his brushes.

But no one could compare with Avery that was his problem. For all that he loved about his art, for all that he'd given of himself to it because there'd been nothing else in his life to give to, nothing compared with giving himself to Avery.

Avery brought to his mind something that he'd never thought of—that being exclusive could actually be satisfying enough for forever if it meant being with her.

Because he found himself caring more than he ever had for another human being, he'd have to avoid her at school and quit going to dance lessons.

Ignoring was juvenile. He saw that reaction every day at school, boys and girls giving each other the cold shoulder because they'd not figured out how to turn someone away with finesse. He laughed. Here he was, twenty-eight and he still didn't know how to get out of a relationship gracefully.

It was loud in the hall, the early morning hour having no effect on the students talking their way to class. He heard his name and turned.

Principle Ackerman was hurrying toward him. The hand the man laid on his shoulder was meant to calm, but Chance's nerves pricked. "Chance, could I steal a minute?"

"Sure." Chance followed the portly man who didn't say much, waving to a student, said hello to a few more.

They were in his office before Chance took a deep breath, remembering other visits to the principal's office a long time ago.

"Have a seat." Principal Ackerman nudged his sliver-framed glasses up his stubby nose, fitting his round body into a too-small chair. "There's something I want to ask you. You realize my first responsibility is to the safety of my students."

Chance's stomach tightened. He nodded.

"I got a phone call at my home over the weekend. I don't know how this person got my private phone number, but they did. The caller, who chose to remain anonymous—I checked my caller ID and it was unavailable, anyway – the caller said you'd been involved in the rape of a sixteen year old girl some years back." He sat forward, clasping his hands. "You want to tell me about that?"

"I never raped anyone," Chance said flatly, seeing his brother's face in his mind. "You're welcome to call the Springville Police Department. There's nothing there."

"I already did and you're right, there wasn't anything. But with any accusation, I have to check it out and that takes more than just a phone call, you understand."

"Yeah."

Principal Ackerman sat back, leveling Chance with a stare he hadn't seen since his own days as a student. "Nasty business this is. Who'd call me out of the blue and say something like that about you? Do you have any idea?"

Chance shook his head. "Sorry, I don't." It was futile defending himself when the signs of dismissal were already in the principal's eyes.

"Unfortunately, I can't keep you on. I just can't take the risk of my parents finding out and coming to me like a lynching mob – and that's just what they'll do."

Though the man's expression was kind, Chance saw flat finality behind them. Still, he was stunned by the news and deep inside the familiar hurt of being pushed aside because of a lie throbbed.

"I'm sorry. From all that I've heard, the kids love you. But you can see my position, I'm sure."

"Sure."

"Now look, if you can settle this I'll bring you back. I'm not even going to say anything to anybody here. No one knows and no one will, this is just a precaution. Get your situation straightened out and then come talk to me. Until then, I need to have somebody else in the classroom."

Principal Ackerman stood just as the first bell shrilled at seven fifty-five. He stuck out his hand. "There's another teacher in the class now. I'll leave it up to you when you want to pack your things."

"I don't have anything that's mine in the room." Chance absently squeezed his portfolio handle tight. He'd planned to share his work with the kids today.

"All right then. Keep me informed."

"Thank you." Chance excused himself and headed down the hall with a pit still in his stomach. He dug out his cell phone and punched in his brother's phone number. The phone rang endlessly and before he knew it, he was at the wall of glass doors that led out of the school. It hurt too much to look any of the kids he passed, so he didn't.

He stuffed the tiny phone back in his pants pocket and walked out the door.

The spacious house where he'd grown up still looked the same—only the landscape had filled out like an aging woman. The one-story brick rambler stretched across the low hill with shading trees and lush oak brush like a house with open arms on an inviting Christmas card.

Chance pulled up the circular driveway and saw that newspapers were still being delivered; they had scattered everywhere and were turning golden brown. The trash barrels had blown over and the place had a look of abandonment. For a moment he stared at it, thinking of the irony.

A black Dodge truck sat near the back door.

Chance's blood began to simmer. He stopped his car next to his brother's shiny new vehicle and got out. They both had keys to the house, always had, though Chance hadn't used his in years. But with the property now belonging to him, Chance strode to the back door and into the house, ready.

He stopped after he entered, the scent of home hitting him like a slap to the face. In the cloistered air he could still smell his mother's heavy perfume, his father's musky scent, as if the walls themselves remembered. He half expected to hear his father cough. He was sure he'd hear his mother on the phone with one of her lady friends.

But there was only the emptiness of silence.

Everything looked the same and he entered reverently. Regimented habits kicking in, he was hesitant to touch anything. He heard nothing, the house so sprawling that he knew unless Kurt was nearby, he would not hear him either.

He treaded softly regardless, his body tense, muscles poised.

The clock his parents had bought the year they'd all gone to Switzerland when he and Kurt were young was still clicking. Chance stood looking at it, recalling the time his mother had taken to choose the timepiece over hundreds of others. The trip had been before the incident with the Drakes. Their family had been intact then, a family flourishing with all of the possibilities of any other.

A thick layer of dust was everywhere and Chance ran a finger along the dining room table where he pictured hundreds of dinners set with his mother's fine silver and imported china. They'd not been dinners like the one he'd shared with the Glenn's, full of laughter and talk, but quiet evenings drilled with table manners, appreciating food, of trading neighborhood gossip, society news and business issues.

His mother's extravagant silver tea set was missing and Chance looked at the large oval spot where the lack of dust had left an imprint on the table. Kurt had no doubt been taking what he wanted.

He heard the undeniable click of a gun and his heart stopped. Cold steel pressed to his temple.

"Almost shot you, little brother," Kurt said without lowering the shotgun. "Thought you were an intruder."

"That what you'd tell the police? That you left the garage door unlocked, then shot your own brother, the one this house and everything in it belongs to, including the gun you used to shoot him with?"

Kurt grinned behind the leveled gun.

Chance wouldn't put it past him. He faced his brother head-on as Kurt held him in the crosshairs for a two few minutes before slowly lowering the weapon. "Just checking out Dad's guns."

"I'll bet."

"All loaded—though I have yet to test them. How about you and me go do a little target shooting up in the foothills, like old times?"

Chance let out a harsh laugh. "Right."

"I always was a better shot than you." Kurt kept the gun

in his tight fists. "You were always whining about Bambi or Thumper."

"What are you doing here? Besides stealing." Chance gestured with a jerk of his head to where the silver set used to sit.

Kurt shrugged. "Just checking things out, getting what's mine."

"You moved out seven years ago, took what was yours then."

"If you think I'm going to make this easy for you you're head's screwed on wrong. Or maybe it's just that pretty little lady I've seen you with. Maybe she's the one fogging your brain."

"Take whatever you've stolen and get out of my house before I call the cops and have you arrested for trespassing."

"It's not your house until the fourteenth." He took the gun and butted Chance in the chest with it. "Still not too late to sign, make it easy on yourself."

With an angry shove Chance pushed the butt aside and strode out of the room, down the hall. Curiosity, pain, had him heading to his old bedroom to see what had become of it. Kurt was right behind him.

"You called the school, opened your big mouth, got me fired."

"Yeah? So? They had the right to know that a—" Kurt's voice trailed off when Chance walked through the door of his bedroom and froze. The room looked just like it had when he'd left. His throat knotted and he took another step inside.

Suddenly he was a fifteen year-old boy, lost in the whirlwind of deception that had surrounded him. His last night in this room had been terrifying as he'd tried to explain to deaf-eared parents what had really happened between him and Chelsea.

He took in everything with a slow scan. Memories shifted as his eyes lit on various belongings he'd been forced to leave behind. Everything was in its place. His art books were neatly stacked on the shelf alongside his yearbooks and other literary favorites from his youth. Soccer trophies, school pictures, travel mementos were all where he last remembered putting them.

"Mom kept the door shut." Kurt stood next to him, looking around. "It was too hard for her to even walk in here. She had to have Maria dust and clean it for crying-out-loud. Dad hated you for that."

A wave of guilt surged through Chance. He'd had no idea any part of him still remained anywhere in his parent's life after they'd banished him from it. The news was unbelievable. The shock cut through bone and ripped open his heart. If he'd been alone, he'd have wept. But with Kurt just a few feet away, he blinked back any show of caring.

He walked in, hands frozen at his sides, afraid of disturbing anything. His closet doors were closed and after a moment's pause he opened them, found some boxes labeled *Chance* stacked inside. If he opened them, he would see what his mother had saved.

He squeezed the doorknobs, averting his face from Kurt's view. "Why don't you leave things alone?" he asked quietly.

Kurt crossed the room, looking around. "You have to have known I'd never let you walk away with all of this."

"It wouldn't have occurred to you that they were trying to make things up to me."

Kurt let out a laugh that cut through Chance's pondering like a hatchet. "They hated you, man. You were an embarrassment. Your little indiscretion cost them their place in society."

Chance still found it hard to believe, even though he'd lived through every dreadfully lonely year since that day. But seeing his room left like he'd died and his mother had enshrined the place resurrected a lifeless hope he'd carried inside that maybe things had been different in her heart.

He believed Kurt, that his dad had hated him. He'd seen the icy hatred in his eyes when his father came to see him the one and only time he had come to the boys' rehab center.

"After that, our lives were never the same. The Drakes—they massacred us." Kurt squeezed anxious fingers together around the gun.

Chance looked at him. Kurt was off in thought for a moment before he snapped out of it, looking over with hardened eyes. "If I heard it once, I heard it a thousand times. Dad kept saying he wished you'd never lifted a brush."

Chance turned his face away, that old emotion fresh and stinging his chest, his throat and eyes.

"I hope it still hurts." Kurt's whisper was so near Chance's ear, he jerked around. Hate glimmered in his brother's eyes as he slowly pulled the rifle into position. "It'd almost be worth killing you," Kurt muttered, the gun steady in poised hands.

Chance's heart pounded. His brother's expression was icy cold, just as his dad's had been that day he'd not even said goodbye, just left him in that place. He figured if this was death, he'd seen it before and lived through the hell of it. He could die and do the same.

Part of him wanted release from everything coming back and clawing at him as he stood surrounded by a past of unhappiness and misery. In a moment of uncertainty, he debated signing the papers and being free of it all.

But his room was untouched, and that had to mean something. The part of him that held onto hope was grasping for something still, even though his parents had been buried. Even sure he would never know his mother's reasons.

He took in a deep breath and walked out of the room. Passing his brother a chill took his spine, he anticipated being struck—or worse. When he wasn't, he headed to the back door, feeling the heaviness of Kurt like a foreboding growl at his heels.

He opened the door and jerked his head. "Get out."

Kurt positioned the gun and grinned as he neared. He cocked it again and Chance didn't back down, not even when Kurt pressed the tip of the barrel just under his chin. "Any way you look at it, your life will be a nightmare. If not from me, from the neighbors."

Chance pushed the gun away and jerked his head. "Out."

Kurt whistled when he passed, his steely blue eyes hard. "Watch your step little brother." He casually tossed the shotgun from one hand to the other. "And watch your back."

Chance slammed the door shut and stood against it, waiting until he heard the rumbling diesel of his brother's engine finally vanish.

It took him a moment of utter silence before he looked around and realized this was his now. Parents he had expected never to see again, never expected to get a dime from, had bequeathed it to him.

He walked slowly into the kitchen, looking at where he'd seen his mother countless times talking on the phone, arranging luncheons and parties. Where she'd shared the latest gossip he would later hear served like dessert at the dinner table. Where he'd painted her. She'd spent hours at the club, hours on the phone. Often he'd tired of waiting with a homework question as she stood here in this kitchen talking to one of her friends.

Chance went to the refrigerator, opened it. It was bare but for some margarine that would last forever. He pulled it out, opened it, looked at where knives had last scraped. Then he put the container back.

The moment was strange, unfamiliar in a way he couldn't describe, being there. He'd grown up in the house but had been ripped from it before maturation was complete, and so what remained in his memories were a mix of a bewildered childhood and the pains of being forbidden to come back.

The rest of the house he took in slowly. They had remodeled. The brown and beige colors he'd remembered had been replaced by idealistic white. The walls were white, the woodwork was white, and the carpet was white. He remembered well how his mother had said she'd remodel once her boys were old enough not to destroy everything. She'd wanted everything to look heavenly.

You got your wish, Mom. He looked at the white carpet where the only tracks came from her last vacuum job, now broken by his footprints.

He slipped off his shoes.

His mother's treasures still sat in ornate glass curios. Her collection of Llyadro was enviable, she'd reminded him of that hundreds of times. They'd gone all over the European continent collecting artifacts which sat around the house or hung on the walls and Chance looked at all of them. Some he remembered from when he'd lived there, others he had never seen and knew she must have gotten after he'd been gone.

The last place he found himself was their bedroom. She had replaced all of the dark, Queen-Anne style furniture he remembered with off-white furnishings—more heaven. The room smelled like both of them. Cologne and perfume was left behind in the bedding, in the upholstery and in the clothes he could see hanging in their closet.

The closet that drew him and he stood just in the door, afraid to breathe. His eyes scanned her side with its sparkly gowns and expensive designer wear. Then his father's side, with his perfectly tailored suits, tuxedos and camouflage clothing he'd worn hunting.

When he'd been a young boy afraid of being far away on the other side of the house, he'd snuck in after he was sure they were both asleep and slept on the floor of this closet. He'd been extra careful to awaken before day broke, before either of them stirred, to get himself back to his cold bed. Once, he'd been too exhausted, hadn't heard them get up. His father had awakened him by pulling him up by the ear.

"Don't ever sneak into our bedroom again," he'd said.

Chance hadn't understood why it had upset him until many years later when he'd known for himself that a bedroom required privacy.

Some of his father's clothes were missing; it was obvious by the holes left where something had hung. Chance could care less. Kurt could have anything he wanted that belonged to his father.

He wouldn't live in this room, he decided as he stood in its center. He'd not keep anything in here. And as he walked out, he thought about donating it to charity. He'd box up the clothing, drop it somewhere – he wasn't sure where, but it didn't matter. None of what was in the house mattered. Somebody would enjoy the opulent bedroom furnishings, the Llyadro collection, the fine china. White was a neutral color, his mother had told him. He'd come to understand that when he'd studied art. Anybody could live with white—except him.

Avery did not consider herself a worrier, but she found herself thinking, feeling, and acting altogether not herself where Chance was concerned, since she'd opened a place for him in her heart.

When she'd heard that he was no longer at the school, she'd immediately sought out Justin, who had no clue what was going on. During her planning period, she'd called Chance's apartment.

He hadn't shown up for dance class. She'd danced alone, and had casually made her way over to Justin and Inessa. Still, Justin had not seen or heard from him.

She knew Chance was free to do and go where he pleased, but she half expected him to make her aware of his plans after what they had shared Sunday afternoon.

She could hardly concentrate now rehearsing with Scott. They had another competition they were getting ready for and Scott had hired Reuben La Bate, one of the most revered dance coaches in the country, for a private lesson. Reuben's enigmatic presence did little to tear her thoughts from Chance.

"You bothered by something?" Scott whispered.

Avery shook her head, absently watching Reuben change from his street shoes into his dance shoes while she did some warm-up exercises. He coached the best, and his fee would be worth it, if she could just concentrate.

"You two ready?" Reuben was all business. He nearly floated to the center of the floor, and Avery marveled at the silky way he moved. His penetrating green eyes made her feel like she wouldn't be able to hide anything from him, her imperfections or her wandering thoughts.

"You're competing in standard, correct?" he asked.

"Yeah," Scott started, "we just want to show you our routine and have you tell us where we can improve."

Reuben nodded and stood back. Crossing an arm over his chest, his fingers held his chin. "On my count."

They began with the waltz. Avery expected the mere familiarity of the steps, of Scott's body moving with hers, to ease her mind into what she was doing. It didn't. She thought of how it felt to be next to Chance. Of how he had kissed her.

"That's a heel lead, Avery," Reuben called from a few tight feet away as he shadowed every move. She flushed, embarrassed that he'd had to remind her of something so simple, so soon.

Fox trot was notoriously challenging and she knew when Reuben shadowed them, she was losing it. For a moment she pinched her eyes shut, knowing it would force her to feel for

Scott's movements. It only made her sloppier.

"Remember CBM, guys."

Another hot flash of shame covered Avery; she knew contra body movement was key to the smooth, linear look of foxtrot; the changing illusion of the dance where upper body faced one direction as legs danced opposite.

"I'm sorry," she muttered but didn't spare Scott a glance, knowing he'd been watching her.

Reuben moved around the room with them. She began to sweat under the pressure. "That's a toe ball flat after the heel turn, Avery. I've seen you two do this and do it well, where are you? Articulate your feet!"

As with competition, they didn't pause for a breath between dances. By the time they had finished all five of the standard dances Avery knew her performance had suffered. She paced opposite Scott, angry with herself.

"Okay," Reuben began. "Here's what I see: Avery, aside from the fact that your mind is elsewhere," his eyes glittered with reproach, "in your waltz routine, when you go into promenade, have that shoulder leading because you're taking the aggressive step there. You're pulling him around." He demonstrated the move, and she nodded.

He turned to Scott. "Scott, make sure your direction on the dance floor is completely accurate on your long side when you start. I couldn't tell if your spin-turn ended straight down the dance floor."

"Other than a few minor things, you guys look ready. We'll go through it again. If the glitches show up, I'll scream at you. Otherwise, we'll figure your heads have cleared."

Scott extended his hand to Avery, whispering as he led her to their starting position. "What's up with you?"

"I'm sorry. I'll work harder."

Slipping his right arm around her waist, his left arm extending theirs together, he said, "I know you'll work harder, that's not what worries me. What's going on?"

"Nothing. Really."

Reuben started them with a count and they began the waltz. Avery's thoughts slowly drifted into the step, finding the relaxation that usually accompanied dance.

When Reuben made no comments, she sent Scott a smile and they moved into tango. Halfway through, she realized she had gotten through almost two dances without thinking about Chance.

"Remember, the sharper the better," Reuben called. "The movement when you switch to promenade should come from how fast you swivel your feet. The more resistance you give each other the better." Avery felt their form unify as they danced.

"Good. Better, much better," Reuben nodded.

When they finally skipped into quickstep, she enjoyed herself, letting go to the fluttering movements. The nods and smiles coming from Reuben assured her.

"Remember," Reuben said between counts and claps, "you want to look like a duck skimming across the water—your feet are moving fast, but from the waist up, your bodies are still—you almost can't tell you're moving. Great. Much better. Yes!"

Reuben told Avery to put on some music then and they ground out the routines for the rest of the hour until both she and Scott glistened with perspiration and Reuben's time was up.

He shook both of their hands. "Good luck guys. I'll probably see you there, I'm judging." He grinned, his teeth gleaming against his black skin.

"Seriously?" Scott asked.

Reuben nodded, then took Avery aside. "I've seen you dance. You're on the up and up, and you just brought it together nicely for me. But whatever's under that skin of yours, get rid of it before comp. It'll weaken you. I've seen it over and over."

Avery nodded but knew Chance was not something she was willing to get rid of, even for a win. "I'm sorry. I should know better."

Reuben patted her arm. "While you're competing, you're not thinking of anything else but competing."

Avery nodded and watched him leave.

"That went pretty good." She turned to Scott, coloring red in the center of the floor.

"It's Savage, isn't it?"

She kept her distance, but her own blood easily roared to a boil. "Don't start."

"We've danced together for seven years, Avery, and not once have you let a relationship interfere. Doesn't that tell you something?"

"It tells me that I should get out more." She crossed to the stereo system.

"It tells me that he's wrong for you. He's poison. Look what he's doing to your head. You can't even think straight. And Reuben was right. He was telling us things he tells his intermediate students, not people that teach for crying out loud!"

She turned on him. "Scott, stop. It's not your place to tell me how to live my personal life. I've given you my dance life, but that's all. You have someone. I've been so cautious, so predictable, and look where it's gotten me. I'm alone most of the time and it's not a satisfying place to find myself."

"You've never been the type to have companionship just for the sake of it, Avery. Now, suddenly you want someone just to have someone? Don't you see how wrong that is?"

"Why is that wrong? And I don't want just anyone. I want one." The admission caused her to stop. Though she'd let her thoughts tiptoe that direction, she knew now that both of her feet had planted themselves in Chance's front yard.

He shook his head, his eyes hard as they stared into hers. "He's a loser. I did more checking—"

"Oh, stop it." She gave him her back and pulled on her sweater.

"I did it because I knew you'd only see it if I had concrete evidence. I found out the name of the girl and she lives here now. Her name was—"

"Chelsea Drake, I know. He told me everything."

"Did he tell you that he got her pregnant?"

Avery's heart skipped then fell to her feet. Her fingers slowed as they buttoned.

"That's why they sent her away and locked him up."

"That's not what happened," she said, the pit in her stomach widening.

"This guy I know knows her. Her child is twelve years old now and lives with Chelsea. Her name's Granger now." He dug in his pocket, produced a yellow sticky note. "Call her. Ask."

Avery's eyes opened wide and she glared at the paper. "I would never call her. Even if that did happen, it's nobody's business, certainly not mine."

"But he lied to you. Whatever story he told you is a lie, and he'll use you just the same."

She rifled through the CDs, her face heating, her heart racing. "I have no intention of getting used, Scott. Or pregnant."

"And I'm sure young fifteen-year-old Chelsea didn't either when he seduced her."

But that wasn't what had happened, Avery was sure. It had been a case of young love, innocent and sweet. Chance told her that they'd barely kissed. But a child—that threw a blanket of doubt over her she couldn't see through.

"Just be careful," Scott said softer now, drawing close.

"Have I ever been anything else?" Her life had been all

about planning, caution, and control. That was part of why she was enjoying it so much lately, the element of spontaneity that Chance and all he was brought with it a freshness she had never experienced.

"Talk to her."

She jerked her head at him. "If you—"

"If you do, I won't."

She tore the paper from his hand. "I'm not giving you permission to do anything like that. It's none of our business."

"You love him," he said quietly, locking her eyes to his. "That makes it your business now." He turned, quietly gathered his things and left.

Avery stared at the paper in her hand, at the name printed neatly - Chelsea Granger, 405-3225. Before Chance, she would have found Scott's loyalty admirable, comforting even. Now she found it annoying and over protective. But Scott was right about one thing, she was in love with Chance.

He'd lived on a diet of Rockstar's and potato chips, hard rock music and painting for days. He'd kept himself alone, just the way it had to be when he was punishing himself. He avoided Justin—not opening the door. Not even talking to his friend who had, at one point, stood on the other side of the locked door for an hour, waiting for him to open it.

The phone had rung endlessly. He'd heard Avery's voice echoing from the answering machine, and she'd left messages on his cell phone. Even Dru had called.

It was just as hard to hear the voices of some of the students who had come over to visit. Justin told them that he wasn't available. Then he pounded on his door and told him he was an idiot.

That, he knew.

He was just biding his time until he could move back into his parents' house, clean it out and sell it.

And move on.

Working on the finishing touches of Avery's painting, he realized that moving back into his parents' house would be like walking back into a lion's den. He wouldn't do it.

Funny, he thought now, absently feathering highlights in Avery's vanilla crème hair, his whole world had crumbled because of what had leaked from a few mouths. But he wasn't the same person anymore and going back, even to start a new life, would be made impossible by those same people.

But he didn't have to fight that fight any longer.

So he'd sell the house, take the money and leave the state for good. He had his parents to thank for his vagabond propensity. When they'd kicked him out, left him to his own genius to survive, he'd gone to living cheap, low, and dirty just so he could go to a junior college, then transfer to the state college, without one cent from them.

Kurt, he was sure, had begun draining his trust fund the minute he turned eighteen.

When the two of them had sat in Frank Nesbitt's office and were told the specifics of the will, Chance had been just as shocked as Kurt, who'd been sure everything had been left to him.

But it wasn't the money that haunted Chance's thoughts now. His mother had left his room untouched. She'd cared for it even in his absence, as if he might, at any moment, walk back into it.

He skimmed some more white to highlight along Avery's bare shoulder and down her arm.

He didn't really know his parents; his perspective spread between a child's and that of a self-absorbed, insecure teenager. Had he lived any part of his adult life with them, he might have the answers to these questions now. But his mother and father, his brother, the house, were all strangers to him.

He was compelled to know why his mother had left his room untouched now more than ever. *Just when you think you can abandon something for good, it comes back to haunt you,* he thought, standing back from the painting.

Like Avery would.

He let out a sigh, thinking of her, of what she must be thinking of him. Time would make her forget. It had been days since he'd enjoyed looking into her face. When he closed his eyes, he saw the way she looked at him there in the tree house: eager desire, infinite promise, untouched innocence. It was the way he was going to leave her.

He was startled to hear movement behind him and he whirled around, found Justin standing behind him with a smile on his lips but simmering anger in his eyes. He held up a spare key. "Dude."

"Hey." Tense, Chance turned back to the painting. "My door was locked."

"Yeah." Justin's tone was sharp. Chance felt him come closer. "And you've been holed up in here for days."

Chance dabbed at the grey on his palette. "And I'm alive."

"And you've been ignoring me, Avery—everybody. What's up with you?"

"I'm working."

"Yeah. What's up with that? Why aren't you at the school?"

Chance let a little displeasure leak out in his tone. "You my guardian?"

"Your friend." Justin shifted into Chance's vision. "I thought. You going to tell me?"

"It's not your business." Severing relationships to avoid disappointing people had been something Chance had done for years. But he'd had few good friends, and this time it ripped him inside. He stroked more grey on the background of the canvas, Justin antsy at his side.

"They didn't need me anymore," Chance told him.

"That's bull."

"I'm just telling you—"

"And I don't believe it," Justin's tone was hard. "You look ready to grovel at the bar, man."

When Justin gestured to his scraggy sweats and torn shirt, Chance shrugged. "I'm not, if that's what you're worried about."

"Okay, that's good." Justin glanced around the room. "I wondered what you'd been doing for food." He reached to the floor and plucked an empty Rockstar. "Why don't we take the girls out?"

"Making it sound like something won't change that it isn't anything."

"She's called every day."

"She's under the wrong impression."

"Are you going to hurt her?"

"I'm trying not to."

"If you think skipping out now won't, you're wrong. I saw the look in her eyes when she asked about you."

Chance's heart twisted. He kept his eyes on her face, reached out with his brush but couldn't touch the canvas. "It can't be anything—for her sake."

"That's a load of crap. Look, I know you better than you think and you just love to punish yourself for stuff that doesn't belong to you. I don't know all of what that stuff is but I have a pretty good idea that a lot of it is completely yesterday."

Chance slid him a warning glare. "We're not right for each other."

"Yeah, right." Justin just laughed, sharp as a spear. "Anybody that makes you happy, brings your life even an ounce of joy is too good for you, right?"

"You looking for some grappling practice?" Chance was

ready to set down his palette and brushes.

Justin took a step closer. "Only to beat some common sense into that thick skull of yours. How long are you going to wallow? You had some crap thrown at you and it wasn't fair, I'll give you that. But you're here now. Good things can happen to you. They *have* happened to you. She cares about you—a lot." He spaced the words. "I can see it. And you feel the same, that's easy to see, the way you're backing away like a cat into a corner."

"A cat?"

Justin grinned, shrugged. "This week I'm working on similes with the kids in class."

"Well don't use weak ones on me."

"It's a weak thing you're doing, bro. There are a hundred guys out there that would give their hands for Avery's time and she's asking for yours."

"Hands?"

"You use yours in your work, don't you? Would you give them up for her?"

In a breath, Chance thought. He looked at her face. Though she would never require anything so drastic, he knew what Justin was getting at. His hands had been the lever through which he'd held onto his fragmented life, through painting. To sacrifice that would be like skinning his heart, leaving it vulnerable, only trusting that she would care for it if he set it in her hands. Could he take that chance?

Justin squeezed his shoulder. "Good. You're thinking."

Chance smiled, noting the glimmer of mischief in Justin's eyes. "I have paint."

He held up his palette, dotted with goopy paint, his wet brush.

"Weapons." Justin's wrist flashed up, flicking the brush into oblivion. His other hand squeezed deep into Chance's shoulder, triggering a pressure point that took Chance to his knees, the palette dropped to the floor.

"And now, it's time to take you down," Justin grunted with a wicked smile.

SIXTEEN

Avery knew she'd gone too far when she asked Alex to look up birth records in the archives at the Daily Herald. They were public property, and she had a right to read what was in the paper – even if it was twelve years ago.

She debated throwing the slip with Chelsea Granger's phone number away, dismissing Scott's warnings, but she'd lived too many years dissecting and analyzing. It was a natural response. She had to admit that decisive quality had kept her life free of ugly entanglements.

She would have preferred talking to Chance about it, hearing firsthand what he had to say, but he hadn't returned her calls and his lack of response was beginning to feel dreadfully cold, like a shoulder turned.

She knew better than to tell Alex anything about the child's birth. Once he got wind of anything suspicious, he was like a bloodhound out for a dead body.

She hadn't gotten the voice of approval from any of her brothers after meeting Chance. Her mother had raved about him, gushing about all of the qualities Avery found interesting as well. Her father had been mildly impressed.

She had something to prove to her brothers.

On her way to dance class, she decided to stop by his apartment. She was anxious when she pulled up, wondering if his sudden absence at school meant he'd found another job. Maybe he'd met someone else or Dru had finally conquered his resistance.

Her reaction was foolish, but she was nervous as a teenager when she knocked on the door. Rock music pounded from behind it. She glanced around. Chance's old green VW sat out front. Justin's SUV was there as well.

She heard laughter, thumping. Knocking harder only hurt her knuckles and she turned the knob, slowly opening the door when she found it unlocked. The living room furniture had been pushed against the walls and she saw a body fly by, heard it land with a thud. Another body flashed after the first, followed by more grunting.

The music was so loud she'd never be heard so she peered in. They were on the floor, the two of them so locked together it was hard for her to see where one began and one ended.

"Hello." Her timid greeting was swallowed up in the guitar licks and drums, and the wrestling going on at her feet. She took a few brave steps near where the two of them writhed on the floor, saw Justin's hand clamp fiercely over Chance's face and she let out a little screech that neither man heard.

She had yet to understand the male need to fight and dominate.

Justin's body heaved; his legs grazed the floor like a blade, and in a fast move meant to further paralyze Chance, one of those legs caught Avery's ankle, sending her crashing to the floor in a frantic thud.

Both men scrambled over to where she laid eyes wide, arms and legs spread like a flattened cartoon character.

Justin reached her first and lifted her so that she was sitting up. Chance came next to her side.

"Avery." Chance's eyes went over every inch of her. Gently he wrapped his hands around her, bringing her to her feet. "Are you hurt?"

"I'm okay." She was embarrassed, and heating with it from head to toe. "I knocked but no one heard me."

"I'll get the music." Justin disappeared down the hall and

she stole the opportunity to look at Chance. The grey in his eyes was wrought with something she couldn't put a finger on but hoped wasn't disapproval for her being there.

"I'm sorry, I tried to knock. I even said hello. I just came by to see if you were coming tonight?" The loud pound of the music died but Avery's heart still thrummed. She so wanted to throw her arms around him, run her fingers along his face and kiss him. "I missed you."

He looked away then, those unsettled eyes lowering, and she couldn't see what was behind them anymore.

Justin appeared, smiling, drenched with sweat. "You sure you're okay?" He came right to her, touched her arm.

She nodded, painfully aware Chance was in a mood that promised nothing pleasant. "I was just on my way to class and came by to see if Chance was coming since he's missed two weeks."

Stepping back from her, Chance drew his arm across his forehead. "I won't be coming back to class."

Both of the looked at him, quieted by the news.

"Dude, why?"

"But you're doing so well."

He couldn't be that near her and not feel an ache in his heart, so he moved. Chance took off to the emptiness of the kitchen in search of a drink. When he heard them follow, his nerves skipped. "I'm going to be busy." He pulled a glass out of a cabinet, stuck it under the faucet.

"Doing what?" Justin asked with a bite.

Chance didn't like being cornered. "Stuff." He drank the entire glass down as they watched then set the empty glass on the counter with a thunk. "I've decided to sell my parents' house."

Justin crossed his arms. "You have?"

"I went out there the other day. There's nothing for me there and no reason for me to go back."

Avery stepped toward him. "Dan's a realtor, he can—"

"I can find my own realtor, thanks."

Avery's brows synched tight and Chance couldn't look at the shocked confusion he saw in her eyes. He reached for his empty glass, stared into it. "Anyway, I'll be tied up in that for who knows how long."

"It only takes a few hours to list a house, dude," Justin said, reaching for his own glass, filling it. He drank, eyes firmly set on Chance. When he'd finished he said, "I'm going to go shower for class." He slid his sharp look toward Avery and it softened instantly. He reached out and patted her arm. "Sorry about earlier. I was kicking his butt."

"It's okay." She shrugged lightly, but her concern was plainly aimed at Chance.

After Justin left, they stood in silence. Avery's feelings were brittle and she didn't like it. "Talk to me," she said.

"I've been meaning to." He rolled the glass between his hands. "Whatever was between us—it was great." It was more than that; it had been the most wonderful thing he'd had happen to him in so long, he was still savoring it. "And I appreciate you trying to make a difference. You have. More than you'll know."

"That won't do for me," she said, keeping disappointment from coating her voice. "I'm not through with you."

A grin flashed on his face but was gone instantly. "Avery, Avery." He dared himself to touch her and moved close, resting his hands on her shoulders. "It can't work between us."

She took a moment to understand the layers behind his words. The kisses, the kindness she'd seen in his face that she would never forget and brought out her defenses now. "You're entitled to your opinion."

His eyes glinted with a smile. He shook his head. "What are you doing?"

"I made that clear some time ago, Chance."

"I'm no good for you."

"I can decide that for myself. Selling or not, you committed to class. Tonight we start learning our formation routine for the show. I need you."

"Nice try but any guy would give their hands to dance with you and they will."

She reached for his. Twining their fingers, she brought his hands to her chest. "These hands will do quite nicely."

"I'm serious," he said, and eased his fingers free with a step back. Leaning against the counter, he crossed his arms.

She refused to let the heaviness in the room and the look of resolve on his face frighten her or weaken her will. But she couldn't excuse the terrifying thought. "Have I done something?"

The shift in his face from resolve to softness gave her a glimmer of hope. He shook his head. "No."

"You're closing up and I want to know why."

"You're making this hard on me."

"Good."

"I don't want to hurt you."

"Then don't." She forced her lips into a smile and waited for his to do the same, but his dark eyes only hollowed with emptiness. So she moved to him, pressing the whole length of her into him as she neared his lips. "You couldn't hurt me." She kissed him then, and her heart soared through the thick heaviness clouding the room.

The fast shudder she felt against her was just what she was looking for; his body confirming what was truth. Gently she slipped her arms around his neck and kept her needy mouth to his.

She would break him of this foolish thing he was trying to do, using every gift she'd been given as a woman if she had to. His mouth took only a breath to respond and when it did his arms snapped around her, stealing her breath, squeezing her so tight she thought her ribs would crack.

The kiss was hungry from deprivation, hard with angst, deep with urgency. She melted under the furious heat from hands taking every inch of her back with that same deprivation that cried from his lips.

Any concern vanished, lost in the whirl suddenly filling the room. An ache started deep in that place in her heart she had carefully given him ownership of, stretching wide with so much love she would do whatever he asked of her at that very moment, whatever his heart desired forever and beyond.

"I love you," she murmured, freeing her mouth from capture. She heard an agonizing sound in his throat and kissed the spot with her lips, skimming rough stubble over hot skin. His grip tightened and she traced soft, fluttery kisses along the side of his neck.

"Avery." Her name grated from his throat.

"It's true," she whispered, then eased back to look him in the eye. "I love you."

Chance's gaze was intense, as if searching would reveal a lie, a joke, or truth, none of which would he be able to believe. All of which could devastate him.

Dark confusion hardened his jaw. Eager to dismiss it, Avery ran her finger there. "You don't have to say anything. You don't even have to believe. But you will."

When his eyes glimmered with tears, her heart swelled. He shook his head, loosened his arms a little. "This isn't right, Avery."

"It is. We both feel it, Chance." She secured her arms around his neck. "I'm not going anywhere."

Couldn't this possibly work? She would have to know that he could only bring her misery. That's all he'd ever given people he'd cared about. Resting his brow against hers, Chance sighed. His body wanted her, his soul already belonged to her and he understood the fight really wasn't with her at all, but with himself.

She shifted in his arms and he thought she was trying to leave. Instinct made him hold her tight, their brows still fused, bodies amalgamated, until she relaxed completely against him again. He knew then that he never wanted her to leave, that he'd been afraid of that all along.

"Are you ready to dance?" she murmured.

Closing his eyes, he nodded.

He didn't know love could feel like this. Filled him with so much hope, waking to each dawn was something he anticipated with his blood jittering the night before.

Chance lay in his bed listening to Justin readying for school. He looked at Avery's painting. It was almost finished. He had yet to put the final glossy touches in just the right places so that when you looked at it, you felt as though you were in the same room with her, that you could reach out and touch her, hear her breathing. He was mesmerized by her eyes, and by seeing in them what had become a reality – the look she'd had when she had uttered the unthinkable – that she loved him. Just hearing her voice say the phrase in his head choked his throat, tightened a band around his heart.

Running his hands over his face, he decided to get up. Two things he had to do today would start the beginning of the end in a chapter he was anxious to close.

A fast knock on the door and Justin peered in. "I'm off, dude."

"Yeah, have a good one."

Justin leaned in the doorframe. "You ever coming back to teach?"

"I gotta settle some things first," Chance said, pulling on some jeans.

"Cool. See ya tonight."

Chance gently covered the painting of Avery, looked around the room and sighed. The place was cleaner than it had been but still left a lot to be desired. He heard the far-off thud of the front door shutting and started in.

A woman appreciated such things, he told himself, and he'd gotten lazy. He could easily recall the way his mother sent his father in once a week for inspection. If things hadn't been House and Garden magazine-clean, he got the belt.

It didn't take long and he stood observing the tidy room with pride.

He showered, dressed and looked at himself in the mirror. Eyes that he'd been unable to face looked back with the clarity and brightness of hope. The swelling of emotion inside grew fast and tremulous, shooting from his heart to every cell, causing him to take a deep breath, echoing one name – Avery.

The smile on his face was involuntary and he let out a laugh. If this was being loved – if this was loving, he'd take it and stop wondering.

He drove out to Springville with that smile still on his face and the oldies channel on the radio. Those songs reminded him of her, and of dancing. The man he saw in his mind whirling her around the dance floor was not Scott. No, he saw himself with her now and it wasn't a dream. The vision was altogether possible.

Dan's small green BMW was already at the house. Chance shook his hand and they went inside.

"Great property." Dan scanned the white marble entryway. "Since I was early, I toured the outside. What is there, about six acres?"

Chance nodded.

"Animal rights with that barn out back. That's the classiest barn I've ever seen."

"Dad sold the horses just before the accident. Thought he

was too old to keep them around anymore."

Chance led Dan through the house one room at a time. Knowing that he was never going to live there again set a strange emptiness in his stomach. They stood in his dad's leather and oak office and Chance thumbed through the file cabinet for pertinent papers. On the walls hung various hunting trophies; the head of a six-point buck, a snarling elk and a commanding moose.

Dan stood just under the massive moose head, its blank black eyes staring out. "You dad was quite the hunter."

Chance didn't even pause in his search. "It's what he loved best, next to work."

"So who's handling the sale of the business?" Dan asked. It was a private question, but with Avery, as with her family, Chance had come to understand that no topic was off limits. That kind of frankness would take some getting used to.

"Dad's lawyer." Chance pulled out the file labeled *House* and looked through it before handing it to Dan.

"May I?" Dan gestured to one of the tufted leather wing chairs facing the heavy oak desk Darrell Savage had used.

"Yeah, of course." Chance hiked his butt up on one corner of the desk recalling that his dad had never allowed such use of the furniture.

This was Avery's brother, possibly someone he would come to know better if fate allowed, and Chance studied the man. He had the Glenn eyes: large, round and deep-sea blue. Dan's hair was light, like Avery's. He dressed well and drove a nice car. That spoke of success.

"How's the market?" Chance asked, unable to come up with anything else.

Still browsing the file, Dan shrugged a shoulder. "It's a buyer's market. I have to be honest with you, houses over four million sit for a while. People figure if they're going to spend that much, they might as well build." He flicked through the papers. "But this place is newly remodeled, sits in a primo area on a fantastic piece of land. I'll bet we'll get a buyer within three months, if we price it right. Ah, here's the latest appraisal. It was done last year. In fact, your parents had an appraisal done every other year, did you know that?"

Chance rose, looked over his shoulder. "No." But he could imagine his net-worth conscious parents continually wanting assurance that their investments were rising in value.

"They were very thorough in their recordkeeping, at least where the house is concerned." Dan looked up at him. "I think you could get twelve million for it. But I gotta tell you, I'd bet my hands that the buyer will be a developer. He'll chop the property and sell it in lots. It's what's happening to older neighborhoods like this."

Chance grinned. It would serve these people right. "Even with it being behind gates?"

"Old gated communities like this are dying under pressure to build new. The newer homes add increased value to an otherwise ghost town area. It's the thing to do and where you'll be the first, I guarantee you won't be the last." Dan stood. "As far as I could see driving in, your property here is the largest, right?"

Chance nodded, recalling how proud his parents had been of that very fact. Others, most especially the Drakes, had been jealous. "Years ago it was a real commandment breaker," Chance said. "Coveting thy neighbor's property? Yeah, there was plenty of that going around."

Dan grinned. "Still is. And you, my friend, will be the benefactor." *Finally,* Chance thought. A little revenge would be incredibly satisfying. Not to mention he'd be exiting in style and with enough rebellion to wipe the smirk off any nosey face anxious to rub in old lies.

"So you think it's the right thing to do?" Chance asked as the two of them walked back into the kitchen.

"Definitely. And I'm not just saying that from a money-making standpoint, for you or for me. Developers are hot for stuff like this but they won't always be. Take the opportunity while it's available, that's when they pay the primo bucks." Dan situated himself at the round table that sat under the large picture window framing the back of the acreage.

Chance stared out like he had so many mornings, afternoons and evenings during the years he'd lived there. A flurry of aspens created a grove to the left, surrounding the white barn his dad had built some twenty years earlier and kept up with yearly paint jobs.

The soft rolling hills had been his play land where he'd sledded with friends, built snowmen in the winter, and ridden the riding mower for fun in the summers. With land to spare, both he and Kurt had begged their parents for a pool. But Darrell and Marva Savage believed in withholding things.

"Regrets?"

Startled, Chance looked down at Dan, who was studying him. He shrugged.

"You know, you don't have to rush into anything," Dan said. "You're adjusting to a huge loss. If it were me, I'd think on it long and hard."

Part of Chance wanted to get it over with. Another part of him was torn. Selling would most definitely put all of this once and for all, away – what smidgen good he still held onto, as well as all of the bad that seemed to never let go of him.

"Yeah, well, your parents are not my parents."

"I don't mean to pressure you in any way."

"I know that." He looked him in the eye so that he'd understand. "But I could tell, from just one afternoon, you have an exceptional family."

"We do." Dan nodded, set aside his pen. "Didn't have a lot, though Dad did well enough, but we managed to come out of it close and still caring about each other."

"I can see that."

"And we've kept an especially close eye on our baby sister."

Chance laughed. "Uh-oh."

"No, it's cool. I think it's great that she's finally out there. She's spent so much time dancing and teaching we almost started to wonder if she was hiding herself."

"She'd never do that." Chance slipped his hands in his pockets, his eyes now on a dozen deer that had wandered into the grove of aspens to forage. "She's just too focused to take the time."

"You know her already."

Yeah, I do. And Chance liked that.

"I've seen a change in her and it's been good," Dan said. "Now I can see where that change is coming from."

"Don't stick me with the credit."

"Avery's always been about doing what's right, what's expected, and that's a good thing. But just the other day she was actually late for my wife's baby shower. That would never have happened before."

"I can't see where making a woman absent-minded is admirable."

"You can't because you didn't see where her mind was before. Man, she got up, did her little thing. Taught school, went to the gym, did her private thing with Scott – there's another guy I'd like to cream – he's done nothing but keep her attached at the proverbial hip, if you know what I mean. It's a strange thing dance partnerships—like a funky marriage. But that's her life, and she's happy with it."

It pleased Chance to know that she was just what he had thought – a beautiful untouched work of art, but that made him uncomfortably aware of how fatal their relationship could be for the picture-perfect future he wanted for her.

"Any guy that can crack the shell of reliability and monotony that has encased my sister for so long, I say—go for it. Now." Dan turned back to the papers but paused, looking up at Chance, saw the ponderous look still on his face and said, "How about we talk in a day or so. I need to look over this stuff anyway and everything I need to write up a listing is in here." He stood, stretched, looked out the window just as the deer's heads all snapped up suddenly and faced north.

"I could never kill one of them," Chance said absently.

"Yeah." Dan nodded. "We Glenn's aren't much for the hunt. Some guys," he gathered his briefcase, "live for it."

The back door swung open and Chance recognized the booming footsteps. Kurt came into the kitchen with a scowl on his face. "What is that Coldwell Banker car doing out there?"

"Hi." Dan stepped forward with a hand extended and a smile on his face. "Dan Glenn."

Kurt ignored him, staring at Chance. His face was already red, now his eyes were splintering with veins. "You'd better not be doing what I think you're doing, little brother."

"Dan, my brother, Kurt Savage." Chance gestured to Kurt who still ignored Dan.

"Okay. I'm out of here." Dan shook hands with Chance. "We'll be in touch." He passed Kurt without saying another word and sixty seconds later the thick silence was broken by the sound of the back door shutting.

SEVENTEEN

"You sell this place and I'll kill you, I swear it," Kurt hissed.

Chance turned and faced the window. The deer were gone. "It's mine. I can do what I want with it."

Kurt didn't say anything, only moved right up behind him, and it sent a sting of ice down Chance's spine. "You think selling will make you more money than just holding onto the property and letting it appreciate?"

"Selling will get me what I want out of something I got very little out of." Chance shouldered past him, striding out of the room.

"Something you don't deserve."

"That's not how I see it. Look. I'm not having this argument again."

"Just what did that realtor tell you? That you should sell it to some developer? Do you know what they'll do to it?"

"Since when do you care? You leeched off Mom and Dad like a bloodsucker. You never cared about roots, home and family."

"I was here, you weren't."

"Yeah, you were. So don't complain about lost opportunities. You had them."

Kurt's body tightened like a balloon filling with hot air. "That's right. I was here for them. I listened to Mom crying her eyes out for months because of you. It was me that Dad beat whenever he got angry thinking about you and the damage you did. Me!"

"I would have gladly stayed and taken those beatings!" *But they locked me out of their lives.* Chance would have taken anger and violence over four blank walls and dozens of kids too screwed up to know the difference.

"All I want to know is was it worth it?"

Chance swallowed a knot in his throat and looked back out the window. "You know damned well nothing happened between us."

"I knew."

"But you didn't say anything."

"I wasn't stupid. I wanted to screw the Drakes."

"What did you have against the Drakes? They didn't do anything to you."

"They let you near her and not me. That wasn't fair. I was every bit as good for her as you. Better, in fact."

Chance sneered. "You?"

"Between her and your paint fumes you couldn't see straight you were so love-struck. Yeah, I liked Chelsea. Your fling with her mother blew any opportunity I might have had into oblivion."

"I never touched her mother."

Kurt snarled out a laugh.

"Why would I lie?" But Chance's innocent pleas had fallen on deaf ears twelve years ago. He knew that would never change, even if his parents were still alive.

"To save yourself."

In a way Kurt was right. He'd wanted to save himself when he'd seen the frightening, precarious cliff he'd been left to stand alone on. Even now the need to vindicate himself was alive.

Kurt peeled off his jacket and threw it aside. "Let's settle this the only way we can."

Chance shook his head. "No way." But his hands began to twitch.

Kurt stepped toward him, flicking out his arms. "Tell you what, you beat me and you can do whatever you want to this place. But if I win, you sign everything over to me and walk away."

"You're out of your mind."

"We still split the sale of the business. That chunk will be plenty for you to crawl into some rat hole again and do your painting, if you can call it that."

The roaring in Chance's blood heated up. Still, he kept his hands at his sides and shook his head. "It's been settled legally. That's going to have to be enough."

Kurt's lip lifted in a sneer. "Come on. You never know, you might survive."

Black hate darkened Kurt's eyes and Chance's stomach knotted knowing he wasn't going to get past him without bloodshed. But if that was part of what he had to do to finally be free, it was worth breaking bones.

He braced himself, his mind flashing every technique Justin had pummeled into his brain over the last few months. He knew one thing; he needed to get Kurt to the floor.

He lunged for Kurt's abdomen. As he took his brother's gut with his head and shoulder, Kurt's arms wrapped around his neck. They toppled to the floor, sending every fragile and ornate trinket on their mother's console table flying.

Chance felt the extra forty pounds Kurt carried in his limbs like a grizzly bear flattening him. Frantically, he twined legs with Kurt's, trying to maneuver his brother's thick body underneath him.

His brother's left arm stayed hooked around Chance's neck, while his right began pummeling his face in fast, hard jabs.

The vise grip Kurt had around his neck drew taut and Chance's efforts to climb on top were dashed by the need to breathe. Clawing at the thick forearm holding him captive, he choked, pulling Kurt over his back as he delivered an elbow into Kurt's gut.

Caught off-guard, Kurt's grip loosened and it was the window Chance was looking for to break away before turning around and diving back into Kurt like a linebacker tackling a guard.

Flying across the white carpet, they careened into the glass coffee table, the corner of it jabbing into the back of Kurt's head. He let out a scream and shoved at Chance with a growl. "You trying to kill me?"

Chance was on all fours, ready for more. Kurt sat up, felt his wound and when his bloody fingers came to his face, his eyes blackened with revenge.

"This can be over," Chance said, gasping for breath. "Right now."

Shaking his head, Kurt lunged as Chance scrambled out of the way, knocking into a chair he shoved aside. No more words were spoken. Flesh fastened to flesh. Fists pounded, skin tore, cloth ripped. Blood shot, streamed. Voices scraped from the gutter of vicious hate, brutally hissing from bodies twisting in fury and agony.

It was Kurt who snagged Chance by the collar and pushed him near the giant glass curio filled with Marva Savage's priceless Llyadro collection. Chance struggled to take Kurt down with a swoop of his legs. He hooked his right under Kurt, and Kurt lost his balance. They both fell into the curio. Glass flew, scattering crystal everywhere. Wood thudded and split. Pale blue and ivory shards sprinkled like rain around them.

Both fell to the ground and stopped, stunned and bleeding. Heaving for breath, Chance heard Kurt somewhere near his left. Every bone was bruised; blood covered his hands and arms. He could barely sit up, the muscles in his stomach screamed when he moved.

He crawled over to where Kurt lay, smeared red and gasping, and straddled him. Kurt's head lolled back and forth as he struggled to breathe, to open his eyes.

Squeezing every bit of energy he could from a body already spent, Chance hooked Kurt's legs in his, wrapped his arms around Kurt's weak neck and squeezed. Still panting, he held him in the chokehold and leaned into his ear. "Submit."

Kurt grunted.

The vise grip Chance had on his neck tightened and he leaned closer. "Submit." With another squeeze Chance waited for Kurt to slap the floor, signaling surrender. At last, Kurt let out a moan and his weary palm bloodied the white carpet.

"It's over." Chance fell to the side, lying in an aching heap, next to him.

Chance stood at the kitchen sink and looked out the window at the darkening yard. Sooty grey clouds hung in the sky with the threat of a late spring snow. The grove in the back looked like it had so many nights when he'd seen the trees vanish into black as night fell over them.

He'd played hide and seek with his friends in those trees. But he'd never played it with his brother.

His arms stung as he ran water over them. Slashes of air cooled where his skin had been cut, scraped and bruised. The joints in his shoulders ached and his head throbbed.

On the sink was a tiny pile of sparkling glass; pieces he gently pulled from raw skin. Splattered with blood, they looked like semi-precious stones of some sort. He picked up a piece, clearly belonging to one of his mother's Llyadro statues, and blinked hard, turning it beneath the water with blood smeared fingers.

Hearing nothing from the living room, he turned his sore

neck slowly to look back where he left Kurt with his own injuries.

Why did it always came down to this?

Kurt demanded his way, and he got it. A sense of relief came over Chance, with the turmoil of the house now over. He couldn't wait to be done with it all and out of this place. There was no reason to ever see Kurt again, something he was sure Kurt was looking forward to just as much as he was.

As night grew darker, Chance's image gradually appeared in the reflected light of the kitchen window. From the smoky shadows on his face and neck, he'd taken a hit.

He dabbed at his face with a cool cloth, but stopped when he saw movement behind him. Kurt stood in the doorway, arms braced. Chance didn't turn. He didn't want to give any idea that he cared because he didn't. If Kurt was suffering, he deserved it.

"Get out," Chance said.

"You learned a few things."

Chance nodded, winced as he pressed the cloth to his lip.

"Never thought you could beat me."

"Yeah, well, I prepared myself."

"You knew this would happen?"

"It always happens, Kurt." Chance eased his aching body around. "But that was the way you wanted it."

Kurt nodded once. Chance tried not to look alarmed; his brother wore blood like an Indian ready for war. Streaks and smudges painted his face, neck and arms. His shirt was torn, the knees of his pants ripped. Oozing gashes in purple and red striped his arms and face. A ripped shred of cloth from the striped shirt he wore was wrapped around one of his bloodied hands.

There was defeat in his eyes. "What was that?"

"Jiu-jitsu."

Kurt gave another nod. "Tough stuff."

"It works."

"You gonna sell?"

"There's no reason for me to stay."

"You got plans for the money?"

"Haven't thought about it yet."

Kurt sneered out a laugh. "That'll kill the neighbors."

"It'd be a toss up, me living here or selling to a developer."

"Somebody coming in and ripping up their perfect little community will be a much bigger pill."

"Good. I hope they choke on it."

"Maybe Ashton Drake will want it."

Chance lifted a shoulder. He'd never knock on that door again, no matter what.

"He'd probably pay more, just to keep you out."

"Probably would."

Kurt shifted, groaned. "Man." His hands assessed the damage on his body. "Well, I guess this is it. It really is over."

Chance nodded.

"I just want to shake before we call it quits."

An uneasy slug hit Chance in the gut. His brother wasn't a gentleman, never had been. "Come on," Kurt came toward him slow and easy. "It's the manly thing to do."

Chance's eyes flicked over him for any signs of a weapon. But Kurt's hands were empty, and no bulges protruded from his pockets. "It's yours now, little brother." Kurt said, extending the wrapped hand.

Warily, Chance took it but saw the flash of glass glittering from the cloth too late as Kurt captured his right hand. The sharp pain dug into the palm of his hand.

For a silent moment, Chance stared into his brother's icy eyes, now glinting with pleasure as the grip turned vise, grinding and twisting, the pain shooting like fire up his arm. In a jerk, he tried to pull his hand free but Kurt's clamped on like the jaws of a shark, the glass thrusting deep.

"Maybe you'll paint better with your left hand," Kurt hissed. "Or your teeth." He released Chance's hand with a vicious shove.

Holding his arm with a hard grip, Chance fought shock, fear and anger and turned his palm. A large shard of glass was embedded in the center. Blood gushed in thick, ruby streams. The hot pain surged in jags up his arm as red trickled through his fingers and down his arm.

Kurt turned and hobbled out.

Sirens screamed through the night and flashing lights lit up the sleepy neighborhood. Chance wondered which of his neighbors had called nine-one-one. Most of them kept a nosey eye on the Savage house, so it was a toss up who to blame. He grabbed a towel, shredded a strip with his teeth and tried to tie it around his aching hand, but the blood was still coming, the pain was still hot.

He couldn't move his fingers.

Paramedics came and settled in to work and he sat, trying not to watch as they examined and assessed. Two policemen followed. One slowly walked around the house, the other asked Chance about what had happened.

He relayed the evening just as it had happened.

"You going to press charges?"

As tempting as it was, Chance shook his head, watching the paramedic work on his nearly lifeless hand. The less contact he had with Kurt the better. Besides, they'd both fought knowing there would be consequences.

"You're going to need surgery for this hand," the paramedics said as he cleaned it. "Right away."

Chance nodded, swallowed to relieve his dry throat. Staring at his motionless fingers, he willed them to move. Only his thumb responded, barely curling. He tried not to feel the flash of panic slapping at his chest. Kurt's icy blue eyes had looked straight into his and crushed that knife of glass into his hand. He still couldn't believe it.

"You want something for the pain?" the medic asked.

Chance shook his head. He just wanted his fingers to move.

That's when he saw her. Ginger Drake. Her auburn hair hung cropped at her jaw line. She wore black jeans and a black blouse. At first he thought shock had brought on a momentary illusion, a horrific dream, but when the police officer asked her who she was, what she was doing there, his heart banged against his ribs.

She didn't even look at the officer addressing her, her green eyes were fastened on him.

"You know this woman?" the officer asked.

"Chance." Her voice was like black velvet. She looked him over with concern in her eyes. "I saw the flashing lights."

Chance had the fleeting thought that it had been her that had made the call to the police. It was inevitable that he'd see her again, the woman who had scarred his life with one single lie. It was a small town after all, and an even more suffocating neighborhood.

"What do you want?" he asked, wincing when the paramedic began to wrap his hand.

"Are you all right?" Her eyes swept him from head to toe. She moved closer. "What happened?"

He had no reason to share anymore of himself than he already had with Ginger Drake. "Nothing."

"I saw Kurt's car here earlier. You two have another fight?"

"Okay. He's ready," the paramedic said. "We need to get you to the ER."

"Your hand." Ginger's voice trailed off when Chance stood and wobbled. The two medics helped steady him. "We'll drive you over," one told him.

"What can I do?" She moved closer.

"Nothing."

"I can drive you," she said.

"Just leave."

He didn't look at her again. The paramedics ushered him out and he was blinded by the streaming lights from the two police cars and the chugging red emergency truck. Just what he needed, he thought, noticing that a small crowd of neighbors had gathered along the bottom of the drive. He wanted to come and go from the neighborhood without notice, leaving the powerful slap of a sold sign in his front yard.

Giving into the aches overcoming his body, he laid his head back in the rear of the police car and closed his eyes as the officer drove through the crowd.

"The shard cut through the flexor retinaculum and the deep transverse ligaments," Doctor Morgan told him. Chance stared at his hand, wrapped now, and propped up on three fluffy white pillows after the doctor had performed surgery. Groggy from the anesthesia, he looked at the man he briefly recalled seeing when he'd been brought in.

It had been a whirl from the speedy drive over to the x-rays and examination once he'd been admitted. They'd insisted on immediate surgery, prepped him and that was all he could remember.

"We were able to reconnect the tissues but we'll have to wait and see if you regain use of your fingers," the doctor was saying, but Chance's brain was too dulled to do anything but feel the phantom echoes of pain where the shard had been shoved deep by his brother's hand.

The doctor lulled some more but Chance just closed his eyes and nodded, nothing registering in his brain.

Sounds around him were soft. A nurse moved quietly. Occasionally he heard the droning voice of a woman speaking over the hospital PA system outside his door, the tinkering of stainless steel. A laugh.

He'd never been in a hospital before, not as a patient anyway.

Silence thickened when he heard the door slide closed. Though his mind was blurry, Kurt's face flashed with regularity, causing his body to startle involuntarily. At one point, he was sure none of this had really happened, that he'd overslept and was just having bizarre dreams.

Avery drifted in and out of his thoughts. Images flowed to dreams and he was dancing with her in that elegant ballroom he'd long ago envisioned her in. He could feel her hand in his and when he looked into her eyes, he was filled with emotion.

He pulled himself out of the thick daze when he heard his voice rasping her name. Blinking heavily, he saw a woman in the dark corner of his room. It was her, it had to be.

Avery.

When the unforgettable scent of sweet perfume filled his head, he knew it was not.

She'd worn it exclusively, Ginger. It had ravaged his senses like a frightening drug when he'd been a teenage boy, scared of what a woman could do.

"Wicked," she'd told him as she'd started undressing in front of him. It was the same afternoon he'd driven her home—saved her, she'd said, from killing herself in the car. "The perfume is called Wicked."

He was there again, his dream had taken him back and his heart was thudding heavily. He stood with his back pressed into a corner.

"I won't do anything to hurt you," she said. He watched shocked and fascinated, frightened and appalled as she slipped out of her clothes and came toward him. "It will be easy, you'll see. And I promise that you will love it. Trust me."

He had trusted her. He'd believed that she was his friend, his mentor. That she would pay him, just like she'd said she would. His heart belonged to her daughter.

His body, he'd never shared with anyone.

He told her it was wrong and asked her how could she do something like this? Didn't she love her husband? What about Chelsea?

"You owe me," she reminded him.

He hadn't been willing, he'd been confused, when he was so loathe to even be near her and yet his body had responded to her touch whether he wanted it to or not. That had filled him with a shame that had thrown him into years of self destructive abuse, hours of useless therapy, and countless casual relationships trying to understand. He hated her for it.

When he'd refused to bow to her continual demands for more, she had administered the final drop of poison that had changed his life forever.

He opened his eyes and she was there, a vision in black, at the foot of the bed. "Why are you here?" he asked.

"I came to see if you were all right."

"I'd be better if you were gone."

She waited in silence until he looked at her again. "You're not in a position to push me away."

Things don't change, he thought. The pit in his stomach filled with anger. "Leave."

"Not until we talk." She moved next to him, sitting in the chair so that their eyes were level.

"You said enough to destroy a lifetime, Ginger. I don't think there's anything left."

He was momentarily surprised when her eyes snapped

closed, when every part of her face drew taut. After she took a deep breath, her eyes fluttered open, resting again with his. "The way you say my name—no one has ever said it like you—no one."

He looked away, disgust throttling his system. "Say whatever it is you came to say and get out!" he rasped, feeling drained afterwards. He closed his eyes. The scent of her was overpowering, pressing his lungs into the bed with the weight of a heavy blanket he wanted to shake off.

He started when he felt her hand touch his arm, and shot her a glare that warned. But she left her hand resting on his helpless one. "I cleaned up the house for you," her tone was meant to calm but didn't. "I hear you're moving back. That's wonderful. I didn't get a chance to tell you how sorry I was about your parents. You, well, I looked for you at the funeral."

He'd vanished on purpose. "No one wanted me there."

She didn't deny his claim, only lightly squeezed his arm and he looked at it. "I wanted to see you."

"You've seen me, now leave."

"Do you hate me that much that we can't talk civilly?"

"Yes."

The compassion and self-pity that had warmed her eyes was starting to cool. "I won't accept your hatred."

"I could care less."

"Don't you even want to know about Chelsea?"

"No." She'd been her victim also, and for that reason, he lied.

"She's married now. She has a child."

Why she would tell him this, he couldn't fathom. He'd stopped caring about either one of them long ago. Caring about Chelsea, what she suffered, had only deepened his wounds.

Ginger lifted her chin. "She blames me."

"Funny how being an adult opens our eyes to the other adults in our lives," he told her.

She studied him. "You were always more mature—"

"I was a kid," he snapped, "a naive kid who couldn't see the signs as they came at him in the form of a beguiling snake."

"You act like what happened between us was bad. It was perfectly natural. Men and women are meant to—"

"Men and women, Ginger, not women and children."

"You weren't a child."

He stared at her with disbelief. "I was young enough to be your son."

"That's ridiculous."

"I was barely fifteen!"

"What we had was consensual."

He let out a harsh but weak laugh, closed his eyes and shook his head. "It was bribery."

"It was two people who loved each other, Chance."

His eyes flew open. "It was rape."

She stared at him long and hard, then slowly removed her hand. "I loved you."

His stomach fisted at the thought. "I had a teenage crush on your daughter. That was all. You're a child abuser, Ginger – a criminal. You promised to pay me money and when I wouldn't do what you wanted, you destroyed me. That's what happened."

It brought him a sliver of satisfaction to see her face pale. He enjoyed it only a moment before he wanted to dissolve in sleep, he was so weary. "Go now," his voice was tattered.

He noticed that she opened her navy reptile purse, brought out a long, narrow piece of paper and held it out. It was a check for fifty thousand dollars.

"Buying some peace of mind?" he asked, but didn't make a move for it.

"I owe it to you, regardless of how differently we see the past." She set it on his immobile hand. "I know you don't need the money now. I've seen your work. It's marvelous, Chance. You're—" She broke off, regret tearing her eyes. "I'm sorry."

They were words he'd longed to hear, words that had not left his mother's lips, or his father's, even after he'd poured out his frightened heart to them. They'd refused to believe him. To hear them from Ginger was too little, too late.

She stood, gripping her purse with whitening fingers. "I'm willing to do whatever you think is fair to make things right."

He couldn't respond, so stunned by her words. The remorse now twisting her classic face created a morbid picture that made it unsightly. "Tell me. Whatever you want, Chance, I'll do it."

Her response had a sickeningly perverse ring to it and nearly took him back, making him wonder if she was genuine or just snaking her way back into his life. He handed her back the check with his good hand. "Take your money."

"No." She stepped into the darkness of the room. "You earned it."

"I won't take it."

"Do you still have them? The paintings?"

He nodded.

Her lips curved a little. "I'd like them, if you could find it in your heart to—"

"No."

"Why?"

He couldn't explain why. In his lowest moments, when his belly had scraped the gravel so long he'd thought for sure his heart would bleed, he had used the paintings, staring at them, hoping the answers he sought would somehow come to him. Letting go would mean finally letting go of what had hung on his back for so long he would be naked without even the ugly excuse to hide behind.

"No," he told her again. He looked at his hand and tried to move frozen fingers.

She moved back into the light. "If you change your mind, you know how to get a hold of me. My number is still the same."

Some things never change, he reminded himself. Except he had, and he wouldn't take even a half-step back, not with Avery in his life.

Chance figured the worst was over. In twenty-four hours, he'd done things he hoped he would never have to do again, he'd gone back home and finally finished the fight between him and Kurt. He'd spoken to Ginger Drake.

And his hand had been severely damaged.

The prognosis was still vague, with too much riding on recovery and rehab for his comfort. He couldn't wait to get out of the hospital. Still feeling lethargic, he sat, dressed now in the battered, bloodied clothes he'd arrived in, and waited.

He wouldn't have called anyone for help had his car been at the hospital, but having been transported there by ambulance left him no choice. It was Justin that Chance phoned, and he arrived with Inessa close behind.

Justin's face showed his shock. "Dude." Letting go of Inessa's hand, he crossed to the bed where Chance sat. "What happened?"

Inessa hadn't moved from the door, her hand was at her mouth, her eyes huge. Chance sent her a half-smile. "It's a lot worse than it looks."

"How could it be?" Justin asked. "You look like you went through a meat grinder."

"Long story."

"I want to hear it."

"Another time." Chance stood, moaned. His bones and injuries wept from lying in bed all night. "You'd have been proud of me. I took Kurt down."

The news didn't even bring a grin to Justin's face. He was staring at the wrapped, elevated hand attached to Chance's chest by a sling. "What happened to your hand?"

"Get me out of here, will you?" Chance grabbed the small bag of pain killers the doctor had issued him and took a few steps, indicating that he was finished with the place—and the topic of conversation.

Begrudgingly he sat in a wheelchair the nurse insisted she escort him out in. The hall smelled faintly of antiseptic and something stale. He couldn't wait to breathe some outside air. Sensing Inessa's apprehension, he looked up at her, partly to avoid Justin. "So how's it going?"

She looked at him through giant hazel eyes. "Fine. We missed you at class last night."

Chance grimaced. "I forgot."

"Looks like you were busy," Justin snapped. Chance didn't meet his friend's gaze, hearing the frustration bubbling in his tone.

The bright noon sun blinded Chance and he squinted. Everything looked like an overexposed negative. Justin's car sat waiting at the curb. He handed Inessa the keys and she went on ahead to unlock the doors.

"Here you go, Mr. Savage." The nurse wheeled him to the car. Justin moved into place to help Chance stand and the nurse wheeled away the wheelchair.

"I feel so out of it." Chance reached for the door but Justin blocked it. "Spend one night in a hospital and—"

"Why didn't you call me?" Justin's voice was harsh.

"I did—"

"Last night."

How could he explain that it was hard to ditch old patterns? He'd been alone, taken care of himself for so long. That was how it had always been. "It was so insane," Chance muttered. "I didn't want to bother you with it."

Justin didn't move. His usually jovial countenance was hard as rock and just as unimpressionable. "When are you going to get it through your head that I'm here?"

"I didn't think you—"

"You're right. You didn't think. I'm tempted to leave you in this place."

Chance smiled and rested his good hand on Justin's shoulder. "You can take me down later. It'll be on me."

A grin finally spread on Justin's lips. He shook his head. "That's nothing. I can do that any day."

"All right then, anything else?"

Justin moved back and jerked his head toward the open car so that Chance could get in. "I want to know what happened."

Chance eased himself in the back seat and sat head back, eyes closed, with a groan. Hanging on the door for a moment, Justin waited. Finally, Chance opened one eye. "All right, all right," he said. "Just get me far away from here."

EIGHTEEN

The studio was empty: no running feet, no laughter, no dancing. Absent were little girls in black leotards with pink tights. The pound of funk music was gone, the smell of sweat no longer in the air.

Avery went to studio A and the cavernous room echoed her footsteps as she crossed to the music system. Only dancing would help relieve her tension and get her mind away from wondering why Chance hadn't called.

What few relationships she'd had had never felt like this, with her heart completely occupied, her mind wholly engaged in someone else. She'd gotten bored and moved on first. She wondered if she was finally getting hers back. But she wouldn't believe that, not when there had been such sweetness between her and Chance.

She knew when a man wasn't interested. Chance had treated her so well she'd started to think he would never touch her like he would touch any other woman.

If she had the opportunity, she would explore that.

She put on "I've Got You Under My Skin." It was incredibly appropriate, since she felt a delicious urge when she thought of Chance. That urge was building with the need to see his face, to hear the smooth, low calm of his voice.

Frank Sinatra's ivory and velvet tone was a temporary fix. Holding a phantom partner next to her, she tried to visualize Chance. She'd become accustomed to the feel of his shoulders underneath her hands, the height of him next to her, the comfortable ease with which they moved together.

Of late, he danced with the confident ease of a dancer who had invested in the sport, rather than simply played with it. She loved seeing that change in people. Dancing, music, brought people an awareness of self few dared to explore under the scrutiny of others. Dance had brought the two of them together and she would forever be grateful for that.

Nothing had ever occupied her mind so completely, except for dance and teaching. She realized that meeting Chance had been what had finally helped her to see that there was room for more in her life.

She and Scott were set to compete again soon. She should focus. She worked at her steps for fifteen minutes, watching her reflection in the wall of mirrors as she moved about the room. Her form was good, her feet doing what they were supposed to, but when she looked at her face, she saw a disgruntled woman whose mind was not going to be tricked just because the other eighty-nine percent of her was doing something different than thinking about the man.

Her cell phone rang and she ran to retrieve it from her purse. She pulled out the phone, hoping she would see Chance's number highlighted in the caller ID. After she laid into him for not calling, she'd string him with some grief. Men earned every bit of grief women dealt them.

Her heart sunk. It was Justin.

Chance lay on his bed staring at the canvas of Avery. After what had happened with Kurt, he wondered if he should reconsider his relationship with her. But that was weak and he knew it. Yet he loved her too much to expose her to anything that would hurt or disappoint her.

He should have expected Ginger would reappear. He couldn't believe she wanted forgiveness. It sickened him to think that it was probably an elaborate lie. One thing was sure, if Ginger Drake were prowling around again, things would get ugly.

His hand throbbed underneath the layers of gauze. He felt like he had years ago, when his world had been like a snow globe suddenly shaken and he was loose inside. But he wasn't stuck in that dome. He'd have more money once the house sold and he could take his new life and do whatever he wanted.

As his eyes settled on Avery's, he knew that it wasn't possible to outrun love.

"You need anything?" Justin appeared in the door, glancing at the painting when he saw where Chance's gaze was fixed.

"No."

Justin crossed to the foot of Chance's bed. "You'd better not be thinking that it's over. You've got a beautiful, talented, caring woman who loves you. And I know you feel the same."

Frustration forced Chance to sit up. "Yeah, but what can I give her? I can't use my hand. I don't know if I'll ever be able to paint again."

"That remains to be seen, yeah. But, correct me if I'm wrong, you're going to be sitting pretty sweetly with the sale of the house and the sale of the business. You can do whatever you want."

"Both of those will take time."

"More excuses. What do you want?"

Freedom. The kind he was just starting to get a taste for as he'd struggled to shed dependency on things that only chained him. *Love.* The kind he'd only tasted in his youth, then had stolen. The kind he knew Avery was intent to give him. He wanted a life with a family, people he cared about who cared about him. Good friends. To teach what he loved at the school.

To dance with Avery.

"I'm tired," he muttered.

Justin nodded. "You know you can stay here as long as you want."

"I know. Thanks."

"Inessa and I are heading out for Chinese. We'll bring back some we can share. You'll be okay till then?"

The lengths his friend was going for him touched Chance, bringing emotion behind his eyes. He turned away. "Yeah. Thanks."

He shifted his aches and got up, gingerly covering the painting with his left hand. His body moaned with the effort. Behind his groan, he thought he heard something and slowly made his way to the front room. There was light knocking at the door. The effort to move brought impatience to the surface and he growled, "Hold on."

He figured Justin had forgotten his keys and locked himself out.

He was speechless to find Avery there. Her eyes shot wide, the blue deepening with shock as they flashed over all of him. He could see that she was working to maintain her composure.

"Chance." For a moment warmth flooded him, just the way she said his name. She wore a light pink overcoat and her hair was pulled straight back like he'd seen her wear it when she taught. Underneath the pink coat she wore black slacks. A black turtleneck peeked at her throat.

"What happened?" Her voice was a whisper.

"You look great." Leaning heavily in the doorway, he didn't even take his eyes off of her long enough to gesture at his wrapped hand, carefully slung against his chest. He so wanted to take her against him and feel her. Her cheeks flushed a raspberry hue darker than her coat but it wasn't from his compliment. She was getting angry.

"Chance. You're hurt—bad."

He stepped aside. "Uh - yeah. You want to come in?" When she passed and he inhaled her, his body nearly tore down the center. "You look great, Avery. Really." All he could do was stare, the very sight of her a salve that sunk to his bones.

"Have a seat." Slowly he moved to the couch, lowering onto it like an old man.

"Tell me what happened."

He closed his eyes, swallowed. "Got in a little fight."

For a moment Avery was so livid, she couldn't say anything. Her heart was just now climbing back into her chest. It had dropped when he'd opened the door. His pale skin was splashed with purple and red, edged in darkening green bruises. Small white strips covered cuts over every exposed part of him. And his hand, something had happened to his hand.

"Why didn't you call me?"

He looked dazed, fading in and out. "I, uh, called Justin."

"Yes. He called me."

"He did?"

Nodding, she lowered herself onto the couch next to him. Her fingers itched to sooth, to comfort and heal. Her eyes began to tear.

When he saw that she was blinking back tears, the gray in his eyes sharpened. "Avery."

"You should have called me. What happened?"

He took her hand. "Nothing."

"Chance, don't." She pulled away, filling with frustration.

"It wasn't anything, Avery. I don't want to hurt you."

"You think being honest will hurt me? Pushing me away, keeping the truth from me, hurts." In one earnest gesture she slid from the couch, dropping to her knees at his feet, leaning her body against him. "Please share with me. I love you, Chance. Tell me."

His heart pulled open by the solemn need in her eyes. He felt weak from consuming pain, lingering drugs, and he didn't have the strength to lie. "My brother and I had a fight."

He waited to see disapproval in her eyes but the love never left. "I went out to the house," he continued, "met Dan there. Kurt showed up and we had it out."

Still, she said nothing. Her body remained poised anxiously over his.

Then she looked at his hand. "Your hand?"

He shrugged. He wouldn't tell her that his hand had been destroyed by the malicious hand of his own brother. "I'll know more in three weeks." He felt her body go stiff against his knees.

He reached out with his left hand and snagged her up between his legs and against him. The pain her body caused when she pressed into his injured hand broke him into a sweat but he buried it by covering her mouth with his.

She opened for him in soft, sweet welcome. The comforting familiar taste of her rushed his blood with a surge of fierce emotion that forced tears behind his closed eyes. So much, he wanted her so much. He needed her even more.

Tears streamed down his face, salt and sweet, as their lips moved together, both taking as much as they could. Suddenly she stopped and pulled back, looking at him. When she saw the tears, her hands framed his face. "I've missed you," she whispered.

He reached up with his good hand and wrapped his fingers gently around the back of her neck to keep her close. "You're here," he murmured.

"I should have been with you, at the hospital." Wearily, he closed his eyes again. "You look exhausted. Why don't you sleep?"

He nodded and with her help, stood. She walked with him to his bedroom where she pulled the sheets back and fluffed the pillows. Patting the bed, she smiled.

"You want me to undress you?" she asked in complete innocence. He tried to laugh but it hurt him in the ribs. He took a deep breath and lowered himself onto the bed. "It's safe for you only because I'm too weak to indulge."

She began by slipping off his shoes.

He closed his eyes and eased himself back. When she reached for the buckle on his pants his eyes flew open. His left hand covered hers, stilling it. "Better not do that."

With a nod, she slid her hand out from under his. Then she pulled the blankets up, stopping when she was at his chest, where his injured hand lay. She sat carefully next to him.

For what grew to be a long and edgy quiet, they looked at each other. Sadness and surrender finally shadowed his face. "I didn't want you to see this."

"Did you think I'd be scared?"

"Do you really want this in your life?"

She studied him for a tense moment with determination in her eyes. Taking his free hand in hers, she ran her fingers over his knuckles forcing words from her lips she hoped would not condemn her. "If you can look at me and tell me that you don't want anything more from me, anything more for us, I'll walk out." Gravity grew thick between them. She kept her firm gaze on his and waited.

"That's an unfair question. I'm still groggy." He couldn't tell her no because deep inside she was already there, filling the emptiness that alone, he'd been unable to fill. Searching her eyes, he found nothing but acceptance, real and unconditional. It seemed unbelievable, and the truth of it tightened his chest with a sob of emotion he fought to hold back.

Leaning closer to him, she laid the sheets and blanket across his chest, smoothing them with gentle care.

"Are you tucking me in?" His voice was a child-like whisper.

She ran a hand over his forehead, leaned over and pressed a kiss there before whispering, "It's settled then. Now sleep."

He was out in a sigh and for a moment she indulged herself in just looking at him. The moment she did, her heart was not her own. It opened and took the rest of him inside. There was no going back.

The dark circles shadowing his eyes were almost lost in the bruises on his face. It was unfathomable, what his family had put him through. She was more determined now to show him that family could love, support and be there for each other no matter how black the night, how gloomy the day.

Quietly she moved around his space, breathing deeply the dusted scent of his cologne, mixed with the smell of paint. Standing out in the middle of the room was his easel, covered with a white cloth. Curious, she went to it and pulled back the cover.

Her hands flashed to her mouth, stifling a gasp. The cover dropped to the floor. A hot flush ran along her spine, springing out to her hands and feet and she looked over her shoulder at him resting, a beaten body amongst the soft white linens of his bed.

Then she stared back at the painting. Slowly her hands fell to her sides. Taken by her own reflection, she was stunned at the realism he had captured in her eyes. She looked shockingly alive, touchable and real even under the delicate lavender sheath that covered her languorously sprawled body. Unconsciously, her hands roamed, as if feeling herself would somehow place her into the painting.

Me, she thought now with rushes of pleasure so strong, she wanted to go and wake him. He had painted her likeness with such perfection she flushed, heating from head to toe again. Self-conscious, she placed the cover back over the likeness and crossed to his bedside, her nerves tingling.

She ran her hand along his face again and kissed him on the mouth, the warm contact of his utterly still lips tingling her blood. She would stay there and care for him. Her heart had no other choice.

Avery left the bedroom, taking off her coat in the hallway. She laid it over the back of the couch and looked around. The place was tidy and dusted, so she decided to watch television while he slept and crossed the small living room to the TV. A soft knock drew her to the front door.

A woman her age looked at her through large blue eyes shades lighter than her own. "May I help you?" Avery asked.

"Is Chance Savage here?"

"He's resting. Can I give him a message?"

The woman seemed disappointed and glanced out into the neighborhood as if in thought before looking back at Avery. "When can I see him?"

"He's recovering from an accident," Avery said, noting the earnest concern on the woman's face.

"Yes, I know."

A little surprised Avery asked, "Are you a friend of his?"

"An old friend. Could I wait inside? I don't live around here anymore. I came in town specifically to see him."

"Sure."

The girl stuck out her hand after she entered the living room. "Chelsea Granger."

Avery froze for a moment before taking the hand extended to her. "Avery Glenn."

"Are you his girlfriend?"

"We're close friends." Avery would never speak for Chance and label their relationship, but she knew what was in her heart. "Have a seat. He's told me about you." Avery kept her tone inviting.

"That must have been some story." Chelsea's light brow went up but she didn't seem averse to continuing the topic. They sat facing each other on opposite couches.

"It wasn't a story, as far as I know."

"I'm sure whatever Chance told you was true. He was never a liar—ever."

The point was taken, and the words settled Avery a little. "So you live out of town now?"

"Yes, my husband works in Park City. I heard about the fight. How is he?"

"He's injured. But I think he'll heal."

"His hand?"

"That remains to be seen."

Chelsea's face grew serious. "They were always at it, the two of them." When she looked up, her eyes were glistening. "It made me feel so bad for Chance, like no one understood or cared."

"He's very private about his family."

Chelsea nodded. "He always was, even when I thought they didn't deserve it. Never once did I hear either one of his parents compliment him, or Kurt for that matter. It was like their children were objects." Seeing the look of disbelief on Avery's face, Chelsea nodded. "I know, it sounds unreal, but that's the way it was. They fed them, clothed them in the best money could buy. Gave them every *thing* they asked for, but that was where it stopped. Their lives were all about how it looked, what everyone saw. That's why things got so bad when—" she stopped herself. "Did he tell you?"

"He did." But Avery wanted more, specifically her side of the story.

"After what happened, I never saw him again. It was horrible. I was crushed. I never even got to tell him how sorry

I was." She looked around the room as if anticipating him somehow. "That's why I'm here. That—and I wanted to see him. Don't get the wrong idea. I'm happily married. I have a little boy I adore. But this part of my life needs closure. I need to make sure he's okay."

There was no way to feel threatened by the sincerity in Chelsea's eyes, but Avery still had questions. "Your son, how old is he?"

"Twelve. He's in school." She lifted her purse, set it on her lap and from there produced a wallet. After Chelsea flipped the leather folder open, Avery looked at a school picture of a boy with dark hair and his mother's crystal blue eyes.

"He's darling."

"He's just like my husband." Chelsea's glow affirmed Avery's deep feelings that the child was not Chance's. Her insides sighed with the dismissal of yet another vicious rumor.

"It's been hard." Chelsea put the wallet back in her purse. "We got married right after I ran away. What my mother did was unforgivable and I wanted nothing to do with her. Nobody wanted to listen to a spoiled rich girl when her mother was paying for anything the community needed. It was much easier to turn a deaf ear and blame a teenaged boy." Chelsea let out a sigh, her perfectly manicured nails now picking at her cuticles.

"It was so unfair to him and his family. But that's what the rich do to each other. When there are too many cocks in the ring, they kill each other until only one is left."

"Not all rich people." Avery thought about her own family. They had money. Maybe not money like the Drakes or the Savages and they certainly did not have notoriety, but their name was untarnished. Nothing would bring them against each other or anyone else for that matter, just for the sake of gain.

"You're right, there are good people everywhere. I'm

jaded. That's why I sought emancipation from my parents. I haven't seen my mother in twelve years. I was surprised yesterday when she called me and told me about Chance."

"Twelve years?"

"She would have destroyed my life if I'd stayed. And I won't let her near my baby. Selfish, I know, but not after seeing what she was capable of."

A rustling sound from the hall startled them both. His hair was mussed, his shirt rumpled, unbuttoned to the center of his chest. His dark pants rode low and baggy. But he looked remarkably rested underneath all of his bruises.

He stopped dead when he saw Chelsea.

She stood. Avery could see the woman's hands were anxious, fingers opening and closing as she kept from going to him too soon.

"Chance."

"Chelsea?" Surprise and shock lined his voice. Quickly, she crossed to him and was gently against him, both embraced in a long hug as Avery looked on.

"What the—" Chance stood back and looked at her. "You—I can't believe it, Chelse. I can't believe it's you."

"It's so good to see you."

"Same here. Wow." Chance looked over at Avery and something changed in his eyes that pleased her. It wasn't the spring of surprise she had just witnessed, but the warm joy of something vital and important. "Avery, you stayed."

"I hope you don't mind that I invited Chelsea in. She's come all the way from Park City to see you."

He moved slowly into the living room. "No, that's okay."

"He got you bad, Chance." Chelsea's face grew dark, her eyes glistened going over his injuries. She shook her head.

"Yeah, well, you know Kurt. Same old, same old."

"But he hurt you." Chelsea touched his slung arm. "How could he do that? You're brothers. I guess I'm the last person that should be asking that question, with my mother the original serpent."

Avery helped Chance lower to the couch then stood in the awkward thickness gathering in the air. "Maybe I'll go for a while."

Chance's good hand wrapped around hers, stopping her. She looked at it, then at him. There was desire, fresh and alive in his eyes. "No," he said. "Please stay."

Unable to refuse, she sat next to him on the couch, pleased that they were facing Chelsea together.

"Chance," Chelsea began, taking a seat on the opposite couch. "I wanted to see you. It's crazy. It's been so long, and yet it feels like just yesterday. In a way it's a miracle, at least for me. But for you it may just be painful. I don't want it to be. If it is, I'll leave."

He shook his head. "It is a miracle. Are you good, Chelse? Happy?"

"Very. I was telling Avery that after everything, I got emancipated from my parents. I haven't seen them for twelve years."

"Wow."

"I had to get away. I got married, had a baby. We're doing well now. It hasn't been easy. I made some mistakes but I've stopped running. That's why I came here. This is part of that. I had to say how sorry I was for everything."

"Chelsea, stop."

"No, let me."

"None of it was your fault."

"I introduced you to my mother. If—"

"Stop, Chelse." Chance was firm. Avery's heart pounded for him—for Chelsea. For what they'd been through. "It wasn't your fault."

"It was my mother."

Chance didn't respond. His gaze flicked uncomfortably

around the room. Avery reached over and laid her hand over his, bringing his lost gaze to hers. His brown eyes softened and settled the moment their eyes met.

Chelsea dug into her purse and brought out a sealed envelope. "She wanted me to give this to you." She held it out to him but he didn't move.

"I don't want it."

"I'm sorry, you know how she is. She thinks money can solve anything. I really don't know what's in it."

Cautiously he took the envelope but didn't open it. "When she told me she was going to bring it over I warned her to stay away. She begged me to bring it, so I met her and had her give it to me."

"That was...wow. That must have cost you."

Chelsea shook her head, her eyes sad with the debt. "It's the least I could do. You don't need permission to toss it. What could she want but more again? Stay away from her, Chance."

He clutched the envelope in his hand. Chelsea stood then. "I should go now. Parker gets out of school in a couple of hours and I need to be there for him. No. Don't get up—rest. You need it." She leaned over and kissed his cheek. "Maybe when you're better we can..."

"Yeah, yeah, that'd be good," Chance said.

"It's so good to see you." Chelsea reached out her hand and waited for his. "I'm sorry. I hope you can be happy, Chance."

"I'm getting there." His eyes met Avery's.

Chelsea's exit left an awkward silence in the air. Not sure what had been discussed between the two women, Chance was uncomfortably reminded of details he had never wanted Avery to know. "You two talk for long?"

"A while." Avery stroked his cheek until the hard line of it softened. "Did you sleep?"

"A little." He let out a sigh and reached for her hand

again. Lifting her knuckles to his lips, he held her gaze for a moment before he pressed a slow kiss there. "You're still here."

"I'm going to take care of you."

"I can do that myself."

"What you can't do is let someone else. That's going to change. Are you comfortable? Do you need more pillows? An itch scratched? A shave?"

He rubbed his scruffy jaw with his hand. "I imagine I look scary by now."

"You look wonderfully masculine."

He let out a laugh. "That's a nice way of putting it."

"Are you going to open it?" With a nod, she gestured to the envelope.

He handed it to her. "Toss it."

Years of suffering were now at an end and yet they had become such a part of him, he couldn't bring himself to believe it was real. But reading whatever was in that letter wouldn't change anything past or present. How different his life would have been had his parents' known the truth, had the small world he'd grown up in, been open rather than closed.

Maybe things would be different now between him and Kurt.

But thinking about what could have been was dangerously close to stepping back and he'd decided not to step that direction again.

Avery tore the envelope into pieces, and disposed of it in the trash before she sat at his side again, quietly waiting. The warmth of her body diffused the whirl of thoughts in his head. There was a future here: he saw it in her eyes, felt it in his heart. He had only to believe and begin again.

He wanted to tell her that he loved her because he did, but he'd never uttered those words to a woman and really meant them. He wouldn't do it now, not in this condition.

Things needed to be in order first.

He watched a sly smile spread on her lips. "What?" he asked.

"When were you going to tell me about the painting?" She took his hand.

His eyes flashed. "You saw it?"

"I admit I peeked while you were asleep."

"You sneak."

"We Glenns—"

"—Are sneaks." He finished her sentence with a good-natured tug of her hand, pulling her over so that her face was inches from his. "I couldn't help it," he whispered against her parted lips. "I had to have you with me."

"It's beautiful."

"Because it's you."

She kissed him, a soft kiss of gratitude and amazement. "But I have to ask why you painted me so…so…"

"Naked?"

Her cheeks flushed and she nodded.

"It's how I dreamed of seeing you some day."

"Well you're imagination was nicely generous."

He reached his hand behind her neck and pulled her lips firmly to his. "I'll be the judge of that." Even with a body barely waking from anesthesia, it didn't stop the hot surge of need racing through his battered system. As she pressed against him, his mind was wont to see her as he'd always dreamed. He wanted to feel her, to run his hands and touch for himself, not just imagine. "I want you."

"You need to heal first."

"I don't need two hands to make love to you."

She smiled and eased back. "I told you, I'm here to take care of you." Her expression brightened with wonder and innocence and he squeezed her hand tight to his chest. In her eyes he saw the most beautiful gift that she wanted to give him. He would wait. If she was at his side, he could do anything.

SAVAGE - *Katherine Warwick*

NINETEEN

Not two days passed and there was a pounding on the door. Chance had just gotten out of the bathtub after a particularly challenging soak. He'd never known how difficult it could be to get wet without getting completely wet. He draped a towel around his waist. He didn't take the time to dry and beads of water dripped down his legs, back and chest as he started for the front door.

Justin beat him to it, wiping off his hands on a kitchen rag. "Rest, buddy. I'll get it. And lunch is almost ready. I made us Little Caesar's." He laughed.

Chance double checked his hand, still wrapped and slung against his chest, making sure he hadn't gotten it wet in during the bath.

"I want to talk to him." Kurt's demand made Chance's head whip up. His brother's bruises were the deep black-purple of his own, only Kurt's were splattered like a paint job gone awry.

Justin didn't move to allow Kurt entrance, but held the kitchen towel twisted between his tight fists as he stood in the doorway.

"It's okay." Chance stepped closer, a chill chasing his bare, wet skin.

Though Justin stepped back, his body was tight as a stretched rubber band and he hung close to Kurt like a hound on a scent. Kurt's defensive gaze shifted from Justin to Chance where it held.

"Can we talk without your Doberman here?" he asked.

Justin reached behind Kurt and whipped open the door. "Out. Now."

Chance smirked. Kurt's lip lifted in a snarl and he didn't budge. "You need this guy to fight your battles? Is that it?" he asked.

"You looked in the mirror lately?" Justin stepped so his nose nearly met Kurt's. "Looks to me like he fights just fine, now get out."

Kurt swallowed, shifted and looked from Justin to Chance. "Call him off so we can talk."

Chance gestured with a slight jerk of his head for Justin to leave and Justin did, shooting fiery glances over his shoulder as he headed to the kitchen.

Kurt kicked the door closed. "And don't kick my door!" Justin boomed, coming through the kitchen opening looking ready to attack again.

"Whatever," Kurt hissed under his breath once Justin had disappeared. His cold stare locked on Chance, on his wrapped hand. Chance searched for regret in his brother's frosty eyes but saw none. In fact, Kurt's lips curled at the edges. "You gonna be able to use that again?"

Chance had crossed the fingers on his good hands and even uttered a few desperate prayers, but he didn't know if he'd regain use of his hand or not. An old anger, hurt and betrayal rose up inside of him, but he held it down. "I don't know yet."

Kurt shoved his hands in his front pockets and stepped closer. "It'll serve you right if you never use it again for keeping what rightfully belongs to me." The air boiled and popped between them.

Chance's free hand clutched at the knotted towel at his waist. "Get out."

"After I've said what I have to say."

Chance sneered. "There's more? I hope you're maimed for

life and I hate the air you breathe and that's not all of it? Its nothing I haven't heard before from you, Kurt."

"Yeah, well, I just wanted to see for myself that you were screwed."

Working to hold in rage, Chance shook his head and let out a snort. "Done?"

Kurt whipped out a laugh. "Why didn't you press charges?"

A decision Chance was beginning to regret, seeing his brother's lack of penitence. Truth was, he just wanted to be done with his past, with Kurt, with the house, and pressing charges wouldn't have given him anything but empty satisfaction. He figured not answering Kurt would drive his brother crazy, so he didn't.

A moment passed with only ugly silence traded between them and Kurt backed toward the door. He snickered, his gaze sweeping Chance from head to toe, and he yanked open the door. "See ya around, little brother."

The door slammed after him. Chance told himself to breathe again. His body had gone to stone—had to—to believe that his own flesh and blood was really pleased he'd possibly handicapped him for life.

Chance looked at his hand, wrapped and pressing against his thudding heart, and he closed his eyes.

"You okay, dude?" Justin's voice came from behind him. At that moment, Chance was glad blood had nothing to do with brotherhood.

He nodded, turned. "Hungry. That pizza still warm?"

The auditorium filled with men in suits, women in dresses and children dressed in whatever they pleased. Chance was in a black suit with a white shirt and black bow-tie, and he stood at the back of the hall, searching the mingling crowd for Avery.

He'd begged out of the performance with the excuse that his still-bandaged hand would be a distraction. Weeks later, movement was still minimal in his fingers, but the doctor had sworn a full recovery with therapy. The only thing better than that news was that Avery had been there with him when he'd heard it.

When his search found her, his heart beat hard. She was stunning in the spring-pink dress sparkling and flowing with diamond-like gems sprinkled in the long skirt. It clung to every soft curve and bared shoulders he couldn't wait to touch.

From his spot in the back corner he marveled at the gracious way she greeted students and the families invited to watch the recital. The moment reminded him of the first time he'd seen her; a classic beauty with dignity that not even his fumbled attempt to meet her could spoil.

He smiled to himself and shook his head. It was unreal that he was standing there. He'd learned how to waltz, tango, fox-trot and quickstep—and enjoyed it. It was unbelievable that he'd fallen in love with the woman who had taught him more than just the steps.

Had someone told him he would be free of the demons that had clung to his back most of his life, he would never have believed it. But the demons were gone now.

Scouring through his parents' house had been difficult, and Chance hadn't kept anything, not even what once belonged to him. The small envelope he'd found from his mother was the only thing he saved.

He still had to close his eyes when he thought about what she had written to him those many years ago—words of sorrow and apology and, most shockingly, love. She'd hoped that someday he would come back home. It saddened him to think she hadn't lived to see that.

His past was at last behind him, and that eased his soul into a place much like a dream. As if the dream couldn't get any better, he'd gotten his wish and been invited back to teach at the high school when another teacher took time off for maternity leave. Principal Ackerman had kindly welcomed him back once the news of Ginger's letter of admission of guilt came out into the open.

The statue of limitations had expired and kept the law from taking any action on Chance's behalf, but the fact that she had stepped forward had helped heal the old wound, closing doors and opening others.

Tonight, Chance would take another step toward the unbelievable.

Avery's family came through the doors, all twenty-eight members. It was tough when that love he felt for her spread to her family. Of its own accord it flourished. He'd fought it, like he fought everything at first, afraid of being hurt or abandoned, but they'd opened their hearts and their home to him and he'd reluctantly entered.

Dan spotted him first and soon the whole lot were smiling and waving. It weakened his knees. It was her mother that came over, smiling that twinkling Glenn smile.

"Why are you hiding back here?" She hooked her arm in his and tugged him from his safety spot.

"Better view." Chance looked over his shoulder and kissed the spot goodbye, unable to refuse Charlotte.

Charlotte eyed him appreciatively, smoothing the lapel of his suit. "You look awfully spicy tonight."

"Spicy?"

"Ask Avery about that. Now." She led him to the rows her family occupied. "You find a seat anywhere in here and you'll be just fine."

That, he was certain of. He took the greetings in stride, still fumbling with names and who belonged to whom.

Chance settled behind Dan and his wife and their brand new baby girl feeling nearly in place. Contentment would come only when he could share his plans with Avery.

The lights dimmed. Avery had vanished. No doubt she was backstage calming nerves in her composed manner, readying the class for their performance. When the song played, a waltz, Chance sat up—eager to see her.

"Moon River's" haunting melody filled the room with Andy Williams's smiling voice. She was there in the back with Scott who had kindly stepped in to fill his spot.

The class was perfect, their timing just right and Chance missed being up there. He counted each step, followed feet with his eyes and found his body moving along even in the confines of the seat. It was clear as he glanced at the proud faces of her family that this was something they were accustomed to; the willingness to support never waned.

It was a miracle to have that kind of love.

After the show, he couldn't wait to find her. She took the compliments as graciously as she had the introductions, and after her family said goodbye, when the crowds fell away, the noise and commotion died, she looked for him.

Avery's heart pumped hard, sending a delicious heat through her body. He was leaning against the back wall, that same dark mystery that had first intrigued her, enticingly dangerous. But he wasn't really dangerous; she had come to understand that he had merely been dangerously lost.

Taking her time to go to him, she allowed her feelings of feminine power to gather. The effect was working; she could tell by the glittering admiration darkening his eyes.

"You look amazing," she said.

He kept his hands in his pockets, his shoulder against the wall, but his gaze moved over her in a burning fire that left her breathless. "I want to take you somewhere."

"Okay. That sounds good." Then she pressed close, nearly melting when the hardness of his body met hers. "I'll just be a second. I can change and—"

Urgency silenced her when he kissed her. Like a rag doll, she fell against him in complete submission. His hand pulled her even tighter to his solid core, and a whimper escaped her throat.

Breaking his lips from hers, he burrowed deep into her hair, inhaling before melting the soft, exposed flesh of her neck with another kiss. "I don't want you to change," he murmured. "I want you just like this."

He drove them in her car because the heater in his hadn't worked for years. Though nights were warming with spring at the fringe of the valley, the heater hummed. Along the majestic foothills of the Wasatch Mountains, a cool breeze teased pines and aspens into a sensual dance. The sky was deep purple. The sun dipped below the rolling western mountains but Avery could see where he was headed and she smiled.

Frank Sinatra serenaded them. Chance parked the car in the dirt just outside of the place he had brought her to months earlier. The lights of the car beamed straight ahead. He left both doors open and cranked Frank up to high before he extended his hand to her.

She set her hand in his and followed him deep into the growth.

"Our place," she said when they came to the clearing. She let out a sigh admiring the twinkling lights of the city, the reflective silver platter of the lake below. "It's beautiful."

"It is." She turned to him, smiled. He was watching her.

His palms were sweating like a school boy, his heart raced against his ribs but he didn't care. He'd waited all of his life for her. Taking her hands, Chance stood in the waltz position. "I couldn't let the night go by and not dance with you. I know there's not a lot of room but we can do it."

"Yes, we can." She waited for him to begin his lead and then followed. "This is wonderful. Thank you."

"I know how dancing relaxes you."

"Except when I dance with you."

"Seriously?"

"But don't stop." Her hand crept up his shoulder to his neck where her fingers played in the softness of his hair, sending soft tremors through his system. "Whenever you take me in your arms, I get nervous. My heart feels like it's going to leap away from me. In the beginning," she hesitated, Chance's heart skipped. "I was afraid that if it leapt, I'd get hurt. Or lose it."

"I'd never hurt you," he murmured.

"I know that now. I knew it then, but you needed to convince yourself."

She was right. All he could do was thank God she'd had the foresight and the patience to wait. In the faint glow of the headlights, her eyes gleamed with pleasure. He imagined kissing her lashes, trailing his lips down her cheeks, finding and capturing her mouth before taking her in the ultimate expression of love. "You said you were right about men ninety-nine times out of one hundred."

Her grin sparkled. "See?"

He moved her in a slow turn and savored a quiet moment. Hope rushed through his system like water finally free from a dam.

His hand tightened at her waist. "Avery." The moment surged with energy, filling every part of him. Behind the determination in her eyes was desire but more, contentment and peace the depth of which he'd spent his whole life searching for.

Avery kept her head against his heart. She wanted to

hear its rhythm when he told her what was inside of him. "Tell me what you want," she whispered, slowing their pace.

He brought their hands in tight and she snuggled more deeply against him. She felt him fight to free words from a heart that had been cautiously kept. "Tell me," she urged.

He stopped suddenly, framing her face with his bandaged hand as well as his warm, whole one. "You," he said. "I want you. Everything is finally over and I need somewhere to begin."

Her heart soared in her chest. "You can begin here." She covered his hands with hers.

"That's what I want."

She smiled, then pressed her head against his chest, the beat of his heart now calm and steady, and they danced.

About the Author:

Katherine Warwick enjoys writing Women's Romance stories that take place in the exciting world of ballroom dance. You can find out more about her and her other works at her websites:

www.katherinewarwick.com

and

www.ballroomdancenovels.com